Just A Game
A Detective Loxley Nottinghamshire Crime Thriller

By
A L Fraine

Copyright & Info

This book is Copyright to Andrew Dobell, Creative Edge Studios Ltd, 2025

No part of this book may be reproduced without prior permission of the copyright holder.

All locations, events, and characters within this book are either fictitious, or have been fictionalised for the purposes of this book.

Publisher - Creative Edge Publishing

Creative Edge Studios Ltd
PO Box 503
KT22 2PL
info@alfraineauthor.co.uk

ASIN: B0D4DYZNKM

Book List

www.alfraineauthor.co.uk/books

Acknowledgements

Thank you to Emmy Ellis for your amazing editing and support.
Thanks to Kath Middleton for her incredible work.
A big thank you to the admins and members of the UK Crime Book Club for their support, both to me and the wider author community. They're awesome.

Thank you also to the authors I've been lucky enough to call friends. You know who you are, and you're all wonderful people.

Thank you to my family, especially my parents, children, and lovely wife, Louise, for their unending love and support.

Table of Contents

Book List 3
Acknowledgements 3
Table of Contents 4
Chapter 1 7
Chapter 2 17
Chapter 3 25
Chapter 4 35
Chapter 5 47
Chapter 6 61
Chapter 7 69
Chapter 8 81
Chapter 9 89
Chapter 10 95
Chapter 11 101
Chapter 12 109
Chapter 13 115
Chapter 14 121
Chapter 15 129
Chapter 16 141
Chapter 17 145
Chapter 18 157
Chapter 19 169
Chapter 20 181
Chapter 21 187
Chapter 22 193
Chapter 23 199
Chapter 24 205
Chapter 25 211
Chapter 26 215
Chapter 27 223
Chapter 28 233
Chapter 29 239
Chapter 30 247
Chapter 31 255
Chapter 32 263

Chapter 33	273
Chapter 34	279
Chapter 35	283
Chapter 36	289
Chapter 37	295
Chapter 38	301
Chapter 39	309
Chapter 40	315
Chapter 41	323
Chapter 42	331
Chapter 43	337
Chapter 44	339
Chapter 45	343
Chapter 46	347
Chapter 47	355
Chapter 48	361
Chapter 49	369
Chapter 50	373
Chapter 51	383
Chapter 52	387
Chapter 53	393
Chapter 54	399
Chapter 55	405
Chapter 56	413
Chapter 57	419
Chapter 58	429
Chapter 59	433
Chapter 60	443
Chapter 61	453
Chapter 62	457
Chapter 63	461
Chapter 64	463
Chapter 65	467
Author Note	474
Book List	475

Chapter 1

20 years ago

Nailer was late home again, and the evening had already drawn in over the city. The streetlights glowed in the evening dusk, reflecting off rain-slicked streets.

It had stopped drizzling for the time being, but there was more inclement weather scheduled for later. At least he'd get home nice and dry. He should be grateful for small mercies, he supposed, especially after the shitshow of the last few days.

Even now, days after taking a potentially career-ending risk, he still wasn't sure if he'd made the right call.

Luckily, everything fell into place, and his gaffer seemed unaware of what he'd done. At least, it appeared that way. He was still being considered for promotion to inspector, after all, which he found reassuring. There was still time for everything to go tits up, though, so he probably shouldn't count his chickens just yet.

Nailer cruised along his road, hunting for a parking space, hoping to get as close to his house as he could. He wrinkled his nose at the pair of Land Rover's parked right outside it and moved on to the next nearest space a few cars further up and eased in. Turning the engine off, he lamented his inability to find a spare moment during the day. It was so busy with the fallout from his current case, he'd been unable to make a phone call, something he'd promised to do.

Nailer pulled out his beaten up 3310 and checked his messages. None. Good, at least the kid could follow orders, he thought with a wry smile. Thumbing through his contacts, he scrolled down to one he'd entered simply as RL, and clicked call.

He climbed out of his car, putting the phone to his ear.

The call connected.

"Hello?"

"It's me," Nailer said, recognising Rob's voice on the other end of the line. "How you doing?"

"I'm bored… But I'm okay, I guess."

"Bored is good. Bored is better than being in prison, remember."

"I know… Thanks."

"My pleasure. Did you have a think about names?"

"I've got a few ideas, but I'm not sure you're going to like them."

Staying beside his car while he spoke, Nailer pulled a face. "I might. What's your idea?"

"You're gonna think it's dumb."

"Try me."

Rob grunted on the other end of the line. "All right, fine. I quite like Loxley."

Nailer felt his eyebrows crawl up his forehead in incredulity. "Loxley? As in Robin of?"

"Aye."

"I think you need to go back to the drawing board."

"I like it."

Nailer sighed. "Well, you're the one who will need to live with it. So, you've not had any visitors, no one's recognised you?"

"Nope. I've not left my room and I still have the 'Do Not Disturb' sign on the door, so…"

"Good."

"I'm grateful for everything you've done, honestly, but how long do I have to stay in this hotel for?"

"Not long, hopefully. I'll get you out as soon as I can. I can't afford to keep you in there for long. My paycheque doesn't stretch that far. I'll find something as soon as I can. But for right now, we just need to keep you away from your family. They're looking for you, you know, after our little stunt."

"No shit. Owen must be pissed. You screwed up his plans."

Nailer smiled. "I know. I was particularly pleased with that, even if it has turned my week upside down."

Leaving his car behind, Nailer marched down the street, making for his front door, when a man stepped out onto the pavement before him and planted himself in Nailer's way. He was tall, broad-shouldered, and stared at him with a scowl.

Nailer slowed and glanced behind him. He had a sense that someone was there, and sure enough, another man had appeared, blocking his primary escape route.

Returning his attention forward, Nailer saw a third man climb out of one of the parked Land Rovers. He recognised him right away.

"You still there?" Rob said over the phone, reminding Nailer he was still on the call.

Nailer grimaced. He stared at Rob's father, Isaac Mason. "I've gotta go. We'll chat later." He hung up before Rob could protest and stuffed the Nokia back into his pocket. "Issac," he began. He took the last few steps towards the man. "How can I be of service?"

"Cute, Sergeant Nailer."

"If you say so. Scores of women would disagree."

Any humour left in Isaac's face instantly drained away. He stared back and said nothing.

"What's this about?" Nailer pressed, keen to get this over with.

"When will you learn to leave my family alone?"

"When they stop breaking the law... probably." He was poking the lion, but he didn't care. He hated these gangsters with a passion. It was why he'd pursued them so relentlessly for years.

"I have no idea what you're talking about. We're a respectable family, Sergeant. Sure, Owen can be a little wild, but he's young. He's just testing boundaries, like all kids do."

"Testing boundaries? You see, it's funny, because I'd call it breaking and entering, theft and assault. But hey, maybe I'm just splitting hairs here."

Isaac took a step towards him, his frown deepening. "Where's Rob?"

"Rob?"

"Don't play games with me, Sergeant. You know who I'm talking about. Where's my son?"

"I don't know," Nailer replied, his tone even and calm, despite his heart hammering in his chest. "Why? Have you lost him? You should keep track of your children more. Your wife, too, if what I've heard is correct."

Isaac lunged and grabbed Nailer by the scruff of his neck and yanked him close. "What did you say?" His voice was a dangerous growl.

Nailer stared back at the man for a long moment. "I said you should concentrate on looking after your own house before you start accusing others. If family members are fleeing the family home like rats leaving a sinking ship, what does that tell you?"

Isaac moved suddenly and punched Nailer in the gut, bending him double. He took a step back having let Nailer go. "You better watch that mouth of yours, John. I know you're a part of this."

Winded, Nailer took his time to catch his breath. He'd pushed Isaac far enough and didn't relish the idea of dying on his doorstep.

"I saw the way you stared at Annabelle, John, back at that charity gala. Don't think I didn't. You're involved in all this, so don't bother trying to deny it. And rest assured, if I find out I'm right, I will hunt you down. You got that?"

Nailer nodded. "Got it." He managed to straighten up.

Isaac adjusted his jacket and sniffed. "Right then, I'm off. I've got a meal with an Assistant Chief Constable to attend."

Nailer raised an eyebrow. "You enjoy that meal." He coughed.

"Don't worry, I will. Right then, boys, let's leave Mr Nailer to his evening."

The car doors closed, and the engines roared. The two four-by-fours drove away, leaving Nailer alone on the pavement. He watched the vehicles disappear into the night while holding his stomach. It still hurt. Isaac packed quite the punch.

Cool spits of fresh rain hit his cheek, breaking his concentration. With a sigh, Nailer turned and walked to his front door. Still in a daze, it took a moment to find the right key and open up. He closed and locked the door behind him, checking it afterwards, just to be sure.

A second later, a face appeared out of a side doorway further up the hallway. "They're gone, right?"

Nailer smiled at Annabelle Mason. "Yeah, he's gone."

"Bloody hell. I thought he'd try to force his way in here," she stated, clearly shaken. She stepped out into the hall, putting a hand to her back and grunting in discomfort. Her pregnancy was quite far along and very obvious.

"That had crossed my mind, too," Nailer agreed. "I think we need to look at other options for you. You can't stay here anymore."

"I know. You're right," she said unhappily. "I'm probably going to do what you suggested and move away for a bit. Maybe to the coast? Cleethorpes maybe?"

"You two should find a place together. You and Rob. You could start again as mother and son..."

"No. That's not what we agreed. You made a promise to me, John. You said you'd be there for him, no matter what. He's going to need you."

"You're going to need help, too," Nailer suggested and glanced at her bump.

"I'll be fine. I've been through this four times already, I think I can handle one more. Don't worry about me. You need to focus on Rob and keep him away from his family. You need to make sure he's all right."

"He is. I just called him before Isaac showed up. He's fine. Don't worry." Nailer bit his lip for a moment in thought before continuing. "I know I agreed to focus on Rob, but things change. You're pregnant with my child and…"

"That changes nothing." She placed both hands on her bump. "You'll be there for her, too, don't worry. But the Masons are dangerous, and Isaac will want Rob back. They will come for him, so it's down to you to keep him safe. But if they do find him, it's better that they don't find me, too." She fixed Nailer with a stern stare. "Me, and your daughter."

"I know." Nailer grumbled under his breath, stressed and frustrated. "I'm just not sure I agree with you keeping your distance from Rob. He's going to need your guidance."

"And that's where you come in. You can be like a father to Rob and keep me up to date on what's going on with him."

Nailer sighed. "I know."

"You know it's the right thing to do." She stepped closer and drew him in for a hug. "I love you."

***

Driving north out of Nottingham, Isaac stared out of the window, his chin resting on his hand as he contemplated his confrontation with Nailer. The sergeant was involved in all this, he knew it. He just knew it. But he had little proof, and killing a police officer was a surefire way to bring way too much heat down on them when they least needed it.

He'd find out, one way or another, that was for sure.

Isaac sat back in his seat and looked at the other passenger. "Guy, I think it's time to talk about your future."

"Of course, sir," Guy replied. "Anything I can do to help, just let me know. What did you have in mind?"

Isaac smiled. "You're going to join the police, son."

Chapter 2

Three weeks ago, Tuesday

The van juddered as it hit another small pothole, Owen's shoulder slamming into the wall of the tiny sweatbox cell he was in.

Shouts went up from some of the other inmates in the surrounding boxes, insulting the skills of the driver and accusing him of hitting the bumps and uneven parts of the road on purpose.

Owen just grimaced, keeping his mouth shut. The journey from Nottingham to Manchester prison would be a long one, and they'd only just set off. Two of the other passengers were already complaining that they needed the toilet, and it wasn't unlikely that at least one passenger would throw a dirty protest and wipe their own waste over the walls.

He hated when they did that. There were no standards these days.

His father came from a different generation of gangster, one that preferred to be seen as respectable by the general community. He'd taught Owen and his brothers the value of respect and honour, urging them to stick to a strict code of conduct, both for their own self-respect but also to hide who they were from prying eyes.

This kind of behaviour was a world away from the brutal, unthinking violence and anti-social attitude that characterised so much of the modern criminal population these days, and it made Owen sick.

He didn't stick as closely to this code of conduct as his brothers did, but he was a far cry from the animals he was sharing this van with.

"Oi, Owen. I've got some mates in Manchester who can't wait to meet you." It was Hadley Watts. He was a thug from the Hyson Green Killers crew, or HGK, as they often referred to themselves. They were fierce enemies of the Masons, and their long-running rivalry would often erupt into violence in the streets when they fought over territory in an ongoing war over drugs. That hatred didn't fade while they were in prison, often leading to fights, injuries, or even deaths while they were serving their time. "We're gonna fuck you up, boy!"

Hadley laughed. Owen reached up and gently touched the fresh scar Watts had given him shortly after being locked up. He still had some aches and pains from subsequent fights that were making this journey more painful than it needed to be, but Owen had promised himself that when the opportunity came along, he'd take his revenge. However, maybe this moment would come sooner rather than later.

After several confrontations with Watts in Nottingham Prison, they were deemed a security risk and were being moved to a high security facility. Owen didn't quite understand the reasoning behind moving both at the same time but assumed they'd be split up at some point.

He sighed and ignored Watts' comments. There was no point getting into a slanging match while they were being moved. It achieved nothing and would only aggravate Watts further.

Besides, Owen had other things on his mind.

Even without windows, he could tell they'd left the confines of the city behind by the style of driving and the sway of the vehicle. Also, it had clearly been long enough by now.

Owen closed his eyes and waited.

When it came, even though he'd been expecting it, it was still a shock.

An almighty bang sounded through the vehicle. Something huge whacked into it, sending the vehicle flying sideways.

Owen braced himself against the walls of his sweatbox. The world briefly descended into slow motion. The van was briefly airborne. It hit the ground with a second massive bang. On its side, it skidded over concrete, the metal panels screeching into the early morning air.

People shouted and screamed, yelling in fear, until it finally came to a halt.

After being slammed against the sides, Owen knelt on the door to his cell. Flipped on its side, the door was now his floor.

Groaning and cursing came from the other passengers. Owen picked himself up. He moved to the edge of the door and waited.

He tried to listen and hear what was going on outside, but it was difficult to make it out; the other prisoners called out, demanding help or an explanation, while continuing to insult the prison officers.

Owen took a long breath. He needed to hold his nerve. It felt like this was taking forever, but it was likely just a few seconds.

Someone banged in a neighbouring cell, and others joined in. They were trying to escape.

Owen allowed himself a wry smile and continued to wait.

Another series of bangs and creaks came from the back of the van before he realised something.

Someone had opened a door.

"Oi, who are you? Get back," the officer inside the van shouted. "Hey, no, get off me. Don't…"

More sudden and violent movement on the other side of Owen's door.

Seconds later, there was a knock. "Owen?"

"I'm in here," he called back. "Third in on the left."

"We've got ya," the man replied. "One moment."

Keys jangled, one was inserted into his door, and the lock turned. Moments later, the door swung open.

Owen stared down to see the familiar face of Mark, one of his crew, looking back.

"Hey, boss. Care to join us?"

"Christ, yes. Get me out of here."

Mark moved out of the way, and Owen jumped down into the gangway, which was now on its side. Ahead, one of the other inmates had managed, through incessant kicking, to partially open one of the cell doors and peered out at Owen.

"Hey, mate. Don't leave me in here. Help me out, yeah?"

Owen pulled a face and shuffled past him.

"Is that you, Owen? Running to hide, are we, Red Man? Fucking pussy!"

Owen froze.

He shouldn't let Watts get to him, but a fire of hatred swelled in his chest. Glancing up, he saw the sidearm attached to Matt's belt.

"Gimme that," Owen said and raised his hand.

"Boss?" Mark placed his hand on his gun. "I thought we weren't killing the guards."

He could see all the prison officers lying facedown on the grassy verge outside, while Gavin and Courtney stood over them. "I said give it to me."

"All right, fine," Mark replied and drew the gun.

Owen took it and held his hand out again. "Keys."

Mark muttered, "Shit, man." But he did as Owen asked.

Owen slid over to Watts' cell. "Hey, Watts," he began and inserted the key. "I said I'd pay you back for this scar."

"Fuck off," Hadley Watts said.

"Gladly." Owen unlocked the door. He kicked it open and jumped down into the cell, right on top of Hadley. Owen grabbed the young man by the throat and jabbed the muzzle of the gun into his face. "Not so fucking funny now, is it?

"Piss off," Watts hissed.

Owen's cheek twitched, then he fired three rounds. Hadley's head deformed as his skull shattered, sending blood and flesh flying. Owen stared at the ruin of the man's face and grunted. "Huh?" He shrugged and climbed out of the cell, feeling nothing. He slid out of the van and tossed the gun to Mark, making for his crew's parked cars. "Let's go."

Chapter 3

Three weeks ago, Tuesday

Rob held on to his mother for what seemed like an eternity, but also, far too short a time than he needed. He couldn't quite believe she was here, after twenty-one years apart. He'd long ago resigned himself to never seeing her again and didn't for a moment believe that this moment would ever actually happen. But here she was, alive and well, and pleased to see him.

"I can't believe it's you," he muttered into her neck, still holding on to her. "It's really you."

"It's me. I'm here, Rob, and I'm thrilled to see you. This hug is long overdue."

Rob laughed and sobbed at the same time. Emotion crashed over him. He felt convinced that he would wake up at any second to discover this was just a vivid dream. Another in a long line of them. He'd fantasised countlessly about finally finding his mother and all the ways it could happen.

But in the end, it had been Mary who'd tracked her down for him.

"Don't ever leave me again," Rob said.

"I don't intend to. Don't worry. I'm not going anywhere."

"You'd better not." He sighed as they squeezed each other. "I've missed you."

"Me too," she muttered.

They finally parted. She held on to his shoulders and got a good look at him. Rob blinked tears from his eyes and could see his mother doing the same.

"You've grown so much, Rob. You're not the kid I left all those years ago."

"I guess not." He sniffed. "You're just as beautiful as ever, though, Mum."

"Aww, thank you, son."

Rob smiled, took a step back, and let his gaze roam around the rustic kitchen. Mary, Nailer, and Erika stood close by, watching, the emotion of the moment clearly getting to them, too. "Have you been here the whole time?"

"Most of it," his mother confirmed. "I moved away for a few years after you got away from the family. I needed some distance, but I couldn't stay away for long. I needed to be close to you…"

Rob smiled and bit his lip to keep his emotions from overtaking him again.

"...and John," she added.

Rob took a long breath. "I have so many questions for you, and so much to tell you, but I don't know where to begin."

She smiled. "I know how you feel. I've been watching you this whole time, through John." She glanced at Nailer. "He's been my eyes and ears, telling me everything you've done and achieved. I can't tell you how proud I am of you, of the man you've become. You're everything your father isn't, and for that, I am eternally grateful."

"Thank you. I had no idea. You've kept the secret well." He glanced over at Nailer. "Both of you."

"It was bound to come out at some point, though," Erika said. "It was only a matter of time."

"Not helped by your moving in next door to him," Nailer muttered, shooting Erika an accusatory glare.

Erika shrugged. "I was curious." She smiled at Rob. "I wanted to get to know my brother."

Fresh tears pricked at the corner of Rob's eyes. "Holy crap, yeah. You're my sister."

Erika smiled. "Guilty as charged. And, um, sorry for the recent... shenanigans. After the Red Room, I wasn't in a good place. I didn't know what to do."

"Come here," Rob said and reached for her. They embraced. "I can't believe I have a sister. I've found my mother and gained a sister."

Moments later, they separated, before Rob turned and hugged Mary, too. "Thank you."

"My pleasure."

"Fancy a cuppa?" Nailer asked.

"I'd love one," Rob confirmed, followed by a chorus of the others agreeing.

They busied themselves by getting the mugs out and boiling the kettle. Somewhere amongst the commotion, a plate of biscuits appeared on the table as well, and Rob found himself feeling suddenly famished. He grabbed a couple of Hobnobs and munched them down before the others settled in around the sturdy wooden table.

"You're a spit of your dad, by the way," his mum commented. "You sound just like him, too. Sean was the same."

"I don't know if that's a good thing or a bad thing," Rob said.

"It's neither, I suppose," his mum added. "It is what it is. I'm just glad you're here."

"Me too."

"At least there's no more secrets," Nailer said. "I hated that they were driving a wedge between us after the Red Room."

"I understand why you did it, though. You were trying to keep me safe. Hiding your daughter was part of hiding Mum from the Masons. It makes sense. I mean, I wish I'd known sooner. If I had, I might have been better able to protect her from Owen. But... Well, what's done is done."

"It's always easier to see where you went wrong after it happens," Mary agreed.

"Speaking of going wrong, I think I need to take a look at our security. If you were able to find out where Annabelle is, what's to stop Isaac doing the same?"

"Nothing," Rob agreed.

"Does he know that I'm your daughter?" Erika asked, glancing at Nailer.

He shrugged. "I don't know."

"I think we have to assume he does," Rob said. "Guy knew about it, and he was working for Isaac this whole time. So, I think it's only reasonable to assume that he told Isaac."

"But that by itself isn't a bad thing," his mum said. "So, he knows that Nailer has a daughter. There are plenty of single fathers with children. As long as he doesn't know about me, then we don't have a problem."

"Which brings us back to keeping you a secret," Nailer said. "I need to review things and make sure we're taking reasonable precautions."

"Why not bring in some help? I think between us we know enough people who hate the Masons who would be more than happy to pitch in and have the skills to make a difference."

"Not a bad idea..." Nailer mused.

"Like who?" Mary asked.

"Calico?" Nailer suggested.

Rob nodded. "I've been messaging that hacker who helped us with the Red Room, Riddle. She's helped us out since, and she despises the Masons. I think she'd be useful."

"You wouldn't mention me, though, right?" Rob's mum asked.

"No, of course not," Rob confirmed. "We just use them to look for Mason interference and bring them in when we need to."

"We'll have to pay them," Nailer added.

"We'll sort it," Annabelle said.

Nailer's phone buzzed. He glanced at it and left the table, moving to the far end of the kitchen.

Rob sipped his tea and listened in to Nailer's brief conversation, trying to work out what was going on. He spoke for less than a minute, then he hung up and returned to the table.

"What's up?" Rob asked.

Nailer glanced around the table before answering. "That was Scarlett. We've just had a report come in that Owen was sprung from custody tonight during a prisoner transfer. His van was rammed off the road, and he escaped. He killed a rival gang member during his escape, too."

"Jesus. So Owen is out and at large," Rob clarified.

"He is," Nailer confirmed and took hold of Erika's hand. "We'll find him. He won't go far. If it's one thing I know from years of hunting the Masons, it's that they always come home in the end."

"You've been after them for a long time?" Mary asked.

"They've been my pet project for decades now, going back to when Manny Mason, Isaac's dad, was in charge. That's how I met Annabelle."

"In the line of duty," Rob muttered.

"Very much so. I used to attend the same events the Masons did, the charity events and such, and it was at one of those that I got speaking to Annabelle and we kind of hit it off from there."

"We had a thing going," Annabelle confirmed.

"Eeeuww." Erika squirmed. "I don't want to know."

"It's nothing to be ashamed of," Annabelle countered. "We just became close, one thing led to another, and then I was pregnant. I knew it was Nailer's, and I also knew that I had to get out. Suddenly I had a time limit. If Isaac found out that I'd been cheating on him and that I was carrying John's baby, then my life would be in danger. I had to leave. So when the opportunity presented itself, I took it."

Annabelle paused for a moment before continuing. "I just wish I could have taken you with me," she said to Rob. "But it was just too dangerous. I couldn't risk it, or my baby. So I got out and I spoke to John. I asked him to get you out of the family as soon as possible."

"Luckily for me," Nailer said, "Owen soon gave me the perfect opportunity."

"And the rest is history," Rob added. "But where do we go from here?"

"I'm staying here for as long as I can," Annabelle said.

"Of course," Rob agreed. "But we need to be much more careful who comes here and when. If you suspect you're being followed, then you do not come here. You do not pay a visit."

"Damn right," Annabelle added.

"I think I'll move back to the flat," Erika stated. "It's better if I'm there, rather than here."

"Are you sure?" Annabelle asked.

"I need to work," Erika said. "We're not that rich."

"I don't care about that. I care about your safety."

"And we all care about your safety. Isaac might know that I'm Nailer's daughter, but he doesn't know you're my mum. But if he follows me back here…" She let the statement hang in the air. "I can't be seen travelling between here and work. Besides, I'm fed up with the commute."

"Good idea," Rob exclaimed. "Also, now that there's no more secrets, I know to keep a closer eye on you." He turned to his mum. "I'll keep her safe."

"Agreed," Erika answered.

"I wish there was a better option, but I think she's right," Nailer added.

Annabelle sighed. "I can't argue with that logic. I just don't like that Isaac knowing about your dad is pushing you away from me."

"I'm not going anywhere." Erika took her mother's hand in hers. "I promise."

"I'll give that key back to you, too," Rob said. "You can use my place any time you like."

Erika smiled. "Muffin will love that. I've missed that naughty fur ball."

"I suspect he's missed you, too."

"Perfect, that's settled then."

Chapter 4

Monday

The first day back to work after the weekend was a chore. After two days of chilling out, doing some jobs around the house, and spending time with the family, the reality of getting back into the office and putting in a day's work was always a drag. Still, Kurt didn't mind his job too much. At least he wasn't dealing with the public like his wife, Sandy, had to.

She'd come home most days with a story or two of someone kicking off or causing problems in the doctor's surgery. But she remained ambivalent about it, or so she said. She'd seen all sorts over the years working on that reception desk, and it used to bother her and ruin the rest of her day. But she was used to it by now, and it didn't bother her as much as it used to.

Honestly, some people were just complete shits.

By comparison, Kurt's job was more business-to-business focused, something for which he was very grateful. He worked for a large construction company in procurement, sourcing materials and tools for the lads out on the sites to use. He spent most of his day on the phone or navigating websites, and that suited him just fine.

He drove through the last few streets of the city towards his home, navigating the evening traffic as best he could. He'd been late to leave due to a mix-up with an order that he needed to put right before he left and hoped this didn't serve as an omen for the week to come.

He waited at another set of traffic lights and grimaced at his phone on the dash. He'd tried calling his wife earlier, to let her know he'd be late, but she hadn't answered. It was both frustrating and a little unusual. Hopefully, nothing was wrong.

Glancing at the lights, Kurt tapped on his phone and called again.

It rang several times before eventually ringing off.

Kurt twisted his lips in frustration. Well, he wasn't far from home now, he reasoned, so the best thing was to just keep going.

Was she annoyed with him for being late? Pressing his lips together in worry, he resolved to apologise as soon as he got in.

The next ten minutes of slow, crawling driving was agonisingly tedious, but eventually he pulled into their reserved parking space and approached the townhouse with his key ready. The door was off the latch, so it was just a quarter turn of the key to open the door and step inside.

"Babe? I'm back. Sorry I'm late," he called out and closed the door behind him. "Things got a little out of hand at work, and I had to finish what I'd started."

Kurt dumped his stuff as quickly as he could. He could tidy up later. But as he removed his shoes, he realised she hadn't answered.

Kurt frowned. That was unlike her.

"Babe? Sandy? Are you in?"

Nothing. Not a sound.

"Breanna?" he called, wondering if his daughter was in the house, maybe with her headphones on so she couldn't hear him.

He listened, hoping to hear a reply, and heard something shift towards the back of the house.

Kurt frowned. He could see the open kitchen door and light spilling from the room. "What the hell?" he muttered and marched down the hallway and into the kitchen. "Sandy...?"

He froze the moment he stepped through the doorway. The sight that greeted him chilled him to the core.

His wife and daughter were sitting at the small kitchen table, facing each other, with red eyes and tearstains down their cheeks. Both seemed frozen with fear as their eyes flicked up to him, pleading for help.

Behind them, facing Kurt, was a man wearing a bandanna across his nose and mouth. He seemed calm, relaxed, and very much in control. Kurt's gaze darted over the scene, and he noticed other details, but none of them were encouraging.

Both his wife and daughter were wearing metal collars with wires, circuits, LEDs, and packs of something attached to them. His mind went instantly to explosives, and his stomach dropped. He could make out wires leading from each collar to some kind of device strapped to the man's chest beneath his shirt which was partially undone. Another wire snaked from that device to another held in the man's hand. It appeared to be some kind of remote control, but it had been heavily modified.

"What the...?" Kurt gasped in shock and took a step forward.

The man raised his other hand, revealing a gun he was holding. "Ah, ah, ah, stay where you are, Kurt. It's my time to speak."

"Who are you?"

The man sighed in frustration. "I understand that this is probably coming as a shock, but you need to concentrate for me, Kurt, okay? You need to listen and do as I say, otherwise… Well, I'll get to that. Just stand there for me, will you?" He waved his gun.

Kurt did as the man asked, sidestepping to the centre of the kitchen. He looked again at the terrified faces of the two people he loved more than anything in the world. His wife sobbed, and his daughter was panicked.

"Now, now, let's all calm down. We're going to play a game."

"A game?" Kurt asked.

The man sighed. "It'll go much easier for you if you just listen. Oh, and by the way, you're on a time limit." He tapped a digital timer on the table before him with the tip of his gun.

Two more wires connected it to the collars around his wife and daughter's necks. The timer was at eight minutes and ten seconds.

"What in the hell...?" Kurt muttered. He was already putting things together in his head, guessing what these various devices were and the danger they were in. He hoped he was wrong, but he had a sinking suspicion he wasn't.

"I'm sure you're wondering what this game is, and it's quite simple really. You have a choice. A or B. Your wife or your daughter. It's that easy. In a minute, I'm going to give you this gun, and you're going to kill either your wife or your daughter. The choice is yours, I don't care. But that's what you have to do."

"Fuck you," Kurt spat. "I'll just shoot you."

"No you won't, Kurt."

"Fuck you, I will."

The man sighed. "It's your time we're wasting."

Seven minutes and twenty-two seconds, the timer read.

"Okay, why? Why won't I kill you?"

"The collar bombs they're wearing are linked to this heart rate monitor on my chest. If my heart stops, the bombs go off. Both of them. So, if I die, they both die. I also have this trigger here in my hand. It's a dead man's switch that if I let go of it, the same thing happens.

Boom. The collars are also rigged to explode if they're tampered with or disconnected. And finally, if you do anything I don't like, I'll trigger it. The only way to save one of them is to kill the other. Also, there's only one bullet in the gun."

"You're insane."

"No, I'm the Games Master, and this is just a game." The man placed the gun on the table and gave it a quick push, sending it skidding over the wood.

Kurt stepped forward and grabbed it before it fell off the end.

"There we go. But that's enough from me. Over to you. You can talk now, ladies. I can't wait to see who you choose, Kurt."

Kurt stared down at the gun in his hand and then up at the man, who gestured with his hand to play the game.

"I can't do this," he said and looked at his wife and daughter. "I can't. I won't."

"You have to," his wife said. "You have to do this. You have to choose."

"But I can't. I can't do this. I refuse."

His daughter was in full floods of tears.

"Then we both die. Is that what you want?"

"No, it isn't," Kurt replied.

"I don't want to die," Breanna sobbed. "I don't. I can't. Please."

"It has to be me," Sandy stated and sniffed back her emotion. "You have to kill me to save our daughter."

"What are you talking about? Kill you? I can't do that." He glanced at the timer.

Just over five minutes to go. He couldn't make this choice in five minutes. There was no way.

"I can't kill you, Sandy. You were always the better parent. You do everything around here. It should be me." Kurt stared into the middle distance and latched on to that idea. Maybe that was the way out of this. Maybe neither of them had to die. If he killed himself, then maybe they could both live!

"I'll kill myself," Kurt stated. "It's the obvious choice. You should be the one to live and to be there for Bree. Not me."

"No, don't. Don't do this, Kurt, please. No."

Kurt took a long breath and raised the gun. He glared at the man, the Games Master. "I'll kill myself."

The Games Master shook his head and wiggled the trigger in his hand. "Sorry, no. If you kill yourself, you forfeit the game, and I kill them both anyway. You all die."

"No," Kurt said and lowered the gun. "Don't kill them. Please. Don't make me do this. Please."

The man shrugged.

"Kill me," Sandy said, her tone serious. "You're the strong one, Kurt. You can be there for her. You can protect her and provide for her. I can't live without her. It has to be me. You have to kill me. Just do it. Just shoot me. Get it done and save our daughter. Kill me!"

"How can you say this?"

"We have three minutes, Kurt, and I've been thinking about this while we waited for you. So I've made my mind up. I've had a good life, been blessed with a wonderful husband and a beautiful daughter. I'm happy and content. You gave me everything I ever wanted. I love you, Kurt…"

"Don't say that."

"But I do. I love you, and if you love me, you'll do this. Do as I say and save our child."

"No, Mummy. Please, don't," Breanna cried.

"You'll be okay, Bree. Your dad will look after you. He'll be there for you. He loves you just as much as I do. But it has to be me."

"No, it doesn't. I don't want to live without you, Mum. I can't. I don't agree with this. I... I think it should be all of us."

"No! Don't say that. You need to live, Bree. I want you to have a life, grow up and meet a boy, or girl, whatever. You need to live."

"Time's running out," the man said.

Less than two minutes, Kurt noted, before he stared at the man, his gaze filled with hatred. "I fucking hate you. Do you hear me? I will hunt you down for this."

"Kurt, focus," Sandy barked at him. "Deal with this now, him later."

"I don't know if I can do this," he whimpered. "I love you."

"If you love me, you'll do it. Put the gun to my head, close your eyes, and do it. Save our daughter. Save Breanna."

Kurt sighed and started to raise the gun. "I... I don't want to. I can't..."

"You can. Go on. Raise it up. That's it."

"Mum!" Breanna cried.

"No shouting," the man barked. "Do that again, and you forfeit the game."

"Breanna. Don't be selfish. You need to live. You need to survive this for me and live your life to the fullest. Promise you will do that for me."

"But, Mum…"

"Promise me!" she snapped.

"All right, I promise."

"And do not blame your dad for this. He's in an impossible situation and doing this for you at my request. Understand?"

"I understand."

Sandy turned to him and fixed her eyes on his. "I love you, Kurt."

"I love you, too."

"Then do it."

Kurt glanced at the timer. There was less than a minute left. He had no other choice.

He raised the gun and gently pressed the end against Sandy's forehead. "I'm so sorry. I'm so, so sorry."

"I know. But this is the only choice. It's the only way. Save our daughter. Now close your eyes and end this."

Kurt closed his eyes. He could still feel the pressure of her head against the gun as he gingerly moved his finger into place. "I love you so much."

"I love you, too. You gave me everything. I couldn't have been happier. Now do it."

"I... I don't know..."

"Do it. Do it now!"

"But..."

"NOW!"

Kurt pulled the trigger. It was surprisingly light and easy to do. The gun went off in his hand, jerking back like a jackhammer. The bullet casing flew across the room. Kurt was deaf, suddenly. The bang was incredibly loud. For a long moment, he thought he'd lost his hearing for good. All he could hear was a ringing sound. A high-pitched whine that cut through his mind like a knife.

Then, the seconds passing, he heard his daughter crying hysterically.

But Kurt stood, unmoving, and couldn't bring himself to open his eyes. He wouldn't. He didn't want to see her like that. He didn't want that image in his head.

The man grabbed him and forced him to the floor, before something hit him in the head and he sank into sweet oblivion.

Chapter 5

Tuesday

"Yeah, there was another gang-related stabbing last night."

Rob nodded as Scarlett spoke. They were driving south through early morning traffic, heading into town from the Lodge along the Mansfield Road.

"HGK again?" Rob asked.

"Yep. They targeted one of the other old-style firms, not the Masons this time." She sighed, sounding exasperated. "It's getting worse. It seems to be spreading and affecting more than just the Masons. They're still getting the brunt of it, and they're hitting back, too, but it looks like anyone who sides against the Hyson Green Killers is considered an ally of the Masons."

"Damn. And of course, the side effect is that even if they weren't friendly with the Masons beforehand, they may well side with them going forward."

"The enemy of my enemy," Scarlet remarked.

"It's stupid. They're just making this more dangerous for themselves. Taking on the Masons is one thing, but taking on two, three, or more similar gangs at the same time? Bloody idiots."

"It's too early to tell if that's happening yet, but if something doesn't change soon, then yeah, I can see things getting worse."

"We're already dealing with what is basically open warfare on the streets," Rob stated.

"Tell me about it. Innocent bystanders have been killed, and more will join them if we don't get a handle on this. I'm working with units across the city to try and coordinate our efforts, but until either we, or the HGK gang find Owen, I can't see this ending anytime soon."

"He's got a lot to answer for. Any leads?" Rob asked, in case there had been any developments overnight.

"No, none. There's nothing, and the Masons are being as helpful as ever."

"I'd expect nothing less," Rob confirmed.

They pushed south. The destination was actually on the Mansfield Road, if they could just make their way through the traffic that was blocking their way. Ironically, it was probably the emergency vehicles further up that were causing the problem to begin with.

"You must be doing a good job," Rob added. "I've heard nothing but praise about how you've been handling this case. Keep going like that, and you might be getting a promotion."

She scoffed at his suggestion. "Yeah, right. I'm just doing my job. I mean, don't get me wrong, a promotion would be nice, but that's not why I do this..."

"Would you turn it down?"

"Nope."

"Then just smile and say thanks," Rob suggested with a wry smile.

"Yes, sir."

"You'll catch me up at this rate, and then I'll be calling you guv. Or would you prefer ma'am?"

"Shut up." She chuckled. "It's not just me. Ellen and Tucker are working just as hard as I am."

Rob smiled. "I'll be sure to tell Nailer to ignore you and give any reward to Ellen and Tucker."

Scarlett smirked. "I wouldn't put it past you. Is this why you invited me on this crime scene visit? Are you trying to stop me getting ideas above my station?"

"Absolutely, yes, that is why I invited you out, to pop that inflated ego of yours," he joked. "I'm struggling to fit in a room with you and your enormous head."

She laughed.

"Nailer just wanted me to take you out, give you a break from the Mason case. He doesn't want you getting bogged down in it. That's all."

"I'm not," she protested, a little too strongly. "I mean... I guess that's not a bad idea. Although, swapping gang violence for domestic violence isn't much of a palette cleanser."

"At least you're out the office."

She sighed. "I guess."

They soon approached the scene and parked as close as they could before climbing out and crossing the final stretch on foot. It was chaos out here, with journalists and the general public all taking tremendous interest in the events of the morning.

Rob led the way, pushing through the small crowd to the outer cordon and the officer guarding it. A quick badge flash later, and they were through, making their way to the crime scene. As usual, the detectives were some of the last people on the scene, after the officers on the initial call-out, and then the Scenes of Crime officers, forensics, and police surgeon, who had far more urgent jobs to do when something like this was discovered.

Beyond the tape, Rob noted the usual collection of emergency vehicles with their blue flashing lights and attendant officers, all of whom were doing their jobs.

Rob got directions from a passing man in uniform and led the way through the chaos to where he spotted Sergeant Alex Soto, who was managing the wider scene.

"Morning," Rob announced as he walked over.

"Aaah, Rob, Scarlett, nice of you to finally join us."

"You know we like to keep you waiting."

"Don't I know it," Alex muttered. "This one's messed up, my friend, are you sure you want to take it on?"

"Worse than the poppets and the Red Room?"

Alex shrugged. "It's certainly up there in the fucked-up chart."

"Sounds delightful. Don't keep us in suspense."

"Don't say I didn't warn you." Alex grunted and took a breath then launched into his explanation. "Mr Kurt Hargreaves, a hardworking family man, got home from work late last night to find a man had broken into his home and strapped bombs to his wife's and daughter's necks. He then handed Kurt a gun loaded with a single bullet and told him to choose between them. Kill one, and the other lives. Anything else, like shooting the man or himself, would result in the deaths of both women. Oh, and he had a ten-minute time limit."

"What. The. Hell," Rob stated in abject horror.

"Yeah, this is so much better than gang warfare." Scarlett rolled her eyes.

"Wait, so what did this Kurt do?" Rob asked.

"He shot his wife in the head." Alex's voice was deadpan.

Rob took a moment to comprehend what Alex had just told him, while staring into the middle distance. Somehow, he hadn't expected that.

"He killed her?" Scarlett asked.

"He did," Alex confirmed.

Rob had seen some crazy stuff on this job, and here was a brand-new contender for the top spot. "How did he stop Kurt from shooting him?"

"The heart monitor on the intruder's chest was connected to the bombs, which were programmed to detonate if his heart stopped. The man also held a remote, in case he needed to trigger the bombs manually."

"And once Kurt had killed his wife, he just let the daughter go?"

"He did. He attacked them, knocking them out, and tied them up so he could make his getaway, but yes, he was true to his word and let the daughter live. Oh, and he referred to himself as the Games Master."

"The Games Master?" Rob repeated. He released a long sigh. He already knew where this was going. "Crap. You don't go to these lengths unless the act itself has meaning. This is not a crime of passion. This took time and planning, and a lot of it."

"Yep," Alex agreed.

"The husband and daughter, are they close?"

"We removed them from the house, but I think they're still here, in this chaos somewhere. You wanna come inside?"

"I do," Rob confirmed.

Alex showed them to the back of a nearby van where they pulled on a set of white forensics coveralls over their clothes. They marched towards the house.

"Who's here?" Rob asked.

"Alicia's inside," Alex answered and waved them through.

Rob kept to the stepping plates that held them above the floor and stopped them either contaminating it or disturbing any evidence. Rob wondered how much evidence there would be, though. Someone who spent weeks, if not months planning a killing like this, wasn't likely to take any chances with his own DNA being left at the scene. Still, it was hard to account for everything, and if this led to more killings, which Rob suspected it would, there was a chance he'd slip up at some point.

They were shown through to the kitchen, where Rob spotted Crime Scene Manager, Alicia Aston, with a clipboard in hand.

Elsewhere in the kitchen, the inert body of a woman was slumped in a chair with a red spatter behind her. Only the small bloody hole on her forehead betrayed the horrors behind her.

There were quite a number of other forensics officers in here, including a couple who were taking a great deal of interest in the metal collars that had been removed from both women's necks and placed on the table.

They were crude but effective devices.

"Rob, Scarlett. Good to see you, despite…" Alicia waved towards the body. "Are you well? I didn't expect to see you here, Scarlett. I thought you were on the gang op?"

"I am. I'm here for moral support."

"Soto filled us in about what happened," Rob added. "I take it this is the wife?"

"Correct. The husband and daughter are outside, they're both a mess. I'm not sure you'll get much more out of them this morning. Response had some difficulty trying to make sense of their story when they arrived."

"Makes sense. So, are those the bomb collars?"

One of the men peering at the devices turned to face him. "They are. They're safe now."

"Bomb squad?" Rob asked, taking a guess.

The man nodded in confirmation. "We'll take the explosive away for analysis and send you the report."

"Thank you," Rob replied and turned back to Alicia. "What else do we have?"

"All sorts. We've got all the electronics, and even the gun he handed to Kurt, so we'll be doing a thorough check of all of it, for DNA and prints. You never know…"

"Fingers crossed."

"We might be able to trace the gun and explosives, and we noticed a doorbell cam, too. So there might be something on there we can use."

"Excellent," Rob complimented her. He took a last look around the room. "Then I'll leave this in your capable hands."

"Thank you."

He nodded to Scarlett, leading the way outside and over to the sergeant. "Are you going door to door?"

"Already started," Soto replied. "Way ahead of you. Do you want to speak to the husband or daughter?"

"Of course, but are they in any state to talk?" Rob peered around and quickly spotted both victims. Kurt seemed in a state of shock and wasn't talking much to the officer who was with him, while the daughter was in floods of tears as another officer tried to calm her down.

"You might get some sense out of the husband," Alex suggested and waved for him to make his way over.

Rob glanced at Scarlett who didn't protest, and wandered over, walking into the man's field of vision.

"Hello, I'm DI Loxley, and I'll be in charge of this case. I wanted you to know that I'll be doing everything in my power to bring this man to justice."

Kurt's eyes flicked towards him. "Huh. Good luck with that," he said dejectedly.

Rob bit his lip. Kurt probably didn't mean to sound ungrateful. He'd just had his life utterly shattered, so it was only natural for him to feel lost with no hope of rescue. Still, it always stung when someone suggested that Rob wouldn't be up to the job. Those feelings were probably linked to his more general experience in the force, and how that, for years, he was treated as little more than a criminal by his fellow officers, all because of his estranged family, the Masons.

"I know you've already given a statement, so I won't go into that too much, but I was just curious to know if you knew why you were chosen? Do you know anyone who might want to do this to you or your wife?"

"Chosen?"

"You were clearly targeted, for whatever reason. Do you know why?"

"No. No idea. I don't know why anyone would want to do this to anyone, let alone us. We don't have any enemies or anything."

"Do you owe anyone money? Have you had an argument with anyone? What about your wife and daughter? Has anything happened in their lives recently to cause this?"

"Not that I'm aware of, no, and we don't keep secrets from each other. We try to get along with everyone. We're good people. I have no idea why anyone would want to cause such chaos and hurt."

Rob nodded, sympathising with this man's complete bewilderment. Even after all these years, and all the crazed murderers he'd encountered, he still couldn't see a reason to visit such horrors on another human being.

"I... I killed my wife last night," Kurt continued. "I shot the woman I've loved for years through her head. I just... I don't know what to do with my life anymore. I'm a murderer, and my daughter watched me do it. How can I care for her after that? How can I even look at her? She's going to hate me. She's not going to come and see me in prison, is she."

Rob sighed. "You were forced into this. You had literally no choice, and through your actions, you saved your daughter's life."

"She asked me to kill her, you know. Sandy, my wife. She demanded that I kill her and save Breanna. I'll never forget her words to me."

"As I said, as far as I'm concerned, you're not a killer. You're a victim who was forced into an impossible situation, and you made the only choice you could. I won't lie to you, though. You'll probably go to court over this, but I will do my best to help you and keep you out of prison."

Kurt snorted in melancholy amusement. "Yeah. Sure. Thank you, Detective. I appreciate that. But if you don't mind, I think I need some time to myself."

"Of course, I understand. Either myself or one of my team will speak to you again later in more detail, okay? We'll look after you and get you some help."

Kurt waved his hand dismissively. "Yeah, sure. Whatever."

Rob bit his lip and stepped away, turning to see Scarlett standing nearby. She'd been listening and fell into step beside him as they walked.

"Poor bloke," she muttered quietly. "I can't imagine what he's been through. I'm not sure I'd want to live another day if I'd been forced to kill Chris."

"Yeah, I hear you," Rob agreed, wondering how he'd react if someone forced him to kill Mary. They were chilling thoughts, and not something he relished giving the time of day. "Seems like I'm going to have my hands full with this one."

"Suddenly, I'm glad I'm dealing with gangs."

"Pfft, I bet. Right, let's get back to the Lodge."

Chapter 6
Tuesday

Walking into the office, Rob motioned to Nailer's office and turned to Scarlett. "I'm going to update the boss," he muttered.

Scarlett nodded and made for her desk. Nick, Ellen, and Tucker were already there, hard at work. Nick nodded to him when he passed, and then headed towards Scarlett. Rob approached the door to the side office. He could see Nailer inside, behind his desk, and knocked on the door.

"Come in," Nailer called and glanced up.

Rob stepped inside.

"Rob. Have you just got back?"

"Yep," he replied, unsure how to launch into the description of what he'd seen and heard in the city. Instead, he took a moment to cross the room and take a seat. He felt like he needed to sit down before getting into this.

"Care to share?" Nailer asked, a note of impatience in his voice.

"It looks like we have a new and inventive killer on the loose, one who doesn't even pull the trigger himself."

Nailer's expression changed to one of surprise and curiosity. "Oh, really?"

"A man broke into a family home, took the mother and daughter hostage, and waited for the husband to return. He put bombs around the two women's necks, which were hooked up to a timer, a heart rate monitor he was wearing, and a remote, and waited. When Kurt, the husband, returned, he was given a gun with a single bullet and a choice. Kill either his wife or his daughter, or both die."

"Bloody hell, that's messed up. I take it that the man killed one of them?"

"He did. He shot his wife, on her insistence."

"Selfless," Nailer muttered. "I hate to say it, but she probably did the right thing. I'm assuming the killer got away?"

"He did, and he stuck to his word and left the daughter and husband alive."

"This sounds well planned to me," Nailer suggested.

"I agree. And now he's free, he succeeded, so I can't help thinking that he's bound to do it again."

"My thoughts exactly. Any obvious leads?"

"No blinking neon arrow pointing to the killer yet, but we have a few leads to follow up on. Unfortunately, from talking to the husband, there doesn't appear to be an apparent motive. Not an obvious one anyway. The husband will be in the building by now, though, so I'll talk to him again and see if he has any new information for me."

"Great. Good luck. How was Scarlett?"

"She's fine. Although, I think she was a bit bewildered about why she came to that crime scene with me, given her workload."

Nailer sighed. "It's not a reflection on her work, if that's what you're asking. She's an incredible officer doing an amazing job."

"She is," Rob agreed.

"I was just concerned that she was getting a little too obsessed with this gang violence operation. After everything that happened to her friend, I'm in two minds about her running these kinds of operations. On the one hand, she's great at what she does, she's given me no reason to think that she's anything but professional, and I want to give her the chance to excel, but part of me is concerned that she'll take this opportunity for revenge somehow."

"I get that, but she's not given either of us cause to doubt her, so far. I've been worried about the same thing, but she's been nothing but professional and hardworking."

"So, you think she's okay where she is?"

"I'm not a psychiatrist," Rob remarked, "but yeah, I think she's okay for now. She should be allowed to continue."

"Fine, let's go with that. Also, the superintendent has been taking notice of her..."

"You mentioned that before. Do you think she's up for promotion?"

"Perhaps, in time. I'm hearing positive whispers, that's all I can say."

"Then I wouldn't want to get in the way of that," Rob said.

"Agreed. Okay, thanks for coming to see me," Nailer said, subtly hinting that he had work to do.

Rob left him and returned to his desk, where Nick was waiting.

"Hey," Nick greeted him. "Scarlett filled me in. Sounds messed up."

"Very." Rob leaned in. "Sorry I couldn't take you, boss' orders."

"Anything I did wrong?" Nick asked.

"No, no, nothing like that. It had nothing to do with you."

Nick's eyes flicked to Scarlett. "Oh, okay. I see. Right then, anything else I need to know?"

"If Scarlett's been over what we saw at the crime scene, then no, nothing really."

Nick nodded. "Great. Well, we're doing the usual work alongside all this, pulling CCTV from public and private cameras, and going door to door. Forensics will also work to trace the gun and the explosives. No idea if they'll get a match, but it can't hurt to try."

"Certainly not."

"I think the victims are here, in the building," Nick remarked.

"I believe so, too. We need to speak to both of them, but let's start with Kurt Hargreaves, seeing as the killer chose him to pull the trigger."

"So, I take it we're referring to this Games Master as the killer?"

"Absolutely. Kurt would not have shot his wife last night otherwise."

Nick nodded. "I hope you're right."

Rob snorted. "So do I."

He made a quick call, soon found out Kurt's location, and the pair set off through the station to find him.

Kurt had been placed in an interview room and was waiting calmly, staring at the opposite wall until Rob walked in and broke his concentration.

"Kurt," Rob began, watching the man closely for any tells or hint of deception. "Thank you for seeing me again."

"Of course, no problem," he replied, his voice croaky and rough. Unsurprising given the circumstances. "I want to help, but I'm just not sure I'll be much help."

"I know, I realise that. I'd like you to go through the events of last night again for me. Is that okay? I have your statement here, and we may well stop you and ask questions, all right?"

Kurt took a long breath and a moment to centre himself before he began. Rob could only imagine what was going through his head as they forced him to relive that night once more, so that sigh was just one outward sign of the stress and pain he was going through this morning.

Rob listened to Kurt going through the day's events, starting in the morning with his departure for work, his workday, and then the return home into a nightmare. Several times Rob stopped and quizzed him on certain details, asking for more clarity or information, or Kurt's own views or opinion on something.

He shed tears several times during the interview, breaking down into sobs partway through when he described pulling the trigger. Rob worked hard to remain impartial and objective, but it wasn't easy with such pain and emotion on display. Once his description of the events of the previous night was exhausted, they moved on to possible motives, probing deep into Kurt's life, hunting for anyone who might be willing to hurt him.

"Listen, I've been over this so many times now. There's no one that I know who'd want to kill or even hurt any of my family. None that I'm aware of anyway. I just don't know anyone who would want to do that. It's madness."

"But you've mentioned that some of the patients at the surgery your wife works at have been horrible to her in the past. Do you think any of those could do this?"

"Is it possible? Sure, I suppose so, but I very much doubt any would," Kurt replied. "She's worked there for years, and no one has ever come looking for her or confronted her outside of the surgery, even if they were upset earlier on. But then, they're not really angry at her, they're upset with the system."

"And there's no one from your work who might have an issue with you?"

"Me?" Kurt asked, sounding shocked. "No, of course not. It's not like that."

"I'm glad to hear it." But inside, Rob was grimacing, annoyed that he was hitting this brick wall already, and it was only the first day. If there was honestly no one who wanted to hurt Kurt or his family, it would mean that the killing was utterly random, which made it much harder for them to trace the murderer.

Chapter 7

Tuesday

Driving through the countryside on the outskirts of Mansfield with the window down and the cool air whipping through the car felt like heaven. After weeks in jail and then several more holed up in a grubby house in Nottingham following his escape, Owen was glad to be outside. He and his crew hadn't planned the escape so he could be a prisoner somewhere else. He wanted to get back out into the world and enjoy his freedom as much as possible.

But he understood his crew's caution and was well aware of the gang war he'd sparked by killing Hadley Watts. He had no regrets about his actions, but didn't enjoy the repercussions that came afterwards.

He'd been careful to keep a low profile as much as possible, but his escape was common knowledge following the news reports and appeals by the police to help find him. He hadn't yet spoken to his father, who was no doubt cautious about calling him in case his phone had been tapped, but he had spoken and messaged his closest ally within the Masons' organisation, Carter Bird.

It had taken some persuading, but Carter had eventually agreed to allow Owen into his spacious home, providing he continued to lie low for a while. The media interest in him had yet to fade, and he was mentioned in either the papers or on the news every few days.

He was sure the media cycle would eventually move on, but it might run for a little while longer yet, even with this new murder being splashed all over the morning roundup.

It was fortunate this killing fell on the day he'd left the house for the first time in weeks and meant that Owen had been absent from the news for a record fourth day on the trot.

Still, it paid to be careful, and he made sure to leave the house wearing a cap with his hood up and his head down. There was no need to tempt fate. After all, people's memories were long, and it wouldn't take much for some nosey person to spot him and report his movement to the authorities.

By the time his driver pulled into Carter's long driveway, Owen was of the belief that he'd pushed it far enough and needed to get out of sight sooner rather than later.

Luckily for him, Carter's home was on several acres of land, surrounded by a tall fence, trees, and patrolled by security with dogs, who allowed Owen's car inside without issue. They directed him around the back of the house into an enclosed courtyard.

The long, winding driveway through the immense garden with scattered bushes and trees reassured him. He'd be able to get out, walk around the grounds and enjoy some freedom until this whole thing died down.

The house soon came into view, reminding Owen that Carter had done quite well out of their business relationship and invested his ill-gotten gains wisely. There were several cars parked up at the front of the property.

"Is anyone else here today, Mark?" Owen asked the driver, wondering if he'd spoken to Carter.

"No idea, boss. That's not something Carter is gonna tell me, is it?"

Owen grunted. "Doesn't mean he shouldn't."

"Well, we'll find out soon enough. Who are you expecting?"

Owen didn't answer, but he wondered if any of his family might show up, as they'd made a point of avoiding him while he was in prison. He knew why, of course. To many in the north Nottinghamshire community, the Masons were a respected and wealthy family who helped worthy causes and invested in the local community. Sure, there were rumours. There were always rumours, especially when money was involved, and the Masons were a rich lot. The press were always hunting for dirt, but so far, they'd been unable to make anything stick.

His father, Isaac, was good at that, and Owen had to give credit where credit was due. Nothing seemed to stick to him, and he always just walked away from any scandal as if nothing had happened. He felt sure something might stick one day, but not yet. The 'Teflon Don' referred to a well-known Mafia boss, but it suited his father perfectly.

It bothered him that his father had not come to see him in prison, even if he did understand why. He hoped to speak to him soon, once he settled in and felt satisfied no one knew where he was. They had business to discuss, mainly about his estranged brother, who Owen blamed entirely for this incarceration.

On reaching the house, Mark turned to the right and made his way around the back. A man directed them into the courtyard and motioned towards their parking spot.

The man nodded once as Owen climbed out. "Boss."

"Where's Carter?"

"Inside. He's waiting for you. I'll take you in." He led them across the courtyard and in through a set of double doors.

They veered right, through a living space to a smaller room in the centre of the house. It was a snug office lit by a warm lamp to one side, which cast shadows across the walls.

Owen spotted Carter inside and walked in, smiling. "Cheers for agreeing to this," he remarked.

"My pleasure," he said.

The moment Owen crossed the threshold, he knew they weren't alone. He could sense the third person in the room and turned to see his father sitting in the corner, watching him with a serious face.

Carter continued. "As long as you follow my rules, we'll be golden."

Owen glanced back at Carter, taking slight offence at his pedantic comment. He grunted before facing his dad. "Father. I had no idea…"

"Good," Isaac replied.

Owen nodded. Of course, his father would have planned this meeting carefully, making sure that no one knew about it other than those who absolutely needed to.

"Dad, we need to…" Owen began, keen to get down to business.

"Shut it," Isaac snapped, cutting Owen off.

He flinched in shock and stared at his father.

"You're a bloody idiot, Owen," Isaac continued. "I have no idea what you're playing at by going on the run, other than causing me a headache. Do you think it's easy to do what we do and keep the image of this family clean?"

Owen curled his lip. "It's not that clean…" he muttered.

Isaac banged his walking stick on the floor, and Owen flinched a second time. Only his father could put him on edge like this. "I don't give a shit what the police think or what the rumours say. In the eyes of the community, we're a respectful, charitable family. We do good work and we help people. That's all I care about. The pigs can run around looking for things they can pin on us all they like, as long as no one fucks with my system." He leaned forward, his eyes fixed on Owen's, and spoke in a guttural tone. "You're fucking with my system, Owen."

"I was being careful," Owen protested, aware he was sounding like a child being scolded by his father.

"Not careful enough. What the hell did you think you were playing at, creating a bloody Red Room, of all things."

"No one knew about it for years."

"Oh, really? Is that why there was all that graffiti around Retford, Mr Red Man?"

Owen shrugged. "Rumours." It was a cheap dig, using his fathers reasoning against him, but he couldn't resist.

"Quiet!" Isaac slammed his stick on the floor again to emphasise the word, before lifting the cane and jabbing it at him. "While you're here, while you're on the run, you keep your distance from me, and from the family, got it?"

He'd angered his father and felt bad. He needed him on his side, so it was not wise to push him too much. "Sure, Dad, I understand."

"I bloody well hope so." Isaac relaxed back into the chair, a scowl on his face.

"Congrats on your escape, that was smoothly done," Carter remarked, clearly trying to break the tension.

"Thanks!" Owen smiled.

"Apart from the gang war you started by indulging yourself... again." Isaac grunted from the corner of the room. "I don't know what goes through your head sometimes."

"He had it coming to him," Owen protested. "Hadley *and* his whole crew. The Killers need to know which gang is in charge around here."

Isaac scoffed at his comment.

"This is an opportunity for us," Owen pressed, wanting to reinforce his point and show his reasoning. "We can crush them and take over their operations. They're just kids playing at being gangsters. They don't do this professionally. They're not like us. We should make the most of this and use it to our advantage."

Carter nodded but seemed troubled. "I get what you're saying, but that's easier said than done. The Hyson Green Killers don't have a centralised leadership or an ordered hierarchy. It's more like a collection of leaders, each with a following that often overlaps with other parts of the gang, and the leadership is always in flux as they fight internally. They only truly unite against a common enemy, like us, but even then, it's a mess."

"They're a hydra," Isaac added. "You cut off one head, and two or more grow back to replace it."

"Exactly," Carter agreed.

"A what?" Owen asked, unsure what his father was talking about. "What's a hydra?"

Isaac sighed. "It doesn't matter. The point is, they're not easy to destroy. They have so many members and affiliated people scattered across the city and beyond, it's almost impossible to keep track of them all."

"Leave it to me, I'll destroy them," Owen replied, confident that he'd be able to do what his father thought was impossible.

"And how are you going to do that while in hiding?"

His father was goading him, trying to get the upper hand, but Owen wouldn't have it.

He sneered. "I have my ways."

"How delightfully vague of you."

Owen turned away, grimacing. "Whatever. That's not want I wanted to talk to you about," he said, keen to move the conversation on.

Isaac sighed and waved his hand, indicating that Owen should speak. "Go ahead."

"Rob," Owen began.

"Here we go."

Owen gritted his teeth before continuing. "You need to do something about him, Dad. He's ruining everything. He'll come for you, too, you know. You watch…"

"He can try."

"You need to do something. You need to end this."

Isaac shook his head. "I'll deal with Rob in my own way. He's my son, and I'm telling you right now, leave him alone. Start hunting down these HGK boys all you like, that's fine. But Rob is off limits."

"But, Dad…"

"But nothing. The subject's closed. I don't want to hear any more about it."

Owen clamped his mouth shut before he started sounding like a spoilt child again, then changed the subject to something more constructive. "Are you investigating Erika? There's something there. I don't know what it is, but she's important to him, or he is to her, I don't know, but…"

Isaac waved his hand again, imploring Owen to stop talking. "Enough. You leave Erika to me. In fact, I have someone looking into her right now."

Owen smiled, gratified that his father was taking him seriously, finally. "Good."

Chapter 8

Tuesday

Rob grasped Kurt's offered hand and shook it with a friendly smile and nod. "Thank you."

"No, no. Thank you," Kurt replied, his other arm around his daughter's shoulders. "I just hope you can find this psycho before he does it again."

"Me too." Rob gave Kurt's hand a friendly squeeze before releasing.

Breanna offered her hand, too. It felt small and limp in his grasp, like he could break or crush it with little effort. He gave it a gentle shake.

"And thank you, too. You've done well."

"Sorry I wasn't much help." There was a deep sadness in her voice. "I wish we could do more."

"I understand, but you've both done enough already. Because of your statements, we know more about how this killer operates, and that's useful."

"But we've given you so little." Her voice sounded weak and croaky.

"That in itself is useful, though. It tells us something about him," Rob continued. "Don't beat yourself up just because you don't have anyone in your life who doesn't want to hurt you. That's a good thing, believe me." His mind briefly strayed to thoughts of his father and brothers and the vile things they'd done.

"If there's anything else we can do, anything at all, just ask," Kurt added, pulling his daughter closer. "We want to help."

"We know," Nick said from beside Rob.

"Thank you," Rob added. "And if you remember anything that you think might be useful, please let us know as soon as you can."

"We will," Kurt confirmed.

"Excellent. Well, if you go with this constable, they just want to go over your statements quickly, and then you'll be on your way. Have you got somewhere to go?"

"I need to make some phone calls, but yeah, I think we'll be fine."

"Great. Take care."

Rob watched them depart with the uniformed officer. He turned, and with a quick nod to Nick, strode back to their office.

"They're squeaky clean," Nick commented as they walked.

"They're normal," Rob replied. "I believe most people don't have anyone in their lives who'd want to kill them. Not that I'd know anything about that based on my own life and the lives of most of the people I meet in this job."

Nick smirked. "Aye."

Rob sighed. "She was right, though. They've not given us much, if anything, to work with. No leads, no jilted family, no vengeful former lovers, nothing."

"But like you said, it gives us some insight into the killer."

"Yeah, but not much. It just tells us that this was random. He picked this family out of the crowd and, for whatever reason, decided to ruin their lives. Not exactly useful information as far as we're concerned."

They entered the office and took their seats.

"So, what do we have?" Rob asked.

"Just the physical evidence at the scene," Nick answered. "The gun, its ballistics, the explosive, and if we find any, maybe some DNA or fingerprints."

"We also have local CCTV and with luck, some witness statements."

"All of which we need to go through," Nick added. "Joy of joys."

"You love paperwork," Rob said with a smile.

"Yeah, like I love a bullet to the head."

Rob grimaced at the mental image and started to work through the files on his PC, until his phone rang. It was Alicia Aston, from the lab, he noted from the caller ID.

"Rob," she said when he answered. "I think I have something for you."

"I seriously hope so," he replied.

"Can you pop over?"

"Yeah, no problem. I'll be glad of a lead if you have one."

"I might... See you shortly."

Rob hung up to see Nick peering over at him. "Sounds promising. Who was it?"

"Alicia. Say's she has something for me."

"I bloody hope so," Nick said, echoing Rob's earlier statement.

Rob smiled. "Hey, that's my line."

Nick grinned. "Want me to come with? I've got plenty to work on here, but if you need a second pair of eyes?"

"Nah, I'll be fine," Rob said and got up from his desk. The lab was in another part of the station, in a connected building, but it didn't take too long for him to find his way.

He walked in, only to be hit with the smells of disinfectant and chemicals in the brightly lit space where Alicia worked. He found her to one side, where there was a cluster of desks. As the CSM, Alicia's was separated off with dividers, but he could see her clearly enough. She spotted him and got up from her desk, meeting him part way.

"Hope I wasn't disturbing you?" she began.

"No, not at all. We're a little light on leads right now, so if you have something, that would be amazing," Rob admitted.

"Maybe. Did the father and daughter give you anything to work with?" She led him across the room towards some workspaces littered with various examination equipment.

"Nope. Neither of them could think of anyone who might want to hurt them, let alone kill them in the manner that this guy did. So, we're back to the physical evidence from the scene. We've got the usual to check through. CCTV, statements from the neighbours, that kind of thing, and whatever you guys can find."

Alicia nodded. It was always a novelty to see her without her ever-present face mask and white scrubs that she wore to the crime scenes. "Right, well, I think you'll be interested to see this." She reached down and picked up something in a labelled clear plastic bag and briefly manipulated it before holding up for him.

Rob peered at the bag. It contained a brass shell casing that gleamed in the light, and on its side, he could make out some markings that shouldn't be there.

He frowned. "What's that?"

"It's two letters. BB. They've been scratched into the side of the casing."

"I take it this is the casing from the bullet that Kurt used to shoot his wife?"

"Unless Kurt was shooting other bullets around his house that we don't know about, yes." She raised an eyebrow.

Rob ignored the sarcasm. "BB. Hmm. Initials, maybe?"

"Could be. But that's for you to find out."

"Have you got a photo of this?"

Alicia smiled. She placed the evidence bag back on the worktop, opening a folder beside it and pulling out an A4 printout. It featured a close-up of the casing, angled to show the scratches, with a ruler beside it to provide a reference for the size. "Here. You can take this."

"Thanks."

"Do you think it's significant?"

Letters scratched into the bullet casing that killed his wife? The only bullet that was in that gun? Rob nodded. "Yeah, I'd say this is significant." He frowned. "I wonder if Kurt's still in the station?" he mused. He turned to Alicia. "Sorry, got to go. Great work."

She smiled as Rob turned and marched out. "No problem."

Chapter 9
Tuesday

Jacob's phone pinged, and a notification appeared on the screen. He picked it up from the table and saw a message from Mr Chowdhury. It was only short, and he could read the whole thing in the notification.

Be there in five.

Jacob sniffed and unlocked his phone. He quickly composed a reply.

See you shortly. I'm on my way. He hit send then pressed the power button, turning the phone screen black.

Taking a deep breath, Jacob glanced round the coffee shop and stuffed his phone back in his pocket. The server was heading over to his table. He smiled at her as she approached.

"All done?" she asked.

Jacob nodded. "I am, thanks. It was very nice." He knew her name but glanced at her name tag anyway. It had a single first name on it. "I've left a tip for you, Erika."

She grinned and inclined her head. "Thanks," she said brightly, taking the small plate with the random selection of coins on it. "Can I get you anything else?"

"No, I'm done. I was just leaving."

"Have a nice day." She grabbed the remains of his coffee and cake prior to walking off.

She was pretty with dark hair and probably of mixed race. He wondered who her parents were and got up, leaving the coffee shop behind. He was only a short walk from Nottingham's Old Market Square, where he'd arranged to meet Mr Chowdhury. It was an obvious and public place to use while he was on the job. He'd still be close to the coffee shop but far enough away that he wouldn't run into any problems.

Marching into the square, he navigated towards the meeting point, and sure enough, there he was, waiting. He recognised Nazir Chowdhury from the photos he'd seen online and took a moment to watch from a distance. He seemed to be alone and a little agitated checking his phone.

Deciding to put the man out of his misery, Jacob approached.

"Mr Chowdhury?" Jacob called out as he got close.

The Asian man seemed relieved to see him. "Mr Beasley?"

"Call me Jacob. Can I call you Nazir?"

He appeared a little surprised but quickly recovered and nodded. "Yeah, sure. What can I do for you? What's this about?"

"I just want to ask you a few questions, that's all. Nothing to worry about."

"About what? Am I in trouble?"

"No, no. Nothing like that," Jacob replied. "It's actually to do with one of your tenants."

"My tenants?"

"Erika Macey? She lives in the apartment you rent out in Trent Bridge Quays."

"Miss Macey. Yes, yes. Is there a problem I should know about?" He sounded agitated.

Jacob raised a hand to calm him down. "No. Not at all. It's more to find out a little more about her, really. I just have a few questions, if you don't mind."

Nazir frowned. "Um, okay."

Jacob directed Nazir towards a nearby bench. "Shall we?"

Nazir nodded, and they quickly sat.

"What do you want to know, Mr Beasley?"

Jacob gritted his teeth at the man's refusal to call him Jacob but said nothing. He seemed more than happy to answer questions, which was useful. Did he think he was with the police? Well, there was no need to dissuade him from that conclusion for now. "What do you know of Miss Macey? Is she a good tenant?"

"Very good, yes." Nazir's eyes were narrowed. "She's been no trouble at all."

"That's good. What about her references? Did you bring them?"

He nodded and withdrew some papers from the backpack he'd been carrying, moving in slow, deliberate motions. "Here you go. They're signed by her guarantor, John Nailer. He's a policeman. A detective, I believe."

"I see." Jacob glanced over the contract. It seemed typical. He pulled out his phone. "Do you mind if I take a photo of this?"

"No. I guess not."

Jacob quickly snapped a picture.

"She had a driver's licence as ID," he volunteered and handed him a printout of that, too.

Jacob photographed that, too, and noted the address. It was a Nottingham one, not too far from here, actually. Was it John Nailer's, he wondered. "Thank you for this. It's very helpful."

"Is she in trouble?"

"I don't think so, no," Jacob answered, unsure if she was or not, given who was paying him. He preferred not to think about that too much, as it just made him feel sick. *Think about the money*, he told himself. *Just focus on the money and get the job done*.

"Okay. But I don't understand, are you police? A detective?"

"No. I'm a private investigator. I've been hired to look into an issue, and Erika has something to do with it. But I must ask you to keep quiet about this meeting. She shouldn't know that we've met, okay? Because that would be bad... for both of us."

Nazir seemed a little worried but nodded anyway. "Of course, I understand. I won't say a word. Is there anything else I can do for you?"

"No, nothing. You've been very helpful. I'll be in touch if I need anything more." Jacob rose from his seat and offered Mr Chowdhury his hand.

Nazir shook it. "Okay, thank you."

"No, thank you," Jacob replied, pleased with his progress. He said goodbye and strolled back towards the coffee shop.

Chapter 10

Tuesday

Rob rushed back through the station, dodging between other officers and civilians going about their working day. He raced to reach Kurt before he left the station. He soon found the room where the victims had been going through statements with a supervising officer and barged in, only to find it empty, with no sign of Kurt, his daughter, the officer, or the statements they'd been going through.

The only logical conclusion was that they were finished and on their way out.

Rob set off for reception. It was a couple of corridors away, and as he approached the door into the main lobby, he spotted the officer who'd been helping with their statements.

"Hey," Rob called out, rushing up to the young man. "Where's Kurt and his daughter?"

"Oh, they're in reception, I think. I just left them..."

"Thanks." Rob darted towards the door and unlocked it with his lanyard. Bursting through, he spotted the pair of them.

Kurt was tapping on his phone, and they wandered towards the exit.

"Kurt," Rob called.

Kurt turned. Rob crossed the lobby and came to a stop before him.

Rob held his hand up and took a moment to catch his breath. "Sorry, I was rushing to find you before you left."

"That's okay, what's up?"

"I need to ask you about something we found at the crime scene."

"At... my house?"

Rob nodded. "Do you know what the letters BB mean?"

"BB?" Kurt seemed confused. "B? B?" He frowned in thought. "I'm not sure. Why?"

"Because they were carved into the bullet casing we recovered from your house. The casing of the bullet that you shot." He held up the printout Alicia had given him.

Breanna came in close to peer at the image beside her dad, who was frowning at it.

"Could it have something to do with you?" Rob asked, pointing at Breanna. "Initials, maybe?"

"My initials aren't BB," Breanna said with a quizzical eyebrow raised.

Kurt sighed, a look of realisation washing over him. "Oh."

"What is it?" Rob asked.

"Okay, so no, it's not Breanna's initials. Not this Breanna anyway. But it might be the initials of another Breanna."

"Explain," Rob pressed.

"Breanna Burke. She was my first and only other girlfriend before Sandy. We were quite serious at the time and were together for a few years towards the later half of my teens. We were very close, and Sandy was her best friend. But at sixteen she caught meningitis, suffered complications, and sadly passed away. I was devastated, and so was Sandy. In the years following that, I grew very close to Sandy, and we eventually became a couple. We both missed Breanna very much, which was why we named our daughter after her."

"I see," Rob muttered as he processed what this all might mean. He glanced back down at the photo of the bullet and tried to make the jigsaw pieces fit. "So, was there any bad blood between you and your wife over Breanna? Was she jealous or anything?"

"No, not at all. We talked about Breanna often and we were always very open about it all. Our love for each other developed after Breanna died, and it was never an issue."

"So, there was nothing about your previous relationship with her that might cause Sandy anguish or upset? Or upset you enough to want to hurt Sandy?"

"No, never," Kurt answered. He sounded hurt.

"Sorry, I have to ask," Rob said quickly, sensing his emotion.

He nodded. "I know. It's okay. It's just… Everything's still really raw."

"Of course. But this doesn't answer the question. Why would the killer carve these initials into the casing? Why would he do that and how does he know about Breanna Burke?"

Kurt frowned again, clearly just as confused and concerned as Rob felt.

"This has to mean something," Rob added. "The killer clearly did this on purpose and wanted us to find it. He wouldn't have left the casing behind along with the gun had he not wanted us to discover this."

"I agree. He went to a lot of trouble over this," Kurt said. "But I'm really not sure what it could mean beyond being Breanna's initials, or why he would put her initials on there."

"Is it a game?" Breanna asked.

"What do you mean?" Kurt asked.

"Well, the killer said it himself. He's the Games Master, so maybe this is a game to him. A clue. He's leading us somewhere, like on a treasure hunt?"

Rob narrowed his eyes at the young woman and her quick reasoning. She might be onto something, and he wanted to keep her going down that path. "And where would BB make you go, if it was part of a treasure hunt in your house?"

"My room?" Breanna suggested.

"No," Kurt replied. "That's not it. No. I know where it would take me. I know exactly where I'd go."

"Where?" Rob asked.

Chapter 11

Tuesday

"Are you sure you want to do this?" Guy asked, tapping the glass of his pint as he sat in the back of the pub. "There are other ways."

Bill shot him a glance that seemed full of contempt. "Are you scared?"

"I'm concerned, yes," Guy replied. "I've not spoken to some of these men in weeks and have no idea how they'll react, or if they're even still receptive."

"Are you changing your position on them? You said they were loyal to you, not the Masons."

"They are… They were. I think."

"Stop being such a bloody wimp," Bill snapped. "We're doing this."

Guy sighed, torn, frustrated, and nervous, but what choice did he have? Isaac Mason, his boss and mentor, had disowned him after Rob and the others in the police had discovered that he was working for the Masons. He understood why. He wasn't a member of the family and his usefulness was greatly diminished now his cover was blown.

Isaac probably saw him as a liability more than anything else and had chosen to cut his losses. So between that and the police hunting for him, his options had been limited. Bill seemed to be the only lifeline he had, the only person who wanted to work with him, and even that was grudging. Bill recognised how Guy had manipulated him and forced him into a situation that had turned him into the very thing he hated.

But Bill still had a fixation on Rob. Still convinced that he was corrupt, despite what Guy had told him, he'd made it his mission to discredit Rob and bring him down, and the way he saw it, the answer to that lay somewhere within the Mason organisation.

This meant that Bill's goals broadly aligned with Guy's. He hated the Masons, and to a lesser extent, Rob. Bill felt the same but with the opposite emphasis.

Their alliance was one of necessity and convenience, and little else, but that was enough for now.

"And if this goes tits up?" Guy asked.

"There's a million ways to skin a cat, Guy. There's always another way."

Guy grimaced and sipped his pint while they waited for his crew to appear. He'd gathered these men into a tight-knit group over the years, working within the Mason organisation to make money through their operation. Guy had been under no illusion that one day his time in the police would end. One day, the police would find out who he worked for, and everything would come crashing down. So he needed to be prepared for that.

But despite his best efforts to keep these five men distrustful of the Masons, they were still embedded within that organisation and subject to its influences. He was surer of some of them than others, but there was always that risk with them. Their ultimate allegiance might be with Isaac, and not him, or it could be with themselves. These men were sharks in their own right after all, and if they saw weakness within Guy, they might turn on him.

There were just too many unknowns to be sure, and there was really only one way for him to find out what the truth of all this was.

He needed to stop being a wimp and find out.

Guy sucked in a long breath and did his best to calm his nerves and centre himself. He needed this to go well, and he needed to be on form.

It wasn't much longer before five familiar men walked into the pub and stopped off at the bar for a drink before making their way over. Oli Taylor led the way. He was the natural leader of the crew and a thick-set man who Guy felt sure could crush him if he wanted to. The others followed. Bruce, Declan, Kris, and Murrey. They all seemed on edge, scanning around the pub as they strode over, hunting for any signs of a trap.

"Oli!" Guy rose to his feet, offering his hand. He fixed Oli with a stare, silently challenging him, wanting to know the man's loyalties.

"Guy," he muttered in reply and shook the offered hand. He moved to take a seat.

The other four followed suit, shaking Guy's hand in turn.

Eventually, Guy retook his seat in the middle of a bench, his back to the wall. Unmoved and watching with interest, Bill sat off to one side, catching sideways glances from the five men. Guy could see them staring in Bill's direction, wondering who the hell he was and what was he doing here.

"We heard," Oli said in clipped tones. "You've been cut loose."

"I have." Guy shrugged. "Doesn't matter. Doesn't change much. Just tells me who the Masons are. Who Isaac is. And now I know."

"Is that why we're here?" Oli asked.

"You want to know what side we're on?" Bruce added.

Guy smiled. "Perceptive. I knew you were good. That's why I created this crew, and why you're on it. Isaac has shown his true colours, and they're not pretty. He doesn't care about me, and he doesn't care about you. He cares only about himself, and he'll cut you five loose at a moment's notice. Hell, if he knew you were here, he'd probably have you killed." Guy smiled. "But we're better than that."

Oli was nodding.

"This isn't the first time you've warned us about them," Kris said.

"I know, but it's always worth reiterating. It's also worth remembering that I am not like that. I am loyal to those who remain loyal to me, and I will protect my friends."

"Great speech," Oli stated.

"Look, we're here, aren't we?" Declan stated. "We're on your side."

"Yeah," Murrey agreed. "If we were working with the Masons, they would have turned up, not us."

"Which brings us back to why we're here," Oli added. "There must be a reason."

"There is," Guy confirmed and took a breath. The moment of truth, he thought. It was now or never. "I've…"

Bill coughed.

Guy glanced at him before continuing. "We've brought you here because, now we know who Isaac truly is, we can make plans."

"Plans?" Oli asked.

"Do you think I'm going to allow Isaac to get away with this?"

"No," Oli stated.

"You're damn right, I'm not." Guy leaned forward. "But I need you guys. I can't do this alone. I just needed to know where you all stand."

"What did you have in mind?" Oli asked.

"The Masons are dealing with some shit right now," Bill stated from the corner.

Oli glanced over and then faced Guy. "Who's this guy?"

"That's Bill. He's working with me on this."

Oli turned back to Bill and scoffed. "Never heard of him."

"Guy and I are equal partners in this endeavour." Bill sat up straight. "This is our mission, and we wondered if you guys wanted in on the ground floor."

Guy found himself pleasantly surprised by Bill's talk of a partnership, although he wasn't sure if Bill actually believed that. He suspected not.

"Fair enough." Oli sniffed.

"May I continue?" Bill asked, his words laced with sarcasm.

Guy cringed at Bill's tone.

Oli waved his hand, indicating that he should continue.

"Like I was saying, the Masons are in the shit, dealing with Owen's action when he escaped from custody. The Hyson Green Killers are on the warpath, and I think we can take advantage of that."

"How?" Oli asked.

Bill grinned and relaxed back into his chair. "Guy here says that one of you has links to the Killers. That you might be able to get me a meeting with them. Was he lying?"

Guy gritted his teeth and scanned the faces of his crew, coming to rest on Declan Lacey. Declan met his gaze and seemed briefly uncomfortable.

"Nah, he wasn't lying," Declan said. "I... might be able to do that."

Bill's smile widened. "Now that's what I wanted to hear."

Chapter 12

Tuesday

The evening was drawing in by the time Rob had driven to Kurt's house. He sighed and took a moment to relax in the driver's seat as he thought back over the day and the small mountain of work he had on. As usual, these new cases always overlapped with old ones, so while he was hunting for clues to find the killer of Kurt's wife, he was still dealing with several other cases, putting together all the evidence for court cases and re-interviewing witnesses and suspects and entering evidence into the casebook.

It was never-ending. One of the recent and time-consuming cases had been the fallout from Guy Gibson, and the revelation that he'd been working with his father all these years. He was an undercover mole for the Mason family, working within the police, and none of them ever had any clue about it.

Hell, he'd dated Erika briefly, which, knowing now that Erika was his half-sister and daughter to his mother, was a terrifying thought. And he didn't even want to think about what might have happened if he hadn't got into that Red Room when he had.

Just the very idea of it sent shivers down his spine.

If he ever needed any proof that his estranged family were utter monsters, that was by far the most damning, even if Owen had done it without family approval.

It didn't matter, Rob concluded. Owen was scum, and so was Isaac and all the others. They didn't deserve any sympathy.

Gathering his wits, Rob jumped out of his black Ford Capri and made his way towards the house. The cordon was gone. Only the police tape on the door and the officer standing outside hinted at what had happened here.

Rob flashed his warrant card.

"Sir?" the officer on guard said.

"I need access."

"Of course." The man fumbled with the door. "Have you made any progress? Any leads?"

"Not really, no. But I'm hoping I might find something inside."

The man nodded. "Oh, okay. Good luck," the man said and stepped out of the way after opening the door.

Rob thanked him and ducked through the tape into the corridor, before closing the door. The sounds of the street outside died, leaving him in the silence of the empty house and the remnants of the crime scene. Stuffing his hands in his pockets, Rob crept down the corridor into the kitchen and paused at the threshold to scan the room where the lives of this family had been destroyed. It hadn't been cleaned yet, and the bloodstains still marked the floor and chair.

Rob grimaced at the scene and tried to imagine himself in Kurt's place, faced with an impossible choice, and wondered how he might have navigated it. But that train of thought led him down a shadowed path that he preferred to stay away from.

He shook those dark thoughts away and turned back to the hallway.

Pulling out the printout, he took another quick look at the image of the marked casing, turning it over and checking the notes he'd made after speaking with Kurt.

He needed to be upstairs. Rob took the short walk up to the first floor, making sure to not touch anything he didn't need to. At the top of the stairs, he peered into the selection of rooms, quickly finding the daughter's room, then what seemed to be a guest room, finally finding the parents' bedroom alongside the communal bathroom. Rob stepped into the bedroom, following Kurt's directions, and headed over to the wardrobe. Reaching into his pocket, he removed a pair of latex gloves and pulled them on, then opened the wardrobe doors.

At the bottom of the cabinet, beneath the hung clothing, was a small dumping ground of more clothes, shoes, old, framed photos, and boxes of unknown detritus. He took some of the stuff out and soon found a small wooden keepsake box towards the bottom of the pile. As Kurt had described, the initials BB had been etched into the clasp.

Rob stared at it for a long moment, wondering if it might be a trap. After a few seconds, he decided to take a risk and carefully drew the box out. It wasn't too heavy and only about twenty centimetres across. Rob carried it to the bed and peered at it for a minute. Again, there didn't seem to be anything suspicious about it, and the clasp wasn't locked.

But still, they were dealing with a man who seemed to relish playing games, and Rob couldn't help but feel nervous. He'd certainly feel something of an idiot if he opened this box and got blown to pieces.

Mary wouldn't be happy with him. He allowed himself a wry smile.

"Nah, he wouldn't," Rob reasoned and opened the box.

The clasp was magnetic and popped open easily, allowing the lid to smoothly lift away and reveal its contents.

Inside were photos, notes, letters, an old troll toy with pink hair, and other treasured things. But, stuck to the inside of the lid, was a scrap of paper that didn't belong.

It was a handwritten note, but the handwriting was different from what was on the other bits of paper. It also seemed newer and fresher.

Rob twisted his head to get a better look and read the simple sentence scrawled on it.

The more Chaotic I am, the more complete I am.

Beneath it, there was a small hand-drawn chaos symbol, and seeing it made Rob's stomach drop.

It was only a few weeks ago, but he was still dealing with the aftermath of the Poppet Killer case and its links to this doctrine of chaos. They had precious little to go on, other than two killers who seemed to be in contact with someone online calling themselves the Ashen King, and their belief in chaos. It was like some kind of weird cult or something, but the one thing that they all had in common was this symbol.

Arrows, all pointing out from a central point, like a star. It had its origins in an unrelated fantasy book, and the symbol had then been taken on by believers in chaos magic.

And now, this new killer might be another believer in this chaos bunkum. Was he a follower of the Ashen King, too, Rob wondered?

With a sigh, he took out his phone to take some photos, only for it to ring as he held it.

The ID on the screen identified the caller as Erika.

Chapter 13

Tuesday

"All right, thanks," Erika said. She stepped out of the kitchen at the back of the coffee shop into the empty dining area. With the lights off, it was dark and eerie in here. Rooms like this needed people in them for them to feel alive and welcoming. But when they were devoid of life and silent, she found them creepy.

She crossed the room and approached the glass front.

"Gimmie a moment," Sarah called from behind her. "I'll be there in a second."

"No worries," Erika replied and waited for her boss to let her out of the locked shop.

She checked her phone, but there was little there that was new or interesting, so she dropped her hand to her side and peered out through the window. With the lights off, she could clearly see the darkened streets. There were still plenty of people walking back and forth, going home or doing some evening shopping in the larger stores.

She scanned over the scene and found her eyes drawn to a man standing on the opposite side of the road, maybe two hundred metres away. He was facing roughly her way and seemed to be waiting for something or someone.

She frowned at the man. He was too far away to get a clear look at him, but she had a feeling she recognised him. Chewing on her tongue, she thought back over the day and glanced into the shop.

Yeah, he'd been in here earlier, and she'd served him, if it was the same person and she wasn't mistaken. She turned back to where he was still standing and grimaced. Was he waiting for her, or was she imagining things?

"Right, here we go," Sarah said. She crossed the dining area, her keys jangling as she walked. "Let's let you out."

Erika smiled at her boss who unlocked the door with practiced movements.

"See you tomorrow," Sarah said.

"Yeah, see ya," Erika answered. She glanced up the street, turned away from where the man was standing, and set off. He was still there. Erika strode away, planning out the route back to her car. She needed to check behind her, to see if the man was following, but she didn't want to make it too obvious. As she walked, she picked out a random shopfront and tried to seem like she was interested in what was inside. She turned her head as she walked, twisting until she could glance up the street and get a good look.

He was there, and he was following her.

Or was he? Was she being paranoid? Was he just a random man who happened to be walking in the same direction she was? Was it maybe not even the same man she'd served in the coffee shop? It had been hours ago, so she might be mistaken.

It was possible that everything that had been going on with Rob and her mother was making her skittish and suspicious of things she had no reason to worry about.

Picking out a random route back to her car, she quickly made a left and hurried up the next street. If he was still behind her after two or three corners, then she'd panic, but not yet. This could all be down to her overactive imagination still, so there was no reason to work herself up into a frenzy just yet.

She made several turns in quick succession along side streets, marching as fast as she could without breaking into a run, until she finally hit another longer straight that took her closer to her car.

She was most of the way down it when she finally glanced back, hoping that she wouldn't see the same man following.

But she was sadly disappointed.

He was there, in the distance, still on her tail. As she watched, he veered down a side street and disappeared from view.

Erika grimaced and pressed on to her car. It was where she'd left it in the car park, and despite scanning around, she couldn't see the man anywhere. He'd disappeared, for now.

She checked the back seat before getting in and locked the door once she was inside. There was no need to tempt fate. She drove away and left the car park behind.

Two streets later, she thought she saw the man again in the same coat and jeans, watching her drive by. She couldn't get a good look at him, and she'd driven past by the time she'd realised.

She scrambled to catch sight of him in her mirrors, only to narrowly miss an oncoming car. Its baring horn snapped her back to the situation she was driving into and saved her from a crash.

"Damn it," she cursed, angry with herself, and still not totally sure of what she was seeing. The drive home didn't take long, but she spent it staring at the cars in her rear-view mirror, wondering if one of them was carrying her new stalker.

If she was right, who was it? Who was following her, and why? What did they want? The obvious conclusion she came to was that of her mother. Did they suspect her links to Rob, maybe even to Nailer, and were attempting to confirm them?

But, who for? Was it the Masons? Were they finally onto her? And, if they were, what should she do?

She eventually parked up outside her apartment block and dashed in through the rear entrance, feeling like she might be grabbed by something at any moment. She felt like a child who was scared of the dark and sprinting to bed after switching the light off in case the monsters got her.

But this was worse than any imagined fantasy creature, this was real. This was a person who might wish her or her family harm.

She reached the first floor and glanced over at Rob's front door and paused. Should she bother him with this? For a moment, she discounted it, and then she changed her mind and walked to his door and knocked.

Seconds passed, but there was no answer.

She cursed, went to her place and let herself in, making sure to lock the door once she was inside. Dumping her bag, she reached for her lights, freezing in place and thinking about what she was about to do.

No, she wanted to see outside. She wanted to know what was going on out there, around her home. She crossed her living space and peered out through the windows, scanning the pavements and roads around her apartment, until she spotted a man walking along the side of the river, approaching her block.

It was the same man, she was sure of it.

As he approached, he glanced up at her building, and this might be her paranoia taking over, but she felt like he was staring specifically at her apartment.

He moved out of sight, around the front of the building, but she'd seen enough and grabbed her phone.

"Rob," she said, when her call connected. "I think I'm being followed."

Chapter 14

Tuesday

Having left Kurt's house as quickly and carefully as possible, Rob had sped home through the city streets to his and Erika's apartment block, pushing his way through traffic and breaking the speed limit most of the way. He relished the acceleration and opening the car up. The feeling of speed he got from the Capri was like nothing else. Certainly, no modern car could give him that same feeling.

But he didn't have the capacity to truly enjoy it tonight. His mind was on Erika and her possible stalker.

His thoughts went immediately to Isaac and the Masons, and what they might do if they knew who Erika really was, and who her mother was. Were they looking into her? Did they suspect she had secrets that would be of value to Isaac?

It was certainly possible, and the thought was a sobering one.

He needed to get home.

The trip seemed to drag out and take forever. It felt like every slow driver in the city had decided that this was the perfect time to clog the streets. He felt persecuted by them, as if they were purposefully seeking him out to impede his journey.

Of course, this was all just his perception and a world away from reality. He knew this deep down, but it didn't stop him from thinking it while shouting and cursing at other drivers, demanding that they get out of his damn way.

Only his concern for the lives of others—and the Capri's bodywork—kept him from forcing his way through several of the junctions.

Eventually he eased into his road and blasted down it, skidding to a halt at a jaunty angle across two spaces. He jumped out and paused for a moment, scanning the residents' parking area for any hint of this stalker Erika had been talking about.

But no one was hanging around, appearing suspicious. The area seemed quiet and unremarkable, as it usually did. Rob bit his lip in consternation. Locking his car, he darted to the entrance and let himself in. On the first floor, he stepped up to Erika's door and knocked.

"Hey, Erika. It's me."

"Rob?" she called from the other side.

He heard something being pulled away from the door, and the lock turn before it finally opened.

"Thank God you're here."

"Are you okay?" he asked, stepping in.

She pulled the door wide. Suddenly, she grabbed him, drawing him in for a sisterly hug.

"Oh, okay. It's all right."

"Sorry," she said, easing away. "I've just been getting myself all worked up. My mind was racing, thinking that someone was stalking me, and… and…"

"It's okay. It's totally understandable." He shut the door behind him. "Shall we sit down? You can tell me all about it."

"Yeah, sure."

They moved to the sofa where she picked up a cushion and hugged it, curling up into a ball. She seemed skittish and worried as she related the brief story of walking to her car from work, and the man she thought was following her. Rob listened intently. She told him she thought she saw the man outside, by the river. She seemed noticeably calmer once she'd finished.

"How sure are you he was following you? Was this a coincidence, or were your eyes playing tricks on you? I don't mean to patronise you, but the brain can do silly things when you're hyped up on adrenaline and scared."

She nodded and attempted a calming breath. "Sorry. But I'm honestly not totally sure. I don't think I was imagining things. I'm about as certain as I can be that someone was following me. That's not very helpful, but I don't know what else I can tell you."

Rob nodded. "That's okay. For what it's worth, I believe you. After everything the Masons have done, this feels very much like something they would do." He sighed. "But if they're following you, I wonder what that means? Do they know that you're Nailer's daughter and think you can lead them to..." He let the sentence hang.

"Mum."

"Or something, or someone. They might not suspect that link between us yet."

"Hopefully not."

"Or, maybe Guy didn't tell Isaac about your link to Nailer, and this is Isaac's way of looking into you... if this man is something to do with the Masons, which he might not be."

"Christ, this sucks." Erika gasped. "I can't live like this."

"We have no choice. We have to. We need to keep mum safe."

"I know. I just, I hate this. Hate it."

Rob nodded and sighed. "I'll see what other options we have, but I think I need to talk to Nailer and discuss solutions. We need to be proactive. We need to fight back."

"Yeah, sure. Sorry I brought you over here."

He smiled warmly at her. "Don't worry about it. I'm happy to come and see you. What are brothers for, after all?"

"It still sounds weird hearing you say that."

"I know the feeling. It sounds odd saying it. But I have a sister now, and I don't want you coming to any more harm."

She smiled and flushed. "Thanks. How was your day?"

Rob grinned. "Busy, as usual."

"I saw on the news about the man who was forced to shoot his wife. Is that your case?"

"Yeah, that's me. We're on it. It's crazy what some people will do."

"I hope you find him."

"Me too." He stood. "Do you want to come over? You can stay at mine, if you like."

She shook her head. "No, I'm fine. I'm feeling better now. I'll be okay here. Thank you, though."

"Any time. And, if you change your mind, you have a key, just let yourself in, okay?"

"Yeah. Thank you." She got up and hugged him again.

He said his farewells, nipped across the landing to his apartment, and let himself in. Halfway down the hall, he pulled his shoes off, and Muffin, his black cat, appeared and nuzzled his legs while meowing loudly.

"You want some food?" Rob asked and walked into the kitchen. He refilled Muffin's bowl and watched the fur ball tuck into his evening meal. Rob took out his phone and called Nailer.

He answered. "Thanks for your text earlier. Is she okay?"

"Erika is fine," Rob replied and moved to the windows that looked out over the River Trent. He scanned the path that ran along the side of the river but didn't see anyone acting suspiciously. "I believe her. She was probably followed, but I don't know by who, or why. I think we need to take this seriously. We both know what the Masons are capable of."

"Agreed. If they thought Erika had some useful information for them, they'd happily do this and more. So, what do you want to do?"

"We've discussed this before, but I think the time has come. We need to bring Riddle and Calico in on this. Get them poking into it."

"Calico I'm fine with, but Riddle? Do you know if you can trust her?"

"I've worked with her a couple of times now on unrelated stuff since the Red Room case, and she's always come through for me. Also, she has no love for the Masons, that's for certain. She was the one who got Mary involved in all that."

"So, you trust her?"

"I do. Mary does, too, and she's had way more contact with her than we have."

"Okay. I still don't like that we don't know who she is, but I suppose actions speak louder than words. I guess we'll be paying her for this, too?"

"Of course. So, shall I bring her in? We need someone like her to hunt online for what we need."

"I know. Okay, yeah, go for it. Bring her in, Calico, too. Let's find out who this idiot is who's following Erika."

"I think you need to keep an eye out yourself, too. If they're onto her, then they might come after you, too. And me."

"I'll be vigilant," Nailer answered. "Make the calls and get Calico and Riddle onto it. Keep me up to date with anything they find, okay?"

"Will do. Oh, and I almost forgot. So, you know the bullet casing with the initials on it? I spoke to Kurt about it, and it led to a box in his wardrobe at his house. I found a fresh note in the box, bearing the chaos symbol. The same symbol from the Poppet case, and that massacre. The note read, *'The more Chaotic I am, the more complete I am.'*"

"Aaah, crap. Really?"

"Really."

"They follow someone, don't they? They have a leader?"

"The Ashen King."

"That's the one. Right, okay. Well, keep digging."

"Will do, sir." He hung up. He had work to do.

Chapter 15

Tuesday

Climbing out of the car and slamming the door shut, Guy strode to the nearby junction and peered along the various roads leading off it. Night had fallen, and the streetlights blazed in the darkness, casting an eerie glow over Hyson Green. Seemingly endless terraced houses hemmed them in, crammed into the street to provide as much low-cost housing as possible. Many of them would be council-owned, creating a variation in appearance that was stark.

Rephrased: Some were immaculately cared for, boasting recent paint jobs and manicured gardens, or what little gardens they had anyway. Others looked like they'd been left to rot and ruin, with no one to care for them.

He turned back to the car, where Bill was standing.

"I don't like it."

"What's to like? This is where we need to be."

Across the street, a little further up, the rest of Guy's crew exited two more parked cars. Declan came over first.

"Ready?" he asked.

"Not really," Guy replied.

Declan glanced at Bill and then back to Guy. "So, are we doing this?"

"We're doing this," Bill said, his tone severe.

"Because we don't have to. I mean, they wouldn't like it, but…"

"We're doing it," Bill reiterated.

"Yeah, we are," Guy agreed. "I just don't enjoy being here, and I don't like their demands."

Declan shrugged as the rest of the crew joined them. "I doubt very much that they trust us either. They're just taking precautions."

"Yeah, if you like. So, where is this Cold Cutz, or whatever his stupid name is? Where are we going?" He scanned around, checking for anything obvious. "We're here and ready, where they told us to be."

"I've just had a text through with some instructions," Declan said, taking out his phone. "I think I know where they are."

"And it's just us three, right?" Guy pointed to Bill, to include him in the trio that the gang had said they'd meet.

"Yeah. Me, you, and Bill. That's it," Declan confirmed.

"Lovely," Guy muttered with no humour. He turned to the rest of his crew. "Right then, you guys wait here, and if we're not back in fifteen minutes, or you don't hear anything, come and find us. Declan, make sure they have these directions and know where we are if things go sour."

"Already done," Declan confirmed.

Guy bit his lip. An idea struck him, and he pulled his phone and called Oli. Oli's phone buzzed. "Answer it, it's me. Keep the line open, and listen in. If things go to shit, you know what to do."

Oli nodded as he answered his phone. "Sure thing."

He addressed Declan. "All right, let's not keep these clowns waiting, shall we?"

He glanced at Bill who nodded and moved to join them. They fell into step with Declan.

"So, who is this Cold Cutz, dude?" Guy asked.

"I know his first name is Thaddeus, but other than that, I just know him as Cold Cutz. He's one of the crew leaders within the Hyson Green Killers. I knew him back when I ran with them, as a teenager. He's worked his way up since then, though. But I kept in touch."

"Useful," Bill remarked.

They walked up the street, turning into the next junction and around the end terrace. They reached a snicket alleyway that led between the houses that backed onto each other.

"Up here," Declan said and dipped into the narrow alley lined with brick walls, fences, and gates on either side that led into the back gardens of each house.

There was the usual collection of bin bags, discarded and rusting bikes, a mouldy sofa that you'd likely catch syphilis from if you sat on the thing, mixed with the occasional hanging basket or planter with depressed shrubs in them. They were a valiant, but ultimately futile attempt to brighten up the place. In Guy's opinion, little could be done—short of flattening the place—to improve the visual of this back alley. As they continued, he spotted bits of foil and discarded syringes scattered about. The telltale detritus of drug taking. They were close.

A man stepped out from an open back gate, wearing a frown. He was thick-set, mean-looking, and sneered at them. "Declan?"

"That's me," Declan said.

"Who are *these* fucks?"

Declan pointed to each in turn. "Guy and Bill, I told Cold about them, he was cool with it."

"A ménage à trois, huh?" He gave them a quick glance up and down, before moving to one side. "Step into my office." He waved at the gate.

Guy followed Declan through into a small, walled back yard. Apart from the weeds growing up through the cracks in the paving slabs, there wasn't an inch of grass or greenery in the space at all. But there *were* six young men, all of whom glared at them when they entered. Guy picked up a strong smell of cannabis and noted the cans of beer scattered around. The yard was lit up by a rear light on the back of the house and some pitiful fairy lights strung around the walls.

The twinkling lights didn't make the scene any more inviting, however. Several of the young men stood as they entered They knew right away that they weren't part of the gang.

Guy kept a stoic face with his eyes level and took in the scene, making sure to give each gang member a second or so of attention as he swept his gaze around. He wanted to keep his wits about him and try to be aware of where everyone was. It was a delicate balance. Glancing down made him appear weak, looking up seemed aloof and not present, but staring at them might provoke them. He needed this to run smoothly with a positive outcome for their goals.

"Frisk them," Gate Man said. He followed Bill in and closed the gate behind him.

Three of the crew approached, one for each of them, and patted them down, making sure they were unarmed.

Guy had emptied his pockets back at the car, anticipating this, and it was good to see that the other two had done likewise.

"They're good," one of them said.

"Is Cold ready?" Gate Man asked.

"I'll check," another stated and disappeared inside, leaving them standing in the middle of the yard.

Taking a second gander around, Guy spotted several guns held just out of sight by the surrounding men and did his best to remain calm. There was no need to suspect that they would use them. They were being cautious, and that was fine. He understood that suspicion of outsiders and would honestly have done the same in the reverse situation.

"What you staring at, fuckface?" one of them snapped, glaring at Bill.

"I don't know, but it's gawping back at me," Bill answered smartly.

Guy sighed and rolled his eyes.

"What you say?" the young man barked, furious.

"Oi," Gate Man barked. "Leave it."

The mouthy kid, who clearly wasn't out of his teens yet, and wouldn't be for a few years, grimaced and backed off. He seemed to be spoiling for a fight.

Guy glanced back at Bill, who briefly met his gaze and mouthed a single word. 'What?'

The young man who'd gone inside returned. "He's ready."

Gate Man stepped forward and waved to the back glass door. "In you go."

"Thanks," Declan replied, leading them in through the rear patio doors.

They navigated through a darkened room with a couple of guys sitting on opposite sofas. Both had sub machineguns on their laps and scrolled on their phones. The pair watched Guy and the others walk through with the cold eyes of killers. Another man waited for them at the door and waved them through to the next room where five men were sitting slumped in sofas and armchairs. Others, a mix of mainly young men and a few young women, were scattered around, standing or perched on furniture. The man in the middle, at the far end of the room, who wore sunglasses and smoked a chunky spliff, caught Guy's eye. Was he the one they were here to see?

The haze of smoke and the keen smell of marijuana on the air told him they'd been smoking for a while, and it felt like he might get high from just standing there.

No one spoke. They all just stared at them with undisguised disgust and contempt.

Declan cut the tension with a cough and nodded to the man Guy had picked out as the one they were here to see. "Cold. Thanks for meeting with us."

Cold waved him off with dismissive gesture, pointing at him and Bill. "What you want?"

"We want to help you," Guy said.

Cold laughed, a deep, mocking sound that Guy didn't enjoy. "You? Want to help us? What the fuck can you do for us?"

There was a chorus of mocking laughter from the others in the room.

"Well…"

Bill stepped forward, barging past Guy. Several of the men who'd been relaxing sat forward. Guns were pulled.

Guy stiffened and held his breath. The room suddenly felt like it was on a knife edge, and any sudden movement might tip it one way or the other.

"Watch yourself, bruv," Cold said, his voice taking on the tone of his namesake. "Wouldn't want to get yourself killed, would yeh. We've got some itchy trigger fingers in 'ere."

"We want to hurt the Masons as much as you do."

"I doubt it," Cold cut in. "That prick, Owen, killed my brother. I want him dead, and I want him to know it was me."

It all suddenly clicked in Guy's mind. "Hadley Watts was your brother?" he asked.

Cold nodded. "I'm his younger brother, Thaddeus Watts."

"Then you know as well as I do that they're colossal pricks," Bill said, taking back control of the conversation. "I think we can work together, towards a common goal. Also, we have something that you don't."

"Oh?" Cold asked. "And what's that?"

"Inside knowledge. Several of my crew used to work inside the Masons' operation until we were thrown out. Now it's time for some revenge."

Cold glowered at him, his top lip twitching.

"Or not," Bill said and turned partially away. "We'll do it on our own anyway and keep all the spoils for ourselves." He took a step towards the door.

Ballsy, Guy thought. Bill wasn't messing about.

"What spoils?"

Bill turned, an incredulous expression on his face. "Are you kidding me? What spoils? They have a lucrative network of operations, from drug dealing to extortion and more, plus contacts and gear. You could take over the Nottingham arm of their operation, doubling or tripling yours in the process."

Guy could tell it was working. The atmosphere in the room had changed, and Cold was clearly interested. He sat forward, pushing away the girl who was sitting on the arm of his chair.

"All right, sure. I'm interested. How do you wanna do this?"

Bill smiled and reached into his pocket.

Several of the guns snapped up.

Bill froze and then slowly withdrew a phone from his pocket. He smiled as the guns dropped, and tossed it to Cold. "Call me. We'll swap intel."

Cold nodded, his gaze fixed on Bill, assessing him. "Will do."

Bill nodded once and turned to the door where the gangster who'd ushered them in stood, his gun by his side, blocking the exit. Bill stepped right up to him and glared at the taller man.

Guy watched nervously.

Bill coughed and politely said, "Excuse me." He even waved his hand dismissively at the man, who looked towards Cold at the other side of the room.

Guy glanced back to see Cold Cutz nod once.

The thug stepped out the way, and Bill walked through the doorway. Guy following quickly, glad to be out of there, with Declan close on his heels. The walk through the house and back garden was tense, but uneventful, and no one got in their way or said anything of consequence.

Hustling up the snicket, Guy felt like the gang might suddenly come running or shoot them, but nothing like that happened. They exited the dark alleyway and returned to the road.

"I bloody hate working with idiots like that," Guy stated, relieved to be out of there. "I get that we have to do it, and give them something at the end, but Christ, I didn't enjoy that at all."

"You promised them quite a lot," Declan added, standing on the other side of Bill. "Do you think they'll uphold their side of things?"

"When it comes to these kids," Bill replied, "I couldn't give a shit about them. I'll use them while they're useful to get what I want, but they're a means to an end and little else. And as for what I promised them," he shrugged, "we'll see. They won't get anything that I want for myself."

Guy nodded, pleased that Bill was thinking ahead.

Chapter 16

Tuesday

Thaddeus relaxed into his seat. The room erupted into low-level discussion and laughter following the visit from Declan and his two friends. He wasn't sure quite what to make of the two clowns who came with him, Guy and Bill, and if it wasn't for Declan, he'd never have given them the time of day.

They'd spoken on the phone earlier that day, after he'd found out that Declan wanted to talk. He'd listened to Declan's proposal and his insistence that his friends were on the level. He knew Declan had links to several gangs, including the Masons, but was basically running with an independent crew who were loyal to no one but themselves and worked with a range of gangs in order to make money. They offered their services, did the job, and split the profit, but now it seemed like they were turning on the Masons.

After Owen had killed his brother, Thaddeus sympathised with the men who'd just paid him a visit. The Masons were becoming more active and prominent in recent months as several of their operations went bad and Owen got arrested.

Declan had neglected to say what had caused this change of heart, but Thaddeus guessed it was something to do with the Masons' recent troubles.

Thaddeus grimaced and considered the offer that Bill had made and wondered if it would be worth it. He was going up against the Masons and their operation anyway, so it wasn't a huge leap for him to team up with someone who might help them, especially when they were running out of leads to follow up on.

Owen Mason had so far remained frustratingly hidden following his escape from prison, and Thaddeus felt no closer to finding that piece of scum. So if they could help him with that, he'd be happy.

Taking a long drag on his spliff, he adjusted his position and enjoyed the gentle high it was giving him, allowing his mind to slow and relax. He knew full well that he'd be back to planning their next attack on the Masons before the night was out, so this was a welcome moment of calm amidst the storm.

He wasn't sure how long had passed when his phone sounded, breaking his trance and ripping him back to the real world.

With a sniff, he raised his phone, but there was nothing on it. He was momentarily confused until he remembered the phone that Bill had tossed to him earlier. He picked it up and found a text waiting for him.

Proof that our word is good, it read and listed an address. *A Mason crack house you might want to take a look at. Keep whatever you find there.*

Thaddeus nodded. Picking up his main phone, he searched for the address. It wasn't far.

Shaking his head, he sat forward. He read through the message a second time while considering his reply. After a moment's thought, he started typing. *Thanks, we'll check it out*.

"What's up, boss?" one of the crew asked from a nearby chair.

"Change of plan, dog," he replied. "Do you fancy fucking up some Masons tonight?"

A chorus of approval erupted from everyone present.

Thaddeus nodded and glanced down at the message from Bill. "This better be legit," he muttered to himself before getting to his feet.

Chapter 17

Tuesday

Sitting at her laptop, Scarlett scanned through the latest statement for the third time with tired eyes, hunting for anything she could use, but there was precious little in there.

It seemed to be a running theme with the statements from most of the people who witnessed any of the gang warfare that was going on, and it wasn't entirely unexpected. The locals who lived closest to them feared the gangs, and they knew if they were discovered speaking to the police, they would face retribution. People had been beaten up, had their legs broken, stabbed, and their houses set alight, all for having the temerity to talk to the police.

The gangs didn't need to do much to enforce this either. Word soon spread once they'd attacked someone, and it was amazing how effective it was. Suddenly, residents who were once helpful and cooperative would clam up and refuse to be seen with an officer.

It forced them to get creative in how they approached the locals, using plainclothes officers, unofficial emails, and coded language just to get a meeting set up, which was usually well away from the area the gang operated in, and conducted in secret.

But even then, after all those precautions, many of them simply wouldn't show up or name anyone.

It made this entire investigation utterly infuriating but also addictive.

Scarlett had a personal stake in taking down the Masons, after they'd killed her friend, Ninnette, and attempted to blackmail her. She would not rest until all the Masons were behind bars, no matter what.

Getting this opportunity to lead an investigation into the gang had been amazing, and she was determined to see it all the way through to a conviction.

That was why she was still working at home, late into the night. She'd eaten with Chris, showered, and had spent the rest of the night sitting at their dining table, sipping on a glass of wine, going through the mountain of paperwork.

She had witness statements, crime scene reports, evidence reports, forensic reports, informant statements, proposed plans of operations, lists of confirmed and unconfirmed gang members, and reports on each, assessing if they might be susceptible to being flipped, and more that all needed her attention.

The background noise of the TV stopped, and out the corner of her eye, she saw Chris get up from the sofa.

"You've been at that all night," he grumbled.

"Yeah, I know. Sorry. I need to crack this case, and it won't do it on its own."

"Can't you just do it at work? Do you have to bring it home and ruin our evening?"

"It's not every night," she protested, picking up her glass as she peered up at him. "You've brought work home before."

He shrugged. "I just wanted to spend some time with you tonight."

She smiled. "That's very sweet of you, but there'll be other nights. It's just really busy right now."

He sighed. "You're doing it more and more recently, and we've only just got married."

"I know. I want to spend some quality time with you, too, sweetie. And we will, just not tonight..."

He sighed again, clearly annoyed. "Just leave it, it'll be there in the morning."

"Less will be there in the morning if I do more now, though." She grinned at him.

"But will I be there in the morning?" he said, spite in his voice.

"Hey!" She frowned. "What is this? What's got into you? Why are you acting like this?"

"Like what?"

"Like…" She hunted for the right words. "Like my career is less important than yours."

"That's not true," he snapped.

She raised her eyebrows at him. "Are you sure? Because that's how it's coming across."

"I didn't mean…"

She decided to press her advantage. "You could always spend your evening round at Austin's, if you prefer? You're always round there."

"Yeah. He's a friend and a good contact to have."

"Better than spending time with your new wife?"

"Ugh, I've had enough of this." He turned and, without a kiss goodnight, stormed out of the room.

She pulled a face at him. "Whatever," she muttered to herself and took a deep breath, trying to calm her nerves. She hated arguing with him, but he was pushing her buttons tonight and she wasn't having any of it. So, if he wanted to be petty and go to bed without saying goodnight, then that was fine with her.

With a shake of her head and a sip of her wine, Scarlett returned her attention to her work, preferring not to over-analyse what had just happened and forget the whole thing. She was perfectly within her rights to want a good, solid career just as much as he was, and he would not take that away from her.

No one would.

Ninette was counting on her, and she would not let her down.

Her phone buzzed. Scarlett jumped, nearly falling off her chair, the name Tucker on the screen. She answered, already taking a wild guess about what this might be about. "Have they been at it again?"

Tucker laughed. "Good evening to you, too."

"Evening," Scarlett answered, smiling. "Well, have they?"

"Yeah, you're right. Looks like the Killers have attacked a Mason operation on the edges of Hyson Green. I'm heading over there now with Ellen. Care to join us?"

Scarlett grimaced and checked the time. Ten-thirty p.m. "Yeah, sure. Why not. Send me the address."

She got up but paused on her way to the front door and glanced down at her shabby tracksuit bottoms and jumper. She considered rushing upstairs to get changed but didn't fancy the idea of talking to Chris again and decided against it. It didn't matter what she was wearing. Grabbing her keys, she exited the house as quietly as possible and dashed to her car. Once inside, she felt her phone buzz.

She looked at it.

Off out? it read. The text was from Chris.

She grimaced. *Work*, she answered and switched to her navigation app.

This was hardly the first, or even tenth time she'd done this since moving up here. Her job, as he was well aware, didn't keep regular hours, and she was always being called out to this or that crime scene. It was just part of the job, it came with the territory. She couldn't really say no.

Starting the engine, Scarlett drove out of her driveway into the leafy, quiet roads of The Park Estate within Nottingham, and headed north towards Hyson

Green. When Tucker's text came through with the address, she stopped and keyed it into her phone before continuing on her way.

Her phone buzzed again as she drove. It was another text from Chris, but she ignored it for now and concentrated on her driving. She'd had half a glass of wine with her meal and couldn't feel any effects to speak of, but it was worth taking things easy.

The roads were mercifully quiet, however, making her drive through the city simple, and it wasn't long before she turned into a street lit up with blue flashing lights. A small crowd had assembled to watch the emergency services go about their jobs. Murders were spectator sports, after all, she mused wryly, or at least, the investigations were.

She checked her phone and read Chris' text. *It's always work.*

She curled her lip in annoyance at the implication. *Would you like a photo of the body as proof?* she typed and hit send.

Jumping out of her car, she made her way over towards the outer cordon and flashed her badge at the waiting officer, who let her through. He glanced at her obviously rather fetching outfit but said nothing.

Scarlett strode through the parked cars and soon found Tucker and Ellen who were talking between themselves.

"Evening," Tucker said. "Going under-fucking-cover, are we?"

She gave her foul-mouthed colleague a sarcastic grin. "Har, har. So, what's the deal?"

"Seems like it was a Mason crack house," Ellen replied, reading her notes and then glancing behind her at the house. It was sporting some broken windows at the front. "It was attacked an hour and a half ago by a group of young men and women who stormed into it and shot up the place."

"We have reports of gunfire," Tucker said. "Looks like there was fucking chaos as people ran to get away from the slimy bastards."

"Have you been inside?"

"Not yet."

"Shall we?"

"Fucking sure, why not? We'd better get suited and booted, though," Tucker suggested.

It didn't take them long to change into some forensic gear before making their way towards the front of the house.

"Stunning fucking joggers, Scarlett. Did we catch you on your way to bed?" Tucker asked.

"Kind of. I wasn't expecting a call-out, so…" Scarlett answered and gave his crumpled suit an askance once-over. "I take it you live in that suit?"

"Hell, he probably sleeps in it," Ellen added. "Have you seen those creases?"

"Has it ever seen an iron?" Scarlett said.

"Yeah, yeah, all right, yeh bastards. Point taken," Tucker remarked.

They approached the front door and made their way into the first tent that concealed the front yard and entrance. Inside, the first body was waiting for them, just outside the house. A photographer was getting his shots, leaning over the body and snapping happily away.

"Work it, work it," Tucker muttered.

The photographer flipped him off but said nothing and continued as if nothing had happened.

Scarlett didn't recognise the body and went through into the house, where she found several more dead young men scattered through the building. At the third body, she stopped and peered down at the young black man who'd lost his life. She recognised him. It took her a moment to place him, but then it suddenly came to her.

"Dodders," she muttered.

"Who?" Ellen asked.

"You know him?" Tucker added and moved round her to get a better view.

"Cedric Dodson, better known as Dodders. He led a small crew that included Ambrose Gordon, better known as Rice to his friends. We arrested them for cuckooing a flat up in Workshop not too long back and got Rice to talk. Dodders looked like he was going down, but the case fell apart, and he was back on the streets. I only remember him because Rice was killed shortly after at the same time and place as my friend, Ninette. He was probably killed by the same people, too."

"Got his comeuppance, then," Tucker muttered. "He fucked around and found out."

"I guess," Scarlett mused.

Someone mouthed off in another room while she crouched beside Dodders and glanced up at her teammates.

"Who's that?" She pointed towards the sound.

"They mentioned there was a survivor," Ellen said.

Scarlett grunted and got back to her feet. "Let's go say hi, shall we?"

She led them towards the back of the house and into the kitchen where they found a young man in baggy clothing sitting on a chair with his hands behind his back. Armed officers stood close, ignoring his near constant spewing of insults.

"Who the fuck are you, bitch?" the young man asked. "Blonde piece of ass? Come to flash me those titties, huh?"

Scarlett grimaced at his hateful bile. He was trying to get a rise out of her, but she'd seen this kind of thing countless times before and ignored it. A nearby officer stepped closer.

"Hi," he said.

She flashed her ID. "Detective Williams. Who's this?"

"Foster Cook," the officer said, while the kid continued his insults and inappropriate comments. "The first officers on the scene found him. He'd been knocked out and left behind. We'll remove him from the property once we've taken his clothes and such."

"Hmm." She turned to him. "What's your deal, then? Can you tell me what happened here?"

"Fuck off, you skanky bitch whore. I ain't talking to no piggy bitch. I've got something in my pants just for you, though, yeah? Come and wrap your lips round this." He pumped his hips as best he could.

Scarlett sighed and spun away. She was getting nowhere. It would probably work better in a custody suite anyway, once they knew a little more about who this guy was and where his allegiances lay.

"All right, I think we're done here," she said, walking back through the house, under no illusions that they'd actually find out who did this. The culture of silence was all-pervasive.

As she stepped back into the cool night air, she checked her phone again, but Chris had not replied. He'd seen her sarcastic reply, though, and she suddenly felt bad. Had she pushed a little too far?

Ugh.

Chapter 18

Wednesday

Zara stirred in her bed as her phone buzzed, vibrating on her bedside table. She grunted and rolled over, preferring to ignore it. It wasn't the alarm, after all. Probably just a notification. In her half-awake state, she briefly thought that it shouldn't do that during the night. It should be set to Do Not Disturb. She was sure she'd set it up like that... She was soon pulled back into blissful slumber, however, her concerns forgotten.

It buzzed again, interrupting her sleep, much to her annoyance. She turned and glanced at the glowing numbers on her bedside clock.

05:03.

"Ugh, no," she grunted and rolled over again. It was too early for this crap.

But her phone wouldn't stop buzzing. Every few seconds it went off again and again, until, with mounting anger, she reached over and checked it. "What, what?"

They were texts, from her dad. Curious, she opened them.

Zara, I need your help.

Can you come and help me?

It listed an address elsewhere in Mansfield, a unit on an industrial estate.

I came here to meet someone but got mixed up, and now I'm stuck.

Please, Zara, come now.

I'm in pain.

I know it's early. I'm sorry. Please come.

"What the hell?" she muttered and hit dial, calling her dad, but he didn't answer. She frowned at her phone, staring at it accusingly. Another message from her dad appeared, and she jumped.

I can't talk right now.

Why the hell not, she wondered? What was this all about? It wasn't exactly the first time he'd got himself in a situation and needed her help, but this one seemed a little odd. She tried calling again, but her dad rejected the call.

He texted moments later. *Don't call. He'll hear.*

Zara stared at the handset in shock. *Who?* she answered.

I don't know, the reply said just seconds later. He sounded in trouble. Zara jumped out of bed. She pulled on her jeans and top while her heart tried its best to burst from her chest.

She texted back. *Are you in danger?*

No. I just need your help.

Huh? *I can call the police*, she replied, wondering if that was the best option. He sounded like he might be in danger. What the hell had he got himself involved in now?

No need. Don't waste their time. I just need a little help, that's all. Just drive over here and pick me up.

She squinted at her phone. This was madness, but she wasn't sure what else she could do and rushed to put her shoes on. She lived in a house share with three other students; each of them had a room of their own. The others were obviously still sleeping, and she didn't feel like waking them up to help her with her dad. She crept through the house and out the front door into the cool morning air. There was a light fog, and the air was damp, making the street feel eerie, like those liminal spaces she'd seen online. It was still mostly dark, but the sky was beginning to lighten, casting everything in dull, grey muted tones.

Zara marched to her car while entering the address into her phone and climbed in. It wasn't far away, just across town, and at this time in the morning, she shouldn't run into any serious traffic.

I'm on my way, she texted.

Thank you, he replied.

She secured her phone and started the car, still none the wiser as to what was going on.

The drive over was as quick as she'd hoped. The roads were mercifully clear, and she'd made excellent time. But she couldn't work out why her dad was at an industrial estate at this time in the morning. She knew that businesses operated from units like these, mechanics and such, so was it something like that? Had he somehow got confused and headed out at the wrong time of day?

Her dad was lovely and quite intelligent, but he could get a bit mixed up occasionally. Losing her mother, his wife, had hit him hard, and he'd never really recovered from it or settled down with anyone new. As a result, it often fell to her to pick up the slack and help her dad when he got into a spot of bother, such as with some modern technology.

She frowned and tried to work out what had brought him to this industrial estate, and wondered if it had anything to do with his job? He was always up early on workdays to get started on his route, so maybe the post office had given him a new one and he'd got lost or stuck somewhere while trying to deliver a letter or parcel? She couldn't quite figure it out, but something to do with his job made the most sense to her.

It wasn't long before she pulled into the entrance of the industrial park and paused at the sign, looking at the listed units. He'd said Unit 4, but there was no business listed for that one.

Odd.

She sighed and drove in, wondering what kind of mess she'd find her dad in, and hoped they'd be able to laugh about it in the weeks to come.

The unit was towards the back of the lot. A smaller building when compared to the other enormous warehouses, but still large in its own right. She drew up to it, the door standing ajar at the front, and a dim light coming from within. Well, she reasoned, he must be in there.

She glanced around to see if there was anyone else about, but the place seemed deserted.

Her phone buzzed. She grabbed it and checked her messages.

Is that you? I'm inside.

"Bloody hell, Dad," she muttered and got out of her car. The hum of the town and nearby roads reached her, but other than that, the area was still and silent. Peering at the door, she started towards it. Hesitantly at first, but with growing speed and confidence, until she reached it and leaned in.

It was one huge open space with a single light hanging from the centre of the ceiling. Below it, in a pool of light, was a large cage made of metal meshing, and something moved inside.

It was difficult to make out what was going on from here, but she had a sinking feeling that her dad was inside it. She stepped into the building, scanning all around, but there was no one else there. She was alone with whatever, or whoever, was in that cage.

"Dad?" she called out, wondering if he'd answer.

Then came noises, voices that were being muffled, coming from the cage. She approached. On hearing the sounds, she sped up and strode across the open space. As she drew close, she could make sense of what was inside, and slowed down. Several people were inside. Three... No, four of them. They were all lying on a table inside the cage. Three of them to one side, and one separated from the others, on the opposite end.

That single person was her dad.

"Dad!" she yelped and dashed to the mesh, gripping and hitting it. "Dad. I'm here. What's all this?"

In her hand, her phone rang. It said "Dad" on the screen, but her father was here, gagged and tied to a table. He strained to look up at her. She ignored her phone. "Dad. Are you okay? What the hell happened? What's going on?"

In rising panic, she tried to work out what was going on and if there was a way in. She spotted a door and darted round to it, but it was locked, and no amount of shaking and pulling on it made any difference.

"Dad!" she yelled and banged on the cage.

He was trying to speak through the gag, but his words were incomprehensible. She moved back to the front of the cage and assessed her dad's situation.

All four people inside were strapped to the table. Three were lying side by side, with a gap between them and her dad. Between them, in a channel that ran beneath all their necks, she spotted a circular saw.

Something mechanical clanked. A light turned red on an instrument panel beside her. She watched it flicker to green, a motor starting, and the saw blade spun. In less than a second, it was little more than a glinting metal blur, making a hell of a racket.

"No, no, no, no, no!"

Zara stepped to the panel with the green light, hoping to find an off button. Instead, she found a countdown. Two minutes. Less than that now. Below it, a note read, *Answer your phone.*

It was still ringing in her hand, but she'd forgotten all about it.

Nervously, she lifted it and tapped the screen and put it to her ear. "Hello?"

"Hello, Zara, and welcome to my little game. You may call me the Games Master, and you have a simple choice to make. Your father, or three innocent young people with their whole lives ahead of them."

She noticed two buttons on the panel before her, one labelled "Dad", the other labelled "3 Strangers".

"You have until the timer hits zero to choose, and if you don't, the saw will kill all of them. Also, if you end this call, make another call, or leave the building, you forfeit the game, and they all die. Make your choice."

Zara stared in mind-numbing shock at the cage, her dad, the three strangers, and the panel. "What the hell? You can't do this. This is madness. I don't want to choose. You can't make me."

The man on the end of the line didn't answer.

"I... You can't..." she protested and looked at the three people she didn't know.

They were all young. Two were male and one was female, and all three of them had twisted their head to stare at her with desperate, pleading eyes. They were trying to talk through their gags, but she couldn't make out anything they were trying to say to her.

"Please, no, please. You can't do this. You can't. Please don't. Please...." No answer. "Are you there?" She could hear him breathing. "Damn you, answer me. Answer me! Please. Goddamn it."

She checked the time. Roughly a minute to go. "This is crazy. Why are you doing this? What did I ever do to you? You can't..."

She stared at her dad. His eyes were trained on her, too. He wasn't trying to speak. He just smiled at her.

She smiled back.

"Dad…"

He tried to talk to her, but she couldn't make it out over the noise of the saw or the three strangers all calling for her attention.

"Quiet!" she barked, wanting to hear her dad. "Shut up."

The strangers settled and stopped shouting at her, allowing her to listen to him. It was tough to make out, but she got the gist from the sounds he was able to make and his body language.

She started to cry. He was saying it was okay. He was accepting his fate and wanted her to save the three strangers. With tears streaming down her face, she shook her head.

"Dad. Please. I can't live without you. Not after Mum… Don't make me do this, please."

He clearly disagreed and was urging her to do it. To save the three strangers and kill him. She understood his rationale, where he was coming from. He was old, he'd lived his life, so it would be better to let the three young people live. What if one of them was destined to cure cancer at some stage in their life?

She glanced between them and her father, and then down at the clock. It closed in on zero, getting ever closer to killing all four of them.

This was an impossible choice. It didn't matter what she did. Someone would die, either her beloved father or these three young strangers who didn't deserve this.

There were just seconds to go. She had no time.

Zara closed her eyes and hovered her hand over one of the buttons. She didn't want to watch what was about to happen.

It was now or never.

She pressed the only button she could, the only one that made any sense to her, and listened to the saw trundle across the table and do its work to the sound of terrified screams coming from within the cage.

Zara sobbed.

The engine stopped, and so had the screams. Zara sank to the floor.

The voice on the end of the phone spoke. "Well done, Zara," he said. "You made your choice. Congratulations."

The call ended, and the cage unlocked.

Chapter 19

Wednesday

The scene in front of the warehouse was the usual mess of emergency vehicles and fluttering police tape as officers stood guard, letting the forensics and Scenes of Crime people do their jobs. The fog had mostly lifted, but the morning was still dull and grey with a damp coolness to the air. That didn't stop a few knots of people from standing around outside the cordon, though, watching proceedings and maybe hoping for a glimpse of something macabre.

Rob grimaced at the spectacle. Another day of seeing humanity at its absolute worst, he lamented.

They'd got the call early on, calling them straight from their homes to the scene before their shift had even started. Rob had picked Nick up on his way out through the city and up to Mansfield. They had precious little information other than it being murder and the location of the scene.

"Do you think it's our guy again?" Nick asked.

"God, I hope not," Rob muttered.

They made their way into the scene, through the outer and inner cordons. Rob spotted Alicia and walked over.

"Morning," he said in greeting.

"It is," she confirmed, deadpan. "Rob, Nick, good to see you. I hope you've not had your breakfast."

"That bad?" Rob asked.

"Worse."

They were at the back of an industrial estate, outside a warehouse that had seen better days, and there was a tent set up at the main entrance to the building, blocking anyone's view of the inside.

Rob could see a young woman and an older man huddled close with blankets around their shoulders sitting on the back of a nearby ambulance. Paramedics were fussing around nearby while uniformed officers stood close. They looked like they were in a state of shock.

"What's the situation?" he asked.

"Triple murder," Alicia stated. "Your guy struck again."

Rob frowned. "Are you sure?"

"Oh, I'm sure."

Rob grimaced. "Jesus."

"We have two survivors, Zara and her father, Peter, they're over there." She pointed to the pair Rob had just spotted. "The killer kidnapped her dad and three other people. He secured them to a home-made automated device that's basically a table with a circular saw set into it. The killer forced her to choose between three young strangers or her dad, otherwise he'd kill all four of them. She saved her dad."

"Bloody hell," Nick remarked. "I don't know which is worse, this one or the first one. Where does he come up with these things?"

"I wish I knew," Rob muttered.

"What do you want to do first?"

Rob glanced between the warehouse and the two victims. "Let's talk to the survivors first, so we can get them out of here."

"Sure thing," she replied and waved in their direction. "I'll be inside, cataloguing the horrors in there."

"Okay."

They turned to the nearby ambulance and headed over.

"Sounds bad," Nick said.

"Yeah…" Rob agreed.

They walked up to the two shaken survivors.

"Hi. I'm Rob, this is Nick, we'll be looking into this case. Do you mind if we ask a few questions?"

Zara sniffed. "No, that's fine. Please, go ahead."

"That's okay," Peter said.

"Do you mind running me through what happened first? Peter, do you want to start?"

"Yeah, sure." He took a moment to himself before launching into his side of the story. "He attacked me in my own home. He just knocked on the door, and when I opened it, he jumped me. I didn't stand a chance. He threatened me with a gun and put me in his van. He gagged me, tied me up, and brought me here."

"What time did he knock on your door?" Rob asked.

"Just after dark, around seven-thirty. Maybe closer to eight."

"Was there anyone else in the warehouse when you arrived?" Nick asked.

Peter shook his head. "No. I was the first. He told me to lie on the table and tied me down. I couldn't move. It was terrifying. There was a heater, but it didn't help much. I was so cold. Then later in the night, he turned up with another person and added them to the table before going out again, until there were four of us. He took my phone, got me to unlock it, and then left. I lay there for hours, all night, until Zara arrived."

"Did you know she was coming?" Rob asked.

"No. I had no idea, not until I saw her."

"And you saw the man who did this to you?" Nick asked.

"Some of him. He hid most of his face. I can try to give you a description, though, if you think it'll help."

"Someone will go through that with you," Rob assured him. "Thank you."

"That's okay."

Rob turned to Zara. "When did things start for you?"

"This morning. Some texts from my dad woke me up at five a.m. He was asking for help, and I was getting text after text. It just went on and on. He told me to come here and help him. It wasn't really clear what was wrong. I thought he was in danger at one point and nearly called the police, but then he said I shouldn't bother you and it wasn't that bad, so I drove over here."

"And you entered this warehouse?" Rob pointed to the building.

"The door was open, so yeah, I just went in. That's when I saw the cage and my dad, with the other three people. Then the guy, he called me, and told me to make a choice."

"And you chose your dad."

"I told her to choose the other three," Peter said. "I've lived my life, I've had everything I could ever want. I don't need anything more." He sighed. "But, I understand why she did it."

Rob nodded to Zara. "Why did you choose your dad?"

She shrugged. "Because he's my dad. He's the only family I have left, my only close family. I didn't know the others."

"What about your mother?" Nick asked.

"She died when I was young. Car crash," she stated. "I couldn't lose my dad *and* my mum. There was no way I was going to be responsible for that. I'm sure the other three were lovely, but I didn't know them." She sobbed.

"It's okay, sweetheart," Peter said and pulled her in close. "Is she going to be charged with murder for this?"

"Hopefully not, no," Rob said. "You had no choice, and you actually saved a life, I'd say. The man who kidnapped you is the killer. He's the one who will be going to prison."

"Good. Has this man done this before?"

"Unfortunately, yes, he has," Rob confirmed.

"Damn. Well, he might do it again."

"What makes you say that?" Rob asked, curious. "Did he say anything to you?"

"He pinned a photo to my jumper that you need to see. I think it's inside."

Rob cringed and suppressed a grimace. It sounded like this man, whoever he was, was far from done. "Thank you for your help. I'm sure we'll be talking to you again."

Rob left them in the care of the various officers on the scene and went with Nick towards the warehouse. "I knew he wasn't done."

"Of course he wasn't," Nick agreed. "But he's been quick."

"Very quick. He must have been planning these for months. You don't do this kind of thing off the cuff. It takes planning."

"Aye," Nick said.

They paused at a forensics van and pulled on protective clothing.

Once suitably covered, they strode into the building through the tent, which served as a concealed entrance. Inside, work lights had been set up, encircling the cage in the centre of the room. To one side, plastic sheeting had been placed on the floor, and the three victims had been laid out, side by side, and covered. Several people in similar white forensic suits were fussing around them, and more were around the cage, taking photos, dusting for prints, and bagging evidence.

Alicia waited for them.

"What's this about a photo?" Rob asked.

She fell into step beside him.

"It's over here," she said and led them to the sheeting where evidence bags were being catalogued by another officer. She plucked the photo from the floor and handed it to them. "Here you go."

The photo had been taken on the street, at a distance, and showed two people, a man and a woman, walking hand in hand down the street. It wasn't terribly clear, so it would be tough to identify who they were. It was also in black and white.

"Next targets, maybe?" Nick guessed.

"That would be my guess," Rob said.

"The interesting part is on the back," Alicia said.

Rob turned the photo over. Two lines of text had been scrawled on the rear in what looked like biro, along with the chaos symbol.

Kill your partner or kill yourself?

"Is that the next game?" Rob asked.

"And the couple who will be playing it," Nick mused. "We know he's serious, so I think we need to take him at his word."

"I would agree." He handed the evidence back to Alicia. "Do you have a copy of that photo?"

"I do, I'll send it over."

"Brilliant."

"These are the other victims, I take it?" Nick asked.

"They are," Alicia said. "I've found some IDs, so it shouldn't be too difficult to confirm who they were."

"Excellent. If we can find that out, it might give up a clearer picture." He said it with confidence, but given the random nature of who the killer had chosen so far, Rob doubted he'd start murdering people he knew. This guy might be a killer and a lunatic, but he was smart and calculating. It was unlikely that he'd start making mistakes now.

"Let's hope so," Nick added.

"Do you want to see them?" Alicia asked, pointing at the three covered bodies.

Rob took a deep breath and nodded, mentally preparing himself for what he was about to see. Alicia and one of the other SOCO guys pulled the sheets back and revealed them. Their heads lay at odd angles that didn't fit with their bodies. Rob's stomach turned.

They were all young, either in their late teens or early twenties, with their whole lives ahead of them.

Rob nodded, and they covered them back up.

"You should see the cage and the device he made, too," Alicia suggested. "If he wasn't such a sick and twisted shit, he'd be quite useful to have around the house."

Rob raised an eyebrow. "If you say so," he muttered.

She led them over to the cage. The whole thing had been hand-made and was quite the feat of engineering. Walking up to the door cage door, Rob peered in at the table inside. The circular saw poked up through a slot in the table, which was awash with dried blood. Crouching, he admired the impressive engineering beneath the table that moved the blade along the slot.

"Remote controlled?" he asked.

"Seems that way. Zara never saw the man, but he must have been close. Close enough to trigger the device anyway."

"All right, thank you," Rob said, standing. He turned to Nick. "Looks like our workload just doubled."

Chapter 20

Wednesday

At the station, Rob leaned back in his chair; it creaked under his weight while he rolled his pen between his teeth. They needed a lead. They needed to get out ahead of this guy before he did it again, which he was sure to do. This second killing just a day after the first told him that the guy, whoever he was, was dedicated and serious. He'd see it through, whatever happened.

He was the worst kind of killer. Focused, dedicated, and on a mission.

The only thing they had was the slightly blurred, black-and-white photo from the latest killing, but little else.

However, the photo also told him that the killer's confidence was growing. He was getting cocky, thinking he could do these things and drop clues without the repercussions. But overconfidence was often the downfall of people like this, thinking they were immune to justice. It often led to mistakes. Hopefully, that mistake came sooner rather than later.

"I hear the Games Master killer struck again," Scarlett said, leaning over from her desk.

"Yep. He gave a young woman another impossible choice. Choose between her dad or three strangers. Whoever she chooses lives, the others die."

"She chose her dad," Scarlett replied, as if it was the most obvious thing in the world. "That's hardly an impossible choice."

"Perhaps not, but she still had to kill three other people, all of them young with their whole lives ahead of them. That's not going to leave her anytime soon."

"True. That would scar anyone for life. I didn't mean it would be easy to do, just that the choice was an obvious one."

"Even with those three innocent faces staring at you, pleading for their lives?" Rob agreed, but he decided to play devil's advocate anyway.

Scarlett shrugged.

"Rob." Nailer walked over from his office. "Have you got an update for me? Is this second killing linked?"

"It is," Rob confirmed and gave Nailer an overview of the crime as he knew it, making sure to hit all the basic details. "We're dusting for prints and searching for any

DNA evidence at the crime scene. We have officers talking to the other companies that operate out of that estate, seeing if anyone saw anything. We'll also hunt down the owner of the building, as we think it was rented."

Nailer nodded. "That could be useful, if he spoke to someone and has their details."

"Hopefully," Rob said. "We'll also do the usual CCTV hunt and local door-to-door stuff. But that's not the most promising lead."

Nailer inclined his head, clearly interested.

"The killer is now telling us who he's going after next."

"Oh?"

Rob lifted the printout from his desk and handed it to Nailer. "That was pinned to the father's chest."

"Kill your partner or kill yourself? Jesus."

"Yeah."

"Do we know who these people are?" Nailer pointed to the photo.

"No. Not yet. We can look into it, try to narrow it down, but maybe going public is the only way to find out."

"Right away?"

"It's an option," Rob said.

"Yeah. We need to be cautious, though. We risk losing the advantage if we go public and he chooses someone else."

Rob shrugged. "We might also save some lives."

"Or seem desperate and out of our depth."

"That's the superintendent talking," Rob remarked.

Nailer shrugged. "True. But these things need to be taken into consideration. The press would have a field day, and my boss would be less than enthused."

"You can worry about them. I don't care about that. I care about stopping people from being killed."

"Of course. But I want you to look into this first. If we can find these people without going public and showing the killer our hand, or that we're clueless, we might be able to set a trap."

Rob nodded. "We can try..."

"Then try. Pass this info to anyone you think might help find this guy. But if you have no luck, we can get this out to the press this afternoon, get it on the evening news, and maybe we can find them that way. I need to run this up the chain first anyway, and that will take some time. I'll keep you posted."

Rob ground his teeth but nodded. He'd have preferred to go to the press right away, but he understood where Nailer was coming from and the issues he wanted to avoid. Also, the evening news was the best chance they had of finding this couple, which gave them several hours' grace to try other avenues anyway.

"Okay, fine, I'll see what I can do."

"Thank you, Rob. And we still have no idea who this guy is?"

"No. We've him caught on the first victim's doorbell and nearby CCTV, but he's always masked, and although we can track him part way, we've not yet pinned him down. We don't know where he lives. We need more to go on."

"Oh, that reminds me," Scarlett said. "I did a little digging on that first note you found. What was it again? The more chaotic I am, the more complete I am?"

"I think that's right," Rob answered.

"It's a quote attributed to a man called Austin Osman Spare. He was one of the founders of the chaos magic movement, but he died in 1956."

"Well, if the chaos symbol on the note wasn't enough, this only serves to link things back to this Ashen King figure we've heard about," Rob said.

Nailer turned to Scarlett. "Have you heard of this Ashen King from any of the gangs you've spoken to? Is he linked to that kind of criminality?"

"Not that I'm aware of, sir," Scarlett replied. "I can do some more digging, though, during my abundance of free time."

"You do that. In the meantime, how's your investigation going? Any closer to bringing this gang war to an end and finding Owen Mason?"

Scarlett sighed. "Not really. The gangs just stonewall me. They don't want to talk, unsurprisingly. They just want to destroy each other. And I've also failed to make much headway on finding Owen. He's proving elusive, for the time being. We do have a witness for this latest attack on a Mason operation, and I'll be talking to him again shortly to see what else he knows. But he wasn't terribly helpful back at the crime scene, and I doubt a few hours in our care will have loosened him up much."

Nailer shrugged. "You never know."

She smiled. "I love your optimism."

"All right, back to work. Let's get some results," Nailer said and left them to it.

Chapter 21

Wednesday

"So you have no idea who it was or what happened?" Scarlett asked.

Slouched in her chair, she glared across the table at the young man sitting opposite with obvious contempt. They'd been over this a couple of times already, pushing him to remember something, but he was being singularly unhelpful, beside his smug solicitor, hiding behind feigned ignorance.

She couldn't be surer that he knew exactly who had attacked that house and why they were there. He had to know. He just had to.

"No. Like I said, I saw nothin'," he repeated, grinning as he spoke, clearly enjoying this game of cat and mouse. "I was just hanging with my mates, having a J2O, you know, like cool kids do, and then we heard a noise. I was scared like, so I hid in the cupboard and waited for it all to calm down. So yeah, I have no idea what was going on." The self-satisfied smile Foster Cook allowed to creep over his face told her way more than his words did. He knew exactly who had been there and why, and he'd clearly been involved.

"But, we found you on the floor."

"Fainted when I came out from my hiding spot, didn't I. It was all too much."

"You fainted?"

"Totally. I'm squeamish. Didn't I tell you that?" He gave her a look that spoke volumes, and even his solicitor smirked.

Gripping her pen in her fist, she wanted to stab him in the eye with it. Him and the solicitor. Scarlett glanced to her right, to where Tucker was sitting, watching the young man opposite. He glanced back and shrugged.

Scarlett rolled her eyes. They were getting nowhere with this guy, and she had no doubt that another hour in here would yield little in the way of results.

"You know we're going over that house with a fine-tooth comb," she pressed on. "If there're drugs in there, or your fingerprints, this might not go well for you."

"I don't know what you're talking about," Foster answered. "You wouldn't catch me taking drugs and ruining my life. But I know some of my mates did sometimes, and they were always in that house."

He was covering his arse.

"Is that right?"

Foster grinned widely. "Totally."

She knew they couldn't hold him for any length of time, not without some kind of proof that he was something more than an innocent bystander. His record wasn't clean, but he wasn't exactly a career criminal either. He'd been picked up for some petty crime, theft, GBH, that kind of thing. Nothing serious. But she wasn't particularly interested in arresting him. He was low level, and taking him off the streets wouldn't make much difference. But what he knew could potentially be much more useful. Who knew what he'd seen or heard while in the company of Mason gangsters. He might have heard whispers about where Owen Mason was.

She decided to take one last stab at it.

"You know, I'm not really interested in arresting you, Foster. You're a nobody, a nothing. No one's going to miss you if you're locked up, and no one's going to go out of their way to get you out. Now, don't misunderstand me. I will have no problem throwing you into jail if we find something in that house that incriminates you. And sure, you can lie and tell me you had nothing to do with anything, you didn't know what was going on in that house, and it was all your friends' faults. Go ahead, sure, why not? You can say these things, but I don't believe a word of it, and I'll lock you up and throw away the key in two seconds flat the moment we get anything that contradicts what you've told me here today. But as I said, it makes no difference to me, and if you were to, let's say, give me something, some kind of crumb. A useful bit of information that I can take to my boss and say, yeah, he's been helpful, useful, then maybe a deal could be struck. Maybe I could overlook any minor infraction that turns up due to DNA evidence. That way, you can be on your merry way, doing whatever it is you do, and I can focus on the real movers and shakers, like Owen Mason, for instance."

His eyes flicked up to her.

"I mean, he clearly doesn't give a shit about anyone other than himself, and he's caused some trouble for you and us in recent weeks, by killing Hadley Watts and kicking off this gang war. So, while you're on the front line, fighting these thugs who want you all dead, killing your mates, Mr Mason is hiding away, nice and safe in some cushy house somewhere. He's not fighting off the Hyson Green Killers, is he? He's not out there on the front line, putting his life at risk. No, he's putting your life, and the lives of your mates at risk, all while getting rich in the process." She eyed him, wondering if she was getting through to him at all. "Doesn't seem very fair, does it?"

Foster sat back with his arms crossed, the levity he was displaying earlier gone, replaced by a calm fury that oozed out of him.

"Sorry, hope I didn't touch a nerve. But you see my predicament? I just want to go after the big dog, the guy at the top who's causing all these problems. So, with that in mind, I was wondering if you knew anything? Something that might be beneficial to you? What do you think?"

With his arms still crossed and his jaw set, Foster glared at her for a long moment before answering. "No comment."

Scarlett sighed.

She pushed him a bit more, firing off some questions, but it was quite clear that they were getting nowhere, and it honestly didn't matter what they said or did. He wasn't going to talk.

In the end, all they could do was let him go, citing no further action.

"You never know, he might come back," Tucker said, standing beside her at the window as they watched Foster leave the building.

"Unlikely," she remarked.

He grunted. "Yeah, probably. But you gave it your best shot, so don't feel too bad." He backed away from the window. "I'm gonna drain the snake. I'll see you back up there, yeah?"

She nodded and waited for him to leave her alone before she pulled out her phone and placed a call.

"Scarlett," Calico said on the other end of the line. "What can I do for you?"

"I've got another one for you."

Chapter 22

Wednesday

"Yeah, he asked a couple of times," Peter said. "'What would you do?' he asked. 'Kill yourself or your partner? What would you choose?' I didn't quite know what to think of that, given my wife died fifteen years ago."

Rob nodded as he listened, making occasional notes while Peter Mayer spoke about his ordeal with the killer, about how he was kidnapped and then strapped to the table by this masked man. He'd tried to speak to the other victims but found that difficult with the gags. They had all been terrified, and justifiably so.

"How did he seem to you? The killer?"

"Calm. Matter of fact. He didn't seem crazy, if that's what you're asking. This seemed… normal to him, as if it was just another Tuesday. Nothing unusual. But that's what made it so odd."

"I understand," Rob said. "We often see people like this as monster, as somehow inhuman. But they're not, and they're often disconcertingly normal and unremarkable."

"You got that right." He sighed and shivered.

"You okay?" Rob asked.

"I just remember turning and seeing that saw for the first time... Ugh, I will not forget that anytime soon."

"I hope you forget it eventually."

"Memories like that fade over time," Nick replied. "It'll never truly leave you. You will be scarred by this for the rest of your lives, but it get's easier." He was addressing both Peter and his daughter, Zara, who was sitting beside him.

She nodded. "I've been playing *Tetris*."

Rob frowned. "Err, okay?"

She gave him a curious look. "It helps," she clarified. "There've been studies about it, and apparently if you play Tetris after a traumatic event, it helps reduce the flashbacks and trauma." She shrugged. "I have no idea if that's true, but I'll try anything."

"I've heard about this." Nick turned to Rob. "It's a thing."

"Sure, why not. Whatever works."

She smiled.

"Thank you anyway," Rob continued. "This can't have been easy for you, so I appreciate you both speaking to us about it in such detail."

"Any time. Anything we can do to help, right, Zara?"

"Absolutely. Anything. Just ask," she confirmed.

Rob noticed a message from Ellen on his phone as he concluded the meeting. He handed the pair off to another officer, reading the text while he and Nick headed back to their office.

"Ellen's tracked the gun from the first crime scene," Rob said.

They marched through the corridors.

"Oh, excellent."

"Unless it's another dead end, of course."

Nick grunted, clearly as optimistic as Rob felt.

They strode into the office and made for their desks. Ellen rose to meet them.

"Don't get excited," she began.

"Pop!" Nick said. "Bubble burst."

"Dead end?" Rob asked.

Ellen shrugged. "The gun the killer used was a police-issue Glock 19 that went missing in Yorkshire several years ago during a sting operation that went a little sideways. It's probably been passed around the criminal underworld for a while now. We found a bullet a year ago that matched the weapon's ballistics, but not the gun. Now we have the gun, too."

"So, we don't know who had it or owned it?"

"Sorry," Ellen said. "No lucky break. But that's not the only lead we've had come in while you were busy. I think we have another witness. A man was found badly beaten last night, and when we finally got an officer to him, he reported that he'd seen a man attack a woman on the street and drag her into the back of a van. He tried to intervene, but the kidnapper attacked him, too, beating him viciously. Apparently he's in a bit of a state. But his description of the young woman who was kidnapped matches the female cage victim."

"He saw the killer kidnap her off the street," Rob summed up.

"So it seems."

"We need to talk to him, see what else he saw. Could he identify the man, that kind of thing."

"I can do that," Ellen suggested.

"Please do," Rob replied with a smile.

Ellen nodded and grabbed her coat, while Rob turned to Nick.

"Have we tracked down the landlord for that warehouse, yet?"

"Yeah, it's just come in. I'm going to call and meet him on the industrial estate. I might visit some of the other businesses while I'm there, try and jog people's memories. Someone has to know something."

"Sure thing. Good luck. Keep me posted. The financials might be our way into this."

The phone on Rob's desk rang. He answered. "Loxley."

"This is reception, sir. I've got Officer Reid on the phone. He wants to speak to you."

"Put him through."

"Sir," Reid said in greeting after the click. "I've been told to get in touch. I think we might have something for you."

"I bloody hope so," Rob said.

"Well, we took a call last night from a man saying he'd seen someone throw a man into the back of a van."

A second witness? "A man into a van? Not a woman?"

"Correct. We went and spoke to him and got a statement, but we've only just linked it to the case you're working on. I'll send over the details and the statement."

"Excellent, thank you." Rob hung up.

Were they finally getting somewhere, or was this a false hope?

Chapter 23

Wednesday

"I don't mind telling you, this has stunned me. I've never heard anything like it before. And it happened in one of my buildings!"

Nick listened to Kevin Emerson, the owner of the warehouse where the killing had taken place, as they stood outside the building. It was still cordoned off with uniformed officers guarding the area, while forensics continued their work inside.

"I understand," Nick said. "I know this is a lot for you to process."

"You're not kidding. I'm not sure I'll sleep tonight." Kevin sighed dramatically. "But you don't want to hear these troubles. What can I do for you, Officer? How can I help?"

"Well," Nick began, getting his thoughts in order. "There doesn't seem to be any sign of forced entry, and in fact, the key to the building was left on the property, which suggests that whoever did this had access. So it's possible that whoever leased this building from you was the killer, or was at least linked to him."

"Aaah, I see."

There was a tension there, Nick thought, when Kevin paused.

"Well, I'm not sure how much use I'll be to you, but I'll try to help."

Nick frowned. "Did you not meet with the lease holder?"

"I met with someone, yes, but it was all a little mysterious. The person I initially spoke to only wanted to converse over email and the phone, saying he lived too far away to visit. Which is fine. That happens sometimes. Anyway, I did eventually meet someone once, but only briefly. He refused a guided tour and only wanted to pick up the keys. That was more unusual, but it does happen occasionally."

"So, he came to your office? Do you have CCTV?"

"I see what you're getting at, but no. We met somewhere else at his request. He said he was busy and couldn't get to me, so I offered to drop them somewhere or meet him, and he gave me a place to meet." He pulled a face. "Looking back, it sounds suss now, but I didn't think twice at the time. I'd been paid so…"

Nick nodded, frustrated. The killer had clearly engineered things to his advantage, while pretending to be just another busy man. Clever.

Kevin continued. "He said he was going to be working there for a few weeks and appreciated some privacy."

"Privacy?"

Kevin shrugged. "I didn't read into it at the time. I would have come here at some point, but he hasn't been renting it for long and he was always early with his payments, so I didn't see the need to be nosey."

Nick grimaced. "The perfect tenant."

"Yeah, I guess. Anyway, here's the lease. It has a name, but I don't know if it's of use to you."

Nick took it and read the name of the leaseholder on the front page. "Austin Osman Spare."

"Yep, that's him."

Nick sighed. Yeah, this wasn't going to be much use. Austin Osman Spare was the long-dead founder of chaos magic, who the killer was quoting in his messages to them.

"No use?"

"Not really. It's a fake name… Well, it did belong to someone, many years ago, but he's long dead now, so…"

Kevin's top lip curled. "Urgh, sorry."

"Not your fault," Nick replied. "We'll look into it, but I don't think it will lead anywhere." He scanned through the papers to the bank statement that listed the payments from the lease holder. They'd come from an offshore account, named as belonging to Chaos Inc. Nick raised an eyebrow. More smoke and mirrors. But an offshore account hinted at some serious backing and more hurdles for them to jump as they tried to figure out who was behind all this.

Was this backer the Ashen King they'd heard about?

Hopefully, the account holder was an idiot and they could track it, but if they were clever, it'd be linked to shell companies and lead only to dead ends... if the account was still open, which it might not be.

Nick could feel a headache coming on. "I appreciate this," he said, holding the lease aloft.

"Well, I hope you find your man."

Nick nodded in agreement and massaged the bridge of his nose. "Me too." He offered his hand to Kevin. "Thank you."

They shook hands, and Kevin left.

Nick watched him walk away, before focusing on the task ahead. Time to interview some workers in the surrounding businesses. It was possible someone had seen something, and it was Nick's job to find that person.

Chapter 24

Wednesday

Murrey's heart hammered as the car moved through Forest Town, Mansfield, along the Clipstone Road, heading north. Contacting Burt Swift had been a gamble, and if he was right, he was very close to finding out if this gamble was about to pay off... or blow up in his face.

Houses streamed past them on either side. Murrey flicked his eyes right to where Swift was driving. He was completely focused on the road and had barely said two words to him since getting into the car.

He assumed Swift was taking him to see someone, to report in about what he'd said. Murrey didn't dare refuse when Swift had ordered him into the car. His reputation preceded him.

Had he done the right thing by meeting Swift and telling him what he knew? He'd been so sure about it leading up to the meeting. Nervous, but sure. It was the right thing to do, he reasoned. Right for him, the crew, and his own future within the family. He knew it.

And yet, doubt was creeping in all the same. Had it been Swift's reaction? The way he'd gone quiet and refused to discuss it further before they reached their destination?

Probably. Had he offended him? Had he accidentally stumbled into something much bigger than he'd realised? Would his desire to advance his own career and standing within the family backfire?

Swift twisted the wheel, and the car veered off down the side of a car wash that had taken over a former petrol station. Here were several other cars and vans parked up, and Swift swerved into a space, skidding to a stop. He jumped out without preamble and slammed the door closed.

Taking a breath, Murrey followed. He didn't want to keep Swift waiting but found him standing behind the car, obviously annoyed that Murrey hadn't been as quick to exit the vehicle.

"Move it," Swift ordered grimly and marched towards the rear of the building.

Murrey followed, keeping pace. Swift slammed his way through an outer door, a man inside jumping.

Swift's actions weren't helping with Murrey's nerves.

"Where is he?" Swift asked.

"Through there," the man answered, pointing.

Swift stalked on into the gloomy collection of corridors and rooms and turned right. A group of men and a couple of women were standing around a central table covered with guns, ammunition, knives, and some drug paraphernalia. Some kind of mission briefing or an execution squad?

"Boss," Swift barked when he walked in.

Across the table, Owen Mason looked up. "Aaah, there you are. I was wondering when you'd show your face. You're late."

"Blame this one." Swift jabbed his thumb towards him.

Murrey stared past Swift to Owen and flashed him a brief smile. They'd met on a handful of occasions, but he could hardly call Owen a friend, and Murrey wasn't sure he really knew who he was.

Certainly, Owen showed no recognition when they briefly locked eyes. Owen frowned.

"Hey," Murrey said, doing his best to sound nonchalant as everyone in the room studied him. They were all holding weapons of one sort or another. He felt incredibly vulnerable and very much at their mercy.

"Who the fuck's that?" Owen asked.

"Murrey Dawson, one of our guys."

"And you brought him here?" Owen waved at the table and the illegal items scattered across it. "I take it you're vouching for him?"

"He'll keep his mouth shut," Swift replied and turned to him. "Right, Murrey?"

He nodded quickly. Now wasn't the time to hesitate. "Absolutely."

"You'd better be fucking right." Owen grunted.

"Tell him what you told me." Swift tilted his head towards Owen.

"Tell me what?" Owen asked and loaded bullets into a magazine.

Murrey coughed. "It's about Guy Gibson."

"That piece of shit?" Owen rumbled.

"He's recruiting. He's joined up with someone called Bill, and they invited me and the lads to a meeting. He wanted to bring us over to their side. He's working with the HGK gang."

Owen paused, freezing in place before glancing up from what he was doing. "He what?"

"They met with them, and they've started swapping intel. They're helping each other."

Owen slammed the gun down onto the table. "That little shit." He grunted and thought for a moment, before looking up again. "But you came to me?"

"Guy hasn't done shit for me."

"And the others in your crew?"

Murrey shook his head. "Nah. They've sided with Guy."

"I see." Owen narrowed his eyes. "Does he know you've come to me?"

"Nope."

Owen smiled. "Good. Let's keep it that way."

"Sure." Murrey wondered what Owen was thinking or maybe planning. But whatever it was, it would be fun to watch the smile drop from Guy's face when he realised what he'd done. "No problem."

"Good." Owen regarded him. He picked up the gun, slapped the magazine into it, and racked the slide, tossing the weapon at him.

Surprised, Murrey flinched but caught the weapon without setting it off. "Whoa."

"You ever used one of these?"

He'd carried one but never shot one. "A bit," Murrey answered, eager to sound tougher than he felt.

"What are you doing this afternoon?"

Murrey shrugged. "Not much."

"Wanna join us? We're gonna pay a visit to some of these Hyson Green shits and give them a piece of our mind. Show them who they're messing with. If you think you're up to the job."

Murrey's throat suddenly resembled the Gobi desert. He found it impossible to swallow, no matter how much he needed to or tried. "Ugh, yeah, sure."

"Good man." Owen turned to Swift. "You brought him here, he rides with you, he's your responsibility."

"Sure, boss."

Sliding another magazine into a different gun, Owen smiled. "Let's go fuck some shit up."

Chapter 25

Wednesday

"Goddamn it," Rob snapped and threw the pen he was holding on to his desk, where it clattered over the keyboard and against his used coffee mug, coming to rest to the left of his monitor. "Bastard."

"Sorry, guv," Nick said, shrugging. "It likely another dead end."

Rob sighed. "Of course it is. They're all just dead ends. None of these clues lead anywhere. They're all red herrings, and it's pissing me off."

"You and me both," Nick agreed. "I'll keep chasing them, but I wouldn't expect much."

"Thanks." Rob sighed and rubbed his hands over his face.

They'd been working this through for hours and hitting roadblock after roadblock, and time was slowly ticking away. He glanced at the clock in the corner of his monitor and grimaced. It was now or never, he reasoned. Time was running short, and they needed to at least try to stop this madman from repeating his psychotic games.

"Right, I'm gonna speak to the guv," Rob said and rose from his seat.

He strode across the room to the side office where Nailer was working. He knocked once and opened the door.

"Guv?"

"Rob. Come in. I was just about to come and get you. What's the latest on this Games Master killer? Where are we?"

"Up shit creek," Rob stated as he stepped into the room and closed the door behind him. "We're no closer to finding him."

"Tell me more."

"Right, well, we got the name of the company paying for the warehouse, but it's an offshore account belonging to a shell company that shut down a couple of days ago. We've been calling them, trying to get more information on who's behind it all, but we're just getting nowhere. Everything's a dead end, and the banks in question are throwing up the usual bullshit privacy regulations. But I don't think it would matter if they weren't doing this. Whoever set this up knew they'd be discovered and covered their tracks. We'll keep on it and continue to follow those leads, but it's not something we're going to be able to do in a day, or even a few days. This will take weeks or even months."

"Not unexpected," Nailer replied.

"No. They work at a glacial pace, and there's little we can do to get them moving."

"Okay, so the money is a dead end. Anything else?"

"Yeah, we've followed other lines of enquiry, but with the same crap results. Nick spent the afternoon interviewing people who work on that industrial estate. There were a few who saw the man come and go, but no one spoke to him as far as we can tell, so that's gone nowhere. We've now got footage of the van the killer used to kidnap the three victims from last night. We've got it on several cameras, both from the Hargreaves murder, and the warehouse murders, and we got the plate. Naturally, it's a stolen plate belonging to a different vehicle from somewhere down in Derbyshire. So we can't trace the owner either."

Nailer gave him a solemn nod. "I see where this is going. Okay, then we do the only thing we can do. Landon approved the use of the image, so we release the photo of the two people he's going after next. Do what you need to do. Send it out, call a conference, the whole nine yards. We should be able to get on the evening news. You've still got a few hours. With luck, someone will recognise them and let them know."

"On it," Rob said and bolted from the office.

Chapter 26

Wednesday

Grim-faced, Scarlett drove through the city towards the latest report of gang violence linked to the war between the Masons and the Hyson Green Killers. The crime scene officers hadn't even finished with the last scene, and now there was another.

The conflict between the two gangs seemed to be intensifying, even now, weeks after Owen had killed Hadley Watts. She wondered if she was missing anything. Had something happened or changed to make things tick up a notch?

Maybe she needed to lean on her informants again and try to find out what has going on, especially now that the gang were conducting these attacks in broad daylight.

Of course, it shouldn't matter whether these attacks happened during the day or night, it changed nothing either way, but somehow, it felt natural for these kinds of things to happen after dark, rather than during the cold light of day.

Beside her, in the passenger seat, Ellen yawned.

"Am I keeping you up?"

Ellen did her best to stifle the yawn. "No, sorry. I don't think I've fully recovered from the gig at the weekend."

"Oh? Who did you see?"

Ellen smirked. "No one. We were playing."

It took a moment for Scarlett to fully register what Ellen had just said, and it snapped her right out of her train of thought. Instantly, she'd forgotten about the case and was totally focused on what her partner had just said.

"You were… You were playing?"

Ellen nodded.

"You're in a band?"

"I am. I'm the singer."

Scarlett was fascinated. "What kind of band? What music do you play?"

"All sorts. Lots of covers. Indie rock and stuff."

"Wow. I had no idea."

Ellen smiled sheepishly. "I don't really announce it. It's my thing. It's something I love."

Scarlett felt the weight of responsibility fall on her shoulders. "I'll keep it quiet, if you like."

Ellen laughed. "Thanks. Tucker knows. I'm not sure if the others do. It's not a big secret or anything, but I like to keep it as my little thing."

Scarlett nodded in understanding. "I get it. Sure. So you were out late at the weekend?"

"Yeah. We had a gig in town. We play at several places fairly regularly and do the occasional wedding and stuff. It's just a side thing, you know?"

"I understand." She twisted her lips in a grimace. "I'm not sure I'd have time to fit that in alongside everything else."

"I'm surprised I do, to be honest." Ellen smirked. "I guess I just make time. We all make time for the things we love."

Scarlett nodded in agreement. "Ain't that the truth."

They arrived at the scene and the chaos that blocked the street. Police were everywhere, trying to preserve the scene from contamination as rubberneckers pressed in. There were knots of youths standing around, their hoods pulled high. Some cycled around on bikes, mouthing off at the officers just trying to do their job.

It felt like a simmering pot of anger that could go either way if they weren't careful. They needed to keep things calm and demonstrate that they were taking the concerns of the locals into consideration.

"These gang attacks always bring out the best in people," Ellen remarked as they climbed out.

"Things seem calm right now," Scarlett muttered. She locked the car and checked it. "If we do our job right, we'll be fine."

"Here's hoping," Ellen agreed. "You can bet the gang will be watching us."

"Oh, they're here all right." Scarlett scanned the crowd. She couldn't pick out anyone she knew from her weeks of investigation, but it didn't take much to spot the onlookers who were likely part of the Hyson Green Killers.

That wasn't why there were here, though, and she needed to stay focused on the job at hand. The pair made their way through the outer and inner cordons, getting signed in, and picked up forensic suits.

Within minutes, they were inside the house, amidst the remains of a nightmare.

The crime scene manager walked them through to the back of the house, past some bloody smears on the walls and signs of violence, where furniture had been kicked over or smashed.

In the rearmost room, they found their two victims, Liam 'Razor' Doyle and his girlfriend. Liam had been tied naked to a kitchen chair placed in the middle of the room and was a blood-smeared mess. He'd been beaten and tortured to the point of unrecognisability. She'd seen pictures of Liam before during her investigations, but there was little left that reminded her who he'd been in life.

Liam's partner, Myra Beckett, lay on the nearby sofa, partially stripped and clearly tortured.

"It appears he was strapped to the chair and forced to watch while they abused her," the CSM related.

Scarlett took a deep breath, having come to the same conclusion. It looked like she'd been raped and mutilated before they'd finally killed her. Whether they wanted information out of Liam or not wasn't clear, but the pain they wanted to inflict was writ large all around the room. They knew what they were doing. They wanted to make this as horrific as possible, and in her opinion, they'd succeeded.

"And when they'd finished with her, they tortured him before killing them both," Scarlett concluded.

"Something like that."

"They're sending a message," Ellen remarked. "The HGK gang killed and tortured people at that crack house, right? So it makes sense that this was retribution."

"It's all retribution and revenge," Scarlett agreed. "They go back and forth like this endlessly. It's a cycle of violence. You kill ours, we kill yours. You torture ours, we torture yours, and on it goes."

Scarlett shuddered at her phone buzzing in her pocket. She plucked it out and glanced at the caller's name. "I gotta take this," she announced and marched from the house as Ellen nodded.

Outside, she answered the phone. "Yes?"

"Our friend from the crack house broke easily enough," Calico said without preamble. She was a woman of few words.

"Well done."

"Once you know the right buttons to push, it's easy."

"What did he say?"

"He told me that Owen has been staying in a house in Newark, or had been until recently, when he moved."

"Moved? Where to?"

"He thinks he went to see Carter Bird and believes Owen is probably still there."

Scarlett scowled. "Carter Bird? I went to see him a little over a week ago."

"Sounds like you were early."

Scarlett grunted. "You have an address for that Newark house?"

"I do. I'll send it over."

"Great, thanks. Well, I guess I need to pay Carter another visit."

"Be careful." Calico hung up.

"Everything okay?" Ellen walked out of the house.

"Fine." Scarlett stuffed the phone into her pocket. Using Calico was not exactly standard procedure, and she preferred to keep such things to herself when she could. It wouldn't be difficult to find a reason to turn up on Carter's doorstep again, but finding a way to search the property was another matter entirely. Well, one step at a time, she reasoned. Maybe she'd get lucky. "Just fine."

Chapter 27

Wednesday

"I hate these things," Rob muttered. He shifted from foot to foot and glanced over his notes. He'd been through them countless times already and knew them back to front, but every so often, his mind would go blank, and he couldn't remember what he was supposed to say in there.

It was just nerves, and nothing unusual, given the circumstances. Speaking at, or even just attending, these things was one aspect of his job he hated.

He'd rather be out there, hunting down clues and throwing the perpetrators behind bars, but that wasn't always possible, and sometimes they needed the public's help.

This was one of those times, and he wasn't looking forward to it in the slightest.

"I can tell," Nailer commented. "You're making me nervous with your constant pacing.

"I just want to get it over and done with and then keep my fingers crossed that something useful comes from it."

"Don't we all, Rob. Don't we all."

Rob grimaced. He walked to the nearby door and peeked through the thin vertical strip of glass into the conference room. It was the room they always used for these kinds of things, and there was a steady stream of journalists, photographers, and camera operators coming in and setting up their stuff.

His phone rang.

Annoyed, he plucked it from his pocket and glanced at the name.

Mary.

Pleasantly surprised, he answered quickly. "Hey. Is everything all right?"

"Hi. Yeah, I'm fine. Um, I just thought I'd give you a call. See how your day was going. That's all."

"Really?" It was odd. She'd never done that before. He frowned. "Why?"

"Well, because I'm here, at the Lodge, about to watch the press conference, and wondered if you were going to be part of it."

"Oh." He turned back to the door and peered through. It was difficult to get a clear view of the room while people moved back and forth as they set up. "Where abouts are you?"

"In the conference room, towards the back. Are you here?"

"Yeah. In the next room. I'll be part of the conference."

"Aaah. I wondered if you might be. Good luck, I hope it goes well."

"I'm sure it will. Do you want to ask a question during it?"

"Hmm, could do. Don't feel like you have to, though. It might be a little odd."

"Nonsense. I'll see how it goes, and if the opportunity presents itself, we'll throw one your way."

"Sure, okay. Thank you. Good luck."

"Thanks."

She hung up. Rob smiled and glanced through the window set into the door again. After a couple of seconds, the room settled, and he finally saw her at the rear of the room, surrounded by other members of the press.

Suddenly, she spotted him and smiled. Rob smiled back, decidedly calmer. She gave him a surreptitious wave and winked.

He waved back, before a fellow journalist got her attention and spoke to her.

Taking a breath, Rob stepped away from the door. He turned to see Nailer giving him a curious look.

"Mary's out there," Rob said, by way of explanation.

"I guessed," the DCI replied. "Feeling better?"

"A little."

"Good. You were doing my head in. So, she wants a question, does she?"

"Only if we're taking them," Rob answered.

"Well, I kind of have to now, don't I." Nailer smiled mischievously.

"Not if you don't want to."

Nailer laughed and waved his explanations away. "It's fine. I was having you on. I'll keep an eye out for her, and if she's got her hand up, I'll give her the chance to ask something. Fair?"

"Fair."

The door to the conference room opened, and a man in a suit appeared. "Ready?"

"Sure." Rob eyed Nailer, who gave his assent. He turned to the civilian. "Lead on."

They walked out of the side room and moved to a table set up at the front, with a pair of chairs behind it. As they sat, the civilian explained how a TV remote on the table would allow them to display the photo on the large TV behind them. Then he backed away, and everyone waited for them to start.

Rob caught Mary's eye. She smiled at him reassuringly. He looked away and took a steadying breath. Nailer launched into the presentation. He began by introducing them both, then got swiftly to the point.

"You will be aware of the recent killing of Sandy Hargreaves on Monday, and Hank Durand, Lulu Purcell, and Darell Salmon yesterday in horrific circumstances. There have been rumours that these killings were linked, and I'm here to confirm that this is correct, and that we need the help of the public to aid our capture of the man who committed these terrible acts of violence before he does it again. So, I'm going to hand over to the lead investigator on the case, Inspector Loxley."

Rob nodded to his boss. "Thank you. The killer, who's referred to himself as the Games Master, has left a clue as to who his next victims might be, in the form of this photo." He pressed the button on the remote, and the photo appeared on the screen.

To either side of the room, civilian workers started handing out copies of the photo to the assembled crowd.

Rob gave the room a moment to calm down before continuing. "We believe that the killer is intending to attack or kidnap, or has already kidnapped, these two people. We don't know their names or anything about them, and we only have this photo to go on. We've attempted to use our forensic teams to track them down, but with time passing quickly, we have decided to go public and enlist the help of the community. So, if you're watching this, look closely at this photo and if you recognise the man and woman you see here, please get in touch using the number on the screen."

Rob glanced at Nailer, passing back to him. "Thank you, Inspector. Now, does anyone have any questions?"

Hands were quickly raised, and the assembled reporters called out, asking their questions anyway. Mary was not yet asking for a question.

Nailer pointed to one of them, and the rest of the crowd fell silent.

The journalist introduced himself then launched into his question. "How close are you to finding this killer?"

"We're doing all we can, and we hope to have good news for you as soon as possible." Nailer pointed to a second reporter.

"How long have you had this photo? Did you find it at the crime scene?"

"A few hours," Nailer replied and moved on, and still Mary didn't raise her hand.

"So, this is a serial killer?"

"Correct." He pointed again.

"Given that it was Sandy Hargreaves' husband who actually killed her, not this Games Master, will you be pursuing charges against him?"

"Not at this time, no. He needs our support after going through that terrible event, and he's a valuable witness."

"Given that the public are at risk, why are you only coming to us with this one? When are you going to do something and find this killer?" another journalist demanded, sounding angry.

Rob grimaced. He didn't like the tone of this question, or the direction this conference was going. Some of the reporters seemed combative. Towards the back of the room, staring at the last reporter in disgust, Mary raised her hand.

"We're dedicating as much of our resources as we can to this, and you can rest assured that we will find him." Nailer glanced at Rob, who, with a tiny movement of his head, directed Nailer's attention to Mary. Or he hoped he had anyway.

Nailer looked over to see Mary with her hand up, waiting patiently. He pointed at her.

"Thank you," she said. "Mary Day, *Nottingham Echo*. We appreciate you coming to us with this, and we'll be sure to publish it right away." She got a couple of groans and muttered comments at that. "Is there anything else that we, as the press, can do to help you find this killer?"

More muttered insults fluttered about the room, directed towards Mary. Rob prickled at them, wanting to shut them down.

Nailer ignored the crowd's response and answered Mary. "Please, get this photo and everything we've told you about this case out to your audience as fast as you can. You could save the lives of these two innocent people tonight." He chose another journalist.

"Is the public at risk?" he asked after giving his name and publication.

"The wider public? No. Not right now. You're only at risk if you think you are the couple in the photo. So, if that's you, please get in touch." He chose another journalist.

Rob noted that it was Vincent Kane, the man who'd taken a disliking to him in a similar way to Bill.

"Vincent Kane, *Mansfield Gazette*. Given that you had these photos hours ago, will you or Detective Loxley take personal responsibility for the loss of life if these two people die at the hands of this killer?"

Nailer gave Vincent a withering glare. "We're working around the clock to find this killer and using all methods at our disposal. Loss of innocent life is always a tragedy we hope to avoid, and every death is felt keenly by our dedicated officers," he answered, then rose from his seat. "Thank you, that's all."

Rob followed suit and stood. He glanced at Mary, who winked at him.

Turning away, Rob smiled to himself and followed Nailer out of the room to the chorus of shouts from the journalists. He was glad to get out of there.

Chapter 28

Wednesday

Following Google Maps on his phone, Jacob drove at a steady pace along Derby Road in Nottingham, heading west. Threading along the north edge of the exclusive Park Estate, the affluent nature of that area spread out into some of the surrounding roads. They might not be inside the estate, but they benefited from being close to it. The crime rate would be lower, but the house prices would be sky-high. Only the wealthy could afford to live in such places.

The Park was on his left, and so was DCI Nailer's house, just a little further along. He'd passed it yesterday to scope it out but hadn't stayed. He'd focused on his primary target, Erika, but it seemed like she was onto him. Yesterday, he'd followed her from the café where she worked to her car, but she'd made it difficult for him.

He didn't enjoy scaring the girl too much, but he had a job to do, and his client wasn't the forgiving type.

After he caught up with Erika this morning, she quickly spotted him, blowing his cover in short order. He'd hung around for a few hours, but she was clearly on guard and was unlikely to do anything useful. He'd need to be more circumspect, he reasoned, although he wasn't sure how he'd achieve that. He'd need to think.

Luckily, she wasn't his only line of enquiry.

Apparently, Erika was somehow linked to two other men, Rob Loxley and John Nailer, both of whom were detectives in the Nottinghamshire police, and it was the nature of her link to these two men that his client was most interested in. He needed to work out what that link was, and gather proof of it. So far, the only proof he'd gathered was that Nailer was acting as a guarantor for Erika's flat. That hinted at a close relationship, maybe a mentor role, or some kind of father figure. Was there a family relationship there? Was it possible that he was her biological parent?

He had no proof of that, and despite putting in a request for her birth certificate, he'd been unsuccessful as he didn't know her full details, such as who her parents were. Ironic, considering that's what he wanted to know.

He needed to do more digging, clearly.

Jacob passed John Nailer's house on the left, on alert for anything that might hinder his investigations or cause him problems if he attempted to stake it out.

But the street seemed normal, and he spotted a couple of places where he could park up and keep watch. Turning back, he picked out a suitable spot and pulled in, slotting his car into the space and turning the engine off.

He did not know if Nailer was in or not, probably not, given it was only late afternoon, so he settled in, getting his camera ready, and waited. It took a surprising degree of willpower to keep his attention on the house and not get distracted by his phone and start doom scrolling through social media. So, to keep his mind focused, he played games with himself, such as picking out colours of passing cars or coming up with backstories for the people who walked by.

But despite his best efforts to pass the time, it seemed to drag on forever, no matter what he did.

An hour and a half in, the passenger door suddenly opened. Someone stepped into the car, picked up his camera, and sat in the seat beside him.

"Hey, what the hell?"

It was a stocky blonde woman with short hair and a severe face. Her cold stare brought him up short, and a pang of fear washed over him. He felt like she was silently challenging him to do or say something.

After a brief moment of hesitation, he found his voice. "What are you doing?"

"I could ask you the same thing."

"You're in my..."

She slapped him across the face. "Shut it. Or next time I hit you with this." She held up his camera by the long lens that was attached to it.

Jacob clamped his mouth shut. Who the hell was this woman?

"ID, now."

"You can't do this..."

The lens of his camera smashed into his face, slamming his head back against the headrest.

"I warned you. ID now."

Jacob hissed at the pain, suddenly scared. She wasn't messing about and was clearly happy to hurt him. He did as she asked and rummaged for his wallet. "I'll report you." He handed her his driver's licence.

She peered at the card. "Go ahead, I'm not the one spying on police and stalking a young woman at night."

Jacob tensed. She knew what he was doing?

The woman pulled out her phone, she snapped a photo of his licence before dropping it into the footwell.

Watching with mounting terror, he blurted out, "What are you gonna do?"

She looked up at him. "Watch you, to make sure you do as I ask."

"Which is what?"

"Go home, right now, and wait for us to call you."

Jacob took a moment to process what she was saying and narrowed his eyes sceptically at her. It was not what he'd expected to hear. "Aaah, okay. Sure. You're going to call me? How? You don't know my nu..." Her raised eyebrow brought him up short. His number was listed in various places. It wouldn't be difficult for them to find it.

"There will be instructions. I suggestion you do as we say."

The woman opened the memory card slot on his camera and popped the card out before throwing the camera into the back seat.

He flinched at her careless attitude towards his expensive equipment and turned to make sure the camera had survived the ordeal. It seemed okay.

He looked back to find her already halfway out the door. She slammed it behind her without another word. He watched as she walked to the nearby wall and put her back to it while making a call. She spoke into her phone, staring at him.

After a couple of seconds, she waved him away, urging him to leave.

Jacob chewed on his lip. He glanced over at Nailer's house and then back to the woman, who wasn't leaving.

She raised an eyebrow and inclined her head.

"Crap," he muttered and started the engine. He didn't think he was going to get away with this. They were onto him and would resist his investigation at every step. He could continue, and his client would likely want him to, but it felt like it would be a futile endeavour from here on out and could also be quite dangerous.

With a final glace at the woman, Jacob pulled into traffic and made for home.

Chapter 29

Wednesday

Rob walked back into the office, drained. Preparing and then hosting a press conference to ask for the public's help at the end of another long day was an exhausting experience.

Following him in, after leading the conference with him, Nailer slapped him on the back.

"Well done," he commented. "You did well."

"Thanks. I just wish we could have got it out sooner."

Nailer nodded. "I know. I pushed it through as quick as I could, and we're well in time for hitting the six o'clock news, which is our best chance of finding a lead, so…"

Rob grumbled. "I know. I'm just frustrated by it all. He's already killed four times now, and I feel no closer to finding this bastard than I did when I walked into that first crime scene."

"With luck, this will change things, and we'll start making some progress."

Rob nodded but didn't feel terribly optimistic. "I hope so," he said.

Nick noticed them walking into the room and rose from his desk.

"Hey, what's up?" Rob asked.

"Reception called. Kurt Hargreaves is downstairs. Says he wants to speak to us."

"Oh, okay. Wanna head down there?"

"Aye, I could do with stretching my legs."

"Let me know if it's anything useful," Nailer said, heading towards his office.

"Will do," Rob confirmed. He turned and made for the exit with Nick beside him. He checked his phone and spotted a text from Mary and opened it. He read it quickly.

Well done. You did great. I'll see if I can come over later and text you if I can. It'll be late, though, I'm working overtime.

Rob smiled and sent a quick 'thanks' back in return.

"How'd it go?" Nick asked, referring to the press conference.

"Yeah, fine. As well as can be expected. Nailer took some questions, I just read from a prepared speech and left it at that. The press has all the details, so, now we wait and hope." But hope was one thing he didn't have much of right now. So far, everything led either to more clues or potential leads, or to a dead end. And it didn't seem to matter what they found out, they were no closer to finding out who was setting these horrific traps. They had precious few leads and even fewer suspects.

Would whatever Kurt had to say shed some light on all this? Would they finally get the break they needed?

He'd like to believe they would, but his optimism was waning. Luckily, his determination was doing the opposite, and Rob felt keener than ever to pin this on someone.

"We seem to be doing a lot of waiting and hoping," Nick muttered. "We need to get ahead of this. We need a break."

"Agreed. We'll find him and stop him, I'm certain of that, but I fear that there's going to be more suffering before that happens."

Nick grunted. "Let's hope not."

Rob grimaced as they approached reception and went through the security door to find Kurt sitting on a nearby chair.

"Mister Hargreaves," Rob said in greeting. "It's good to see you again."

"Hi. Sorry to bother you, I know you're busy…"

"We are, but we're always happy to speak to you. How are you and your daughter holding up?"

He shrugged and seemed to sag a little. "We're… taking each day as it comes, you know?"

"Of course. Sorry to bring it up."

"No, no. It's fine. It's been tough, but we'll get through it. Breanna is finding it hard. I think she blames me for… what happened, and… I don't blame her really."

"You had no choice. Remember that, Kurt. You chose to save your daughter's life, and one day she'll come to terms with all this. But she's going to need time."

"I know. Anyway, that's not what I came here to talk about."

"Of course not. What can we do for you?"

"I remembered something today, which I think might be related to what happened."

"Okay, how about you come through," Rob suggested and led him back through the security door, along a corridor, and into a side room where he directed Kurt to a nearby sofa.

Nick set his phone to record what Kurt said, and Rob pulled out his notepad.

"Please, go ahead," Rob said. "What have you remembered?"

"It was something that happened a few months ago. I was mugged."

Something slotted into place in Rob's mind. He recognised this piece of information. "I think we know about this," he said. "I saw it on your record."

"Yeah, I reported it at the time."

"Good man. So, do you think this is connected to your wife's murder?"

"I do now, yes. It's been niggling away at the back of my mind, and something just clicked today, you know? I realised what it was."

"Okay, why don't you take me through what happened."

"Sure. So, we were in town doing some shopping, and when we got back to the multistorey carpark, Sandy and Breanna went up to the car, and I went to pay. There was a pay station at the bottom of the stairwell. So I set about paying for my parking, and as I finished up, a man attacked me. He threw me against the wall, held a knife to my throat, and demanded to have my wallet."

"I presume you gave it to him?" Rob asked.

"Of course. He took it and ran out the door. Scared me to death. I quickly cancelled my cards and stuff, so he only got what was in the wallet. When reported it, the officer I spoke to said he thought it was odd, because the mugger didn't take my phone."

"That is a *little* strange. So, he just took your wallet?"

"Yeah. He didn't get much from me, really. Just some cash."

"What else was in your wallet?"

"Well, that's the thing. Because now I think back, I think the voice of the mugger and the Games Master were similar. So, maybe he didn't want money. Maybe he wanted my details. He wanted my address."

Rob pursed his laps and thought it through. "That's certainly possible. I take it he was wearing a mask?"

Kurt nodded. "A beanie hat and a mask, so I could only see his eyes." He paused and seemed to think for a moment. "I'm sure they were the same eyes. I'm convinced it was the same guy."

"Then you're probably right," Rob stated. "It probably was. Did you notice anything odd in the lead-up to the other night? Anyone hanging around your street? Anything odd in the house, like stuff moving or going missing?"

"Maybe, once or twice. I think Sandy noticed a couple of things that went missing, but I can't be sure with her gone."

"Of course. Don't worry. Was there anything else?"

"Not really. But I figured you could try and trace the mugger or something. It might help you out."

"You're right, it might. Thank you."

"I saw the news," Kurt said. "About the three killed in the warehouse? Is it the same guy?"

"Yeah, it is," Rob confirmed, seeing no reason to hide that from him. "We're working day and night to find him."

"I know. I know. Don't worry. And thank you. I appreciate all the support you've given me."

Rob smiled. He was grateful for the tip, but he wasn't sure it was going to suddenly solve the case for him. They finished up, taking as much detail as they could, before sending Kurt on his way.

With Kurt gone, Rob walked with Nick back to the office.

"It's not much, but it's something." Rob said.

"Something's better than nothing, and now we know he thinks it's linked, we try to link it all up. You never know, we might catch a break."

"One can but hope."

Chapter 30

Wednesday

Ryan stared out of the car window towards the pub, squeezing and releasing his fist as he nervously shifted position again. He'd been staring at the door for several minutes, while the others were getting impatient.

"What are we doing, Coops?" Jamie said, practically bouncing in the forward passenger seat. "Come on. We need to get in there. We need to get this done. You can't let these bastards get away with this."

"I know. I know. They won't. Trust me. We'll do this. I just need to be sure."

"Sure? Sure of what? We know they're in there."

"I know, but this needs to be done right. We can't screw this up.

Turning his head, Ryan glanced up and down the street again. He'd been to Retford before, but he didn't know the town terribly well. It was enemy territory, after all, so it wasn't somewhere he would choose to casually visit. But that last attack on Liam and his girlfriend was a step too far.

The Masons had crossed a line with that one, and they deserved to suffer for what they did.

He'd heard of others planning similar revenge attacks, but Ryan wanted to get in there first. Liam was a mate, and there was no way he was going to let these idiots get away with what they did to him and his girlfriend.

Satisfied that the road was quiet, Ryan looked back over at the pub and grimaced. The Hangman's Noose. He'd heard of it and knew it was a hangout for the Masons. It was one of their regulars, where the gang's Made Men came to kick back and relax.

So, where better to deliver their message? No one fucks with the Hyson Green Killers! And what a coup, to strike right in the heart of Mason territory.

They'd never see it coming.

"Coops, man, let's do this!" Theo raged in the back seat. "I wanna kick some arse."

"Come on," Jamie agreed, along with the two others in the car.

Each of them brandished a weapon, including a couple of blades, a hammer, and other makeshift melee items.

Cooper held a wheel wrench that he'd plucked from the boot of his car and felt the weight of it in his hand.

"Cooper!" Jamie called, clearly desperate to do something other than just sit there.

The nervous energy in Ryan's legs built, his left one bobbing up and down like a jackhammer. Suddenly, it was too much. "Fuck it, let's do this." He jumped from the car, unable to resist the urge to show these fools who they were messing with. His nervousness and apprehension screamed at the back of his mind, wailing, desperate to be heard, but he couldn't listen to it. Not now. He pushed it away, forcing it into silence, and led his crew over the road to the pub. He slammed the door open and stormed inside.

An aroma of warmth and hops washed over him. He moved inside, into a modest room of wooden beams, old framed photos, and well-worn tables. A quick headcount revealed eleven people in the room, scattered around various tables, including a man behind the bar.

Several of them, most of whom were men, could be part of the Masons. The couple sitting to his left were almost certainly not, and he couldn't be sure about the man at the bar, but the rest? Maybe.

"Evenin' lads," the server said, leaning on the bar. "What can I get yeh."

Spotting some glasses on the table closest, he brandished his wrench. "Which of you *fucks*," he smashed the glasses, "is a Mason then, hey? Which of you is gonna get fucked up first?"

Behind him, his mates issued a chorus of affirmations and spread out.

To his left, the couple stared at him in horror, but everyone else remained surprisingly calm and stoic. Several of them exchanged glances, and Ryan's confidence wavered, just a little. There was a curious mood in the room, and it wasn't one of fear. They seemed... offended and incredulous.

One of the men closest turned square on to him and frowned. A couple of the others adjusted their position to something more ready as they gave him and his mates the once-over. They didn't seem impressed.

"Are you sure you wanna do this?" the barman asked. "Do you know where you are, boy?"

"Boy? Boy?" Ryan took a step towards the bar.

Several of the men shifted moving to block him, but didn't attack.

"I suggest you start talking, old man." Ryan hesitated but quickly regained his composure. "The Masons. Where are they? Now!"

Furthest away, a man was sitting on a stool reading a local paper. He'd not yet looked up but shuffled his paper. "You know, they say print is a dying form of news. Especially local papers like this." He turned a page and then closed it to inspect the front. "The *Retford Times*. You should read it, it's good."

"What the…?" Ryan began.

"But for me," the man raised his voice, "it's more than just a paper. It's one of the linchpins of the local community. It's part of the vibe and feel of the town, you know? It brings us together, a bit like this 'ere pub."

"What are you talking about?" Ryan eyed the other men suspiciously but took a threatening step towards the man.

He rustled his paper again, before folding and rolling it up. Newspaper Man sighed and looked up. He was older, maybe in his fifties? Stocky and virile, but several decades older than Ryan and his mates.

The man shook his head. "You come in here, into our pub, think you can threaten us and get away with it?"

"We're gonna do more than threaten yeh, old man."

Newspaper Man grimaced and then glanced over to the scared couple. "You two, leave." He waved the rolled up paper at them.

Ryan frowned and peered back.

"Err, no!" Jamie protested and turned towards the couple as they rose from their table.

One man appeared out of nowhere and smashed his fist into Jamie's face.

Jamie staggered. "Fucker."

"Out. Now," the man who'd hit Jamie ordered the couple.

The pair clattered out of the establishment as quickly as they could. Another man closed the door behind them and locked it.

Ryan's stomach lurched.

"Now, you asked me what I was going to do about your visit and rudeness, right?"

Ryan turned to Jamie, who was bleeding from his nose. Deep in his gut, he felt his anxiety grow. Were they out of their depth? Would he come to regret this?

"You think this changes anything," Ryan snapped, pointing at where the couple had been sitting. "You've just evened the odds."

"Yeah, sure. You can believe that, if you like. But I like to think I'm a reasonable man, and I think you might have a few doubts about what you've walked into."

Around him, a few of the men had pulled weapons of their own. He swallowed and did his best to ignore the voice in his head telling him to run.

"So I'm going to give you one chance, and only once chance, to walk out of here, right now, and no more will be said. Besides, I don't want to damage any of this beautiful building and cause Mister Mercer any trouble." Newspaper Man waved his paper at the barman.

Ryan glanced right, just as the barman lifted a shotgun into view. He released the break action and slotted two rounds of buckshot into the two exposed barrels, before clicking it shut.

"No trouble at all." He eyed Ryan and smiled.

Newspaper man nodded. "Now then, children. What's it to be?"

"You bastards. You killed my mate, Liam. I ain't just walking out of 'ere. Someone's gonna pay, and that person is ye—"

Newspaper Man smacked him across the face with the paper, snapping his head to the side.

Ryan paused and then slowly looked up at Newspaper Man. His rage roiled and frothed; he knew there was no going back, even if he'd wanted to. Not now. His pride and his friendship with Liam wouldn't let him leave here without getting what he wanted. But the time for words was over. Tightening his grip on the wrench, he lunged for Newspaper Man.

Chapter 31

Wednesday

Jacob turned into his estate and made his way through the familiar series of roads towards his home with a feeling of trepidation. He sported a huge bruise on his face that both ached and would need explaining to his wife, and he still hadn't heard from the woman who'd inflicted this injury upon him. She'd promised that either she or someone associated with her would be in touch, but he'd been at his office for several hours and heard nothing. But he needed to get home. His wife, Tessa, would be waiting for him.

Surely, they'd have been in touch by now?

Had they forgotten or changed their minds? Maybe he could continue with the investigation?

Not with his luck.

But if he did pull out of the investigation, that was likely to be just the start of his problems, because he'd still need to somehow explain to his client why he was off the case and would not be returning to it. He dreaded that call and the repercussions of it.

Which meant it came down to a choice.

Should he stand by his client, who'd given him occasional but lucrative work for several years, even though he knew that Isaac Mason was involved in some shady dealings, and referred him to others Isaac knew needed someone like him? Or, should he do as the crazy woman asked and pull out?

As the hours had passed and the pain in his cheek faded, his initial submission to the attacker's threats and his fear of what she might do had waned, and he was starting to ask himself why he was agreeing to her demands.

Maybe he should tell his client about this. Isaac might be able to help. He certainly had connections.

He couldn't very well go to the police. Isaac and others had always been very clear about keeping them away from their dealings and paid him handsomely for his discretion.

Besides, it was the police he was looking into.

By the time he'd left the office, he was feeling much more self-assured and bolshy towards these thugs who thought they could bully him into stopping what he was doing. Why should he stop? Why should he let these people throw their weight around?

As he neared his home, his phone rang.

He glanced at it and sneered at the unknown, withheld number.

"Screw you," he muttered and declined the call.

Seconds later, it rang again. He declined it for a second time and turned into his driveway.

It rang once more.

With a sigh, he grabbed the device and answered.

"What?" he snapped.

"I advise you not to hang up, if you know what's good for you," said a digitally altered voice.

"And I advise you to stop harassing me."

"Stop your investigation into Erika Masey, effective immediately, otherwise…"

"Piss off," he barked and hung up. With a grunt, he stuffed his phone into his pocket, climbed out of his car, and made for the house.

His phone rang again.

Jacob sighed, plucked the device from his pocket, declined the call, and set it to vibrate only. "Get lost," he muttered, unlocking his front door and stepping inside. Light and warmth enveloped him. He shut the chilly night air away. Sounds of movement came from the kitchen.

"Hi, honey," Tessa called out. "How was work?"

"Yeah, good, thanks. Busy, though. You?"

"Yeah, all right. I've made a start on dinner."

"Excellent, I'll be right there." His phone buzzed once in his pocket. A text? He checked. It was from the same withheld number.

Answer the next call, otherwise steps will be taken.

Jacob sighed at his phone ringing again. It didn't seem like they were going to give up.

"Are you coming through?" Tessa asked. "I could do with a hand."

"I've got to take this call. Sorry, I won't be long." He turned into the front room and answered in hushed tones. "What do you want?"

"You know what we want. We need you to stop the investigation right away, and if you don't, we will make it public that you work with known criminals."

"Isaac Mason is an upstanding member of the local community," he protested. It was worth trying. To those who knew little about the Masons, it was easy to believe, but to those in the know, to those privy to certain information, the Masons were far from innocent.

"Sure, some will believe that. But he's not your only client, is he?"

Jacob clenched his teeth. "Don't you dare."

"Oh, I dare. How about I call your wife and tell her all about your work habits and where your income comes from? I have some fun images and investigative journalism I could email to her and her family that might colour their impression of the Masons and others."

"You wouldn't…" Jacob's wife's ringtone sounded in the kitchen. "Wait, don't."

In the other room, his wife answered the phone. "Hello? Hellooo? Anyone there?"

"Should I tell her?" the voice asked.

"No," he said and then called out to his wife, "Hang up, sweetie, it's probably just a spam call."

"Spam? Me? That's offensive," the voice said.

"Why are you doing this?"

"Because you're harassing people, and they don't like it. I've got your business bank account open here. It makes for interesting reading. Hmm. Oh yes. Right. I'll just screenshot that. Lovely.

"Leave me alone," Jacob pleaded.

"Absolutely, I'd love nothing better than to never speak to you again, but that very much depends on you, doesn't it. So, what's it to be? Shall I call your wife again? Or maybe I'll take out an ad somewhere and let all of Nottingham know what you're up to."

He was trapped, and he couldn't see any way out of it. Jacob's breath caught in his throat, and weighed up the options, but there was only ever really one option.

"Honey?" his wife called out. "Everything okay?"

He covered the phone with his hand. "Two minutes." He stared into the middle distance. There was nothing else he could do. There was no way he was going to sacrifice his business and his marriage to this.

With an exasperated sigh, he placed the phone back to his ear. "Okay, fine. You win. I'll stop."

"Thank you. And remember, we're watching you." She hung up.

Defeated, Jacob lowered his phone and groaned. Now he needed to speak to Mr Mason. But that could wait until tomorrow. No need to get into that now.

"Hey. Are you all right?"

Jacob spun to find his wife standing at the door to the living room. He went to answer, but Tessa's jaw dropped when she saw his face.

"Oh my God." She rushed closer. "What happened to you?"

He'd forgotten about the bruise.

Chapter 32

Wednesday

Leaning back on the wooden kitchen chair, Rob sighed contentedly and smiled across the table at his mother. She matched his smile and sipped at her glass of wine.

For the first time today, Rob felt relaxed and happy. Over the course of the meal, he'd slowly forgotten his troubles while his mother talked about inconsequential, everyday things that weren't about to shatter anyone's life, and it was an utter delight.

Having her back in his life after all these years was amazing, and he couldn't be happier about.

Of course, it came with certain precautions because of the circumstances they found themselves in, but with a full belly and cool glass of wine, those concerns slipped away easily enough.

He had no idea he was coming here tonight. As usual, nothing had been planned, because it was best if these visits were spontaneous. But once he'd been invited, he went through a rigorous series of checks and precautions. He'd called Riddle to get an update on the Masons, looking for reassurance that there was no suspicious activity and that he wouldn't be followed. It appeared that she and Calico had convinced the private investigator to back off from poking into Erika, which was another weight off his shoulders.

But once his various checks were complete, he took a roundabout route to get here, going through a series of switchbacks and using a few techniques designed to highlight and then throw off anyone who might be following him.

As far as he could tell, though, no one was. He was clean and free to see his mum.

"I remember when you left, you know," Rob said. "I remember waking up the following morning and realising you were gone and what that might mean for me."

"Sorry," she began. "But..." she waved towards Erika who was sitting to Rob's right, also enjoying her drink.

"No, don't be. You did what you needed to."

"Because I *was* pregnant at the time and knew it wasn't Isaac's," his mother explained. "I was beginning to show. I hid it for a while, but..."

"Of course, I get it. I didn't know that then and remember being upset and angry with you. I couldn't understand why you'd done it, why you'd spent all those years protecting me from my dad and brothers, only to vanish. It was why I slipped so easily into working with my brothers. I was acting out."

"The choice to leave you there has played on my mind for so long," she said. "You can't imagine the guilt I felt over that, but I knew that if I took you, he'd hunt me down and follow me to the ends of the earth. I didn't want that for you."

Rob nodded, aware that she'd tasked Nailer with watching out for him, and in time, extracting him from the family when the moment presented itself. Her desire to give him freedom and let him live a full life, rather than stay in hiding for the rest of it, was why she'd never approached him. That and because if she ever revealed herself, her life would be in danger.

"That's okay. You did what you needed to. I know that now," Rob comforted her. "And it all would have continued on quite happily had Erika not stuck her oar in."

"Oi," Erika sniped, eyeing him reproachfully before smiling and shaking her head. "I guess you were just too dark and mysterious for me to stay away."

"Trust me, there's nothing mysterious about me," Rob stated.

"I hope Isaac didn't treat you too badly, after I left," his mum said.

"Not too bad, no. He was upset, but he wasn't the worst. That was Owen. I truly think he hated me and had it in for me the whole time. Although, his desire to punish me is what led to getting out of there."

"He locked you in at a crime scene, right?"

"Yep. Left me to take the fall. Luckily, Nailer had been following me and knew something was up. He got me out of there and saved me. Another night I'll never forget."

"A more positive one, though," his mother suggested.

"Of course."

"Speaking of more positive things, tell me more about this pretty lady you're seeing. Mary, is it?"

"Yeah, Mary." He grinned at the thought of her. "She came out of nowhere, honestly. I'd been seeing someone else, on and off for a while. Mainly off." He thought of Matilda. He saw her occasionally, but it had certainly become less frequent in recent weeks. She probably knew about Mary and made a choice to keep her distance. He couldn't blame her, really. "But when she found out about my family, she backed off. Then that whole Red Room thing happened, where I was working with Mary, and it really threw us together."

"She seemed nice when I met her."

That was the night Mary had brought him here for the first time. She hadn't been back since, though, mainly due to calendars not lining up.

Rob nodded. "I like her."

"That's always a good place to start," she answered.

"Even though she's a journalist?" Erika asked.

Rob smirked. "Yeah, even in the face of that, I still like her. I can't hold that against her. They're not all bad, after all."

"How very diplomatic of you," Erika said.

"Don't get at your brother," their mother said to Erika. "I've only just got him back. I don't need you driving him away."

Erika rolled her eyes. "Looks like you can do no wrong."

Rob grinned at his half-sister. "She's probably sick of the sight of you."

A single finger was raised in his direction.

"Ignore her," his mum said and reached out, taking his hand in hers. "Don't you go messing Mary around, now. You hear me?"

"Yes, Mum."

"Good."

"Christ, I'm getting more crap sitting here than I do at work, and that's saying something."

"How is work?"

"Frustrating," he answered, the tightness of anxiety and concern over the case gripping his heart once more. "But we'll get there."

"Are you still dealing with that anti-corruption man? I know you've struggled at work over the years."

"Jesus, Mum," Erika said. "I thought this was supposed to be a nice relaxing meal, not the third degree."

"I'm curious."

"It's okay," Rob said. "I don't mind." He turned to his mum. "Things are better at work now. The man you're talking about was Bill Rainault, but he's left the force in disgrace, mainly for doing dodgy stuff to get to me, and from what I know, he's turned fully to the dark side."

"You mean...?"

"He's a wanted man," Rob clarified. "A criminal. I don't really want to go into it, but he's screwed himself quite badly recently."

"Oh, I hope you're not in any danger."

He dismissed her concerns. "Nothing I can't handle."

"Okay. Fair enough," his mother answered and changed the subject.

As they chatted, Rob got a text from Mary saying she'd let herself in back at his and would see him when he got home. He let her know he'd be a little while longer, but it wasn't too long before the evening came to a natural end and Rob was saying his farewells.

Enjoying the ride home in his 1985 black Ford Capri Mark 3, he blasted through the countryside surrounding Nottingham, then plunged into the lit streets of the city.

Driving through the shadowed suburbs, he wondered if the killer was out tonight, somewhere, luring another victim or two into his third twisted game, or would he leave that for another night?

He pulled into his parking space behind his apartment building, his mind filled with imagined horrors that might await him at work tomorrow. Rob climbed out of the car and locked it, running his hand appreciatively over the paintwork.

"You're out late tonight," said a voice from close by as something grabbed his head and smacked it into the side of his car.

Rob grunted and flailed. He tried to pull away. He staggered between his and a neighbour's car, out into the quiet back road, and turned. He'd recognised the voice and looked up at the familiar face that leered down at him. "Bill."

"Where have *you* been this evening?" Bill asked.

Rob narrowed his eyes and peered up at his building. His head spun, and his vision swam from the pain. Something warm and wet trickled down his brow, and he saw deep dark blood on his fingers when he pulled them away from his temple. Was Mary okay? How long had Bill been waiting here? He took a long, deep breath and squeezed his eyes shut. It didn't quite banish the vertigo, but it helped. Rob squinted up at Bill and formulated an answer.

"Out," he groaned. "My job keeps me busy."

Bill sneered. "While you still have a job."

"Really?" Was he still angry that he was a serving police officer?

Bill shrugged. "I wouldn't want you to think that I'd forgotten about you. I've been busy..."

"No shit. You're a wanted man."

"I was framed... Not that you care, I'm sure."

"Whatever. You killed someone. That tells me everything I need to know."

"Does it? How convenient." Bill lashed out and punched Rob in the face.

Pain, sharp and angry, flared as he tried to back away. The world tilted and spun. How far was the door to his building? He glanced over and cursed. Too far. Bill would never let him get there, let alone unlock the door and get inside.

Rob cursed himself for letting his guard down. He should have been more aware. "You're a murderer."

"I guess so. So, what are you gonna do about it?"

"Well, back up, give me a minute, and I'll slap some cuffs on you as soon as the world stops spinning."

Bill lunged again. Rob raised an arm to block him. But he was sluggish and uncoordinated. Bill slammed his fist into Rob's jaw.

The next thing Rob knew, he was on the cold, hard ground, having fallen.

"Fat chance of that," Bill said. "You're not taking me in." He kicked, burying his foot into Rob's side, and then did it again.

"Just do it, kill me. Kill a police officer. I'm sure your dad would be proud of you."

"Shut up," Bill roared and kicked him again before backing up. "No. I'm not going to kill you. I'm going to ruin you, like you did to me. This..." He held his arms out wide. "You did this. Who I am today is your fault, and I will make sure you suffer the same fate. Mark my words."

"Whatever," Rob grunted, but when he looked up, Bill was gone.

Chapter 33

Wednesday

Darius navigated the last few roads out of Hucknall, towards their home, satisfied and comfortably full after a very pleasant evening with his partner, Fraya, at a small Italian restaurant in town.

It was one of Fraya's favourite places to eat, and he'd wanted to treat her. She'd been grafting hard recently, putting in extra hours and working in the evenings at home, but that client's contract had ended, and he'd decided he wanted to spoil her.

"Thank you so much for this," Fraya said, reaching over and squeezing his thigh. "That was lovely."

"My pleasure," he answered, a little embarrassed.

"You're not *too* full, I hope. It was a massive pizza you had." She plucked her phone out of her handbag as she spoke.

"Nah, I'm fine. I enjoyed it." He'd have chosen a grill or burger joint as his eatery of choice, but he was always happy to tuck into a pizza. "Your pasta salad wasn't exactly tiny."

"It was more than enough for me."

"That's okay then."

"Huh, my phone has been going crazy. I've got a load of missed calls…" It suddenly buzzed in her hand. "Oh, hold on." She answered it. "Holly, hi. Are you okay?" Fraya paused and listened to her friend. "What? Are you sure? You're kidding. Are you sure it's us? Okay. All right, yeah, we can… Okay. Yes, I will. I promise. Don't worry, we're fine. Yes. Okay. Okay, bye."

Darius pulled into their shared driveway off a country road. "What's up?" he asked while driving towards the back of the house and the parking area.

"Holly said the police want to talk to us."

Darius braked. "What?"

"Yeah. Apparently there's been an announcement or something on the evening news, and they want to speak to us in relation to those killings that happened in the last few days. They think we're in danger."

"Us?"

"Well, they didn't name us. They showed a photo of a couple, and Holly thought it looked like us."

"Is she sure?" He parked and turned the engine off.

"I don't know. That's what she said. We're all over the news, apparently."

"That's crazy." He took out his phone and did a quick hunt online. "Let's get inside. Maybe she got it wrong."

"I think we should go to the police," Fraya suggested. "We can go straight there."

"Really?" Darius sighed and shifted in his seat. "I'd quite like to go inside first. It's cold, I need the loo, and I'd like to get changed."

"But… We're already in the car."

"I really don't want to drive to a police station right now if we don't have to. We should call them." He found the news article on his phone and saw the blurry black-and-white photo that was supposedly of them. Darius peered at it, unconvinced. "Are you sure that's us?"

He showed Fraya his phone.

"I think so… Maybe…" She didn't seem certain.

"It's hard to tell. The photo's rubbish."

"That's your jacket, isn't it? And I think I recognise my coat."

Darius scanned the article. "There's a number to call. Let's go and do that. It might not be us, but if it is, and they say to come in, then we can do that. Okay?"

She glanced at the house and then up the driveway. "Okay, yeah. I need the loo myself, actually, so…"

"There you go then," he said and climbed out of the car. He waited for Fraya and drew her in for a hug. "I don't want to go haring off to some random police station only to find out there was no need for it. It would ruin an otherwise great night." He kissed her.

"Yeah, it would," she agreed.

Lights flashed over the house as a van turned into the driveway and accelerated towards the parking area. It was similar to Greg's. They hurried to get out of the way and made for their apartment door.

Behind them, the van skidded to a stop as Darius unlocked his front door. He heard the door shut and turned to greet his neighbour.

Silhouetted by the van's light, the man marched towards them.

"Greg?"

Somewhere deep in his head, an alarm bell rang. This wasn't right. It didn't look like their neighbour.

The man raised his hand and stepped into the edge of the porch light's range. He was carrying a gun and pointed it at Fraya.

She yelped. "Oh my God!" She raised her hands in surrender.

"What the…?" Darius said in shock.

"Quiet!" the man hissed. He wore a mask over his nose and mouth, a beany hat, and weirdly, blue latex gloves peeking out from his sleeves.

"Sorry," Fraya whimpered in surrender, her knees buckling in terror.

"Wha… what do you want?" Darius whispered, holding his hands up, his voice catching in his throat. The world had gone mad all of a sudden.

The man reached for Fraya. "Come 'ere." He yanked her close by the scruff of her neck and then wrapped his arm around her throat, putting the gun to her temple.

"Don't hurt her," Darius pleaded, utterly helpless and lost.

The man glared at him. "Get in the van, now."

Seeing no other option, and completely terrified, Darius nodded. On wobbly legs, with a sinking feeling in his stomach, he crossed the driveway, cursing himself for not just driving straight to the police station as Fraya had suggested.

"I'm sorry, Fraya."

"I said quiet," the man barked under his breath and jabbed the gun into the back of his head.

"Ow," Darius complained.

"Open it, get inside."

Darius opened the van's rear door and climbed inside.

"On the floor, facedown, hands behind your head."

Darius did as the man ordered. There was an odd smell in here, and the bed of the van was cool against his skin. Beside him, the man pushed Fraya to the floor of the vehicle. She stared across at him, tears streaming over her cheeks.

"I'm sorry," he muttered.

"I love you," she answered.

Something pricked his arm. He looked up. A syringe! Seconds later, his vision faded.

"Darius! Darius. Don't leave me..."

The darkness took him...

Chapter 34

Wednesday

Following the strobing blue lights of the police car, Nick sped through the dark countryside to the outskirts of Hucknall and pulled into the property their tip off had given them the address for. Coming to a stop, he jumped out and marched towards the house. Uniformed officers from the patrol car joined him.

"Darius? Fraya?" Nick called, hoping that they weren't too late. "Go that way," he ordered one of the officers around the side of the house as he made for the front door to number 47B. He noticed three separate front doors, designated A, B, and C beside the number 48. The large house had been divided into three properties, apparently.

He knocked on the door. Keys hung from it. Nick frowned and tried the door. Why would keys be in it?

Already unlocked, it opened easily. With a frown, Nick moved to step inside, when a neighbour's door opened suddenly.

"They're not there," the man said.

Nick stepped back outside. "Are you sure?"

He pointed to his doorbell camera. "I'm sure. You got here quick. I only called a minute ago."

"Really? I wasn't aware of your call. We had another tip-off, though, earlier on. So, this is the house of Darius and Fraya, right?"

"Yeah, it is," the neighbour confirmed.

"And you are?"

"Greg. Greg Fairburn. I'm their neighbour. I heard some commotion outside and saw a van shoot out of here in a hurry, so I checked my app and saw what had happened. That's when I called you."

"Would you care to show me what happened?" Nick asked.

"Sure." He took out his phone and tapped at the screen, turning it sideways and holding it up.

Nick watched Darius and Fraya, who paid a passing resemblance to the couple in the photo they had, walk up to their front door. They unlocked it and turned when a man stepped into the frame and pointed a gun at Fraya's head.

"Jesus," Nick hissed under his breath.

The man dragged Fraya closer, wrapped his arm around her neck, and then moved out of frame while directing Darius to join him. Then they were gone.

"Damn it." Nick sighed, realising he was too late.

Chapter 35

Wednesday

With Bill gone, and the parking area quiet, Rob rolled to his back and stayed there. His face and side ached, and his pride had taken something of a beating as well.

He couldn't believe he'd allowed Bill to get the jump on him. He wasn't sure how he'd live this down. Nick was sure to comment on it. Bill was slimmer and shorter than he was, but there was a scrappiness to him that belied his size.

It was as the old saying went, he guessed. It's not the size of the dog in the fight; it's the size of the fight in the dog.

Whatever the case, he just needed a moment to let the pain subside before he attempted to get up and make his way inside.

It was a bizarre encounter. It seemed that Bill just wanted to remind Rob that he was still out there and had not yet moved on from his personal vendetta against him. The man, it seemed, remained as petty and obsessed as usual.

Wonderful.

He wasn't sure how long he lay there, probably no more than ten minutes, but it felt like a lifetime. Eventually though, he resolved to get up and quit moping around. Rolling to his good side, Rob got to his front and pushed himself up to his knees, where he took a moment to catch his breath before attempting to stand.

As he got his feet under him, he felt momentarily wobbly but soon steadied himself and rose to his full height. A sudden blood rush gave him a few seconds of tunnel vision, before that faded too, and he started to feel a little more normal, despite the lingering pain.

Taking a deep breath, he focused on putting one foot in front of the other and slowly made his way towards the building's door.

His phone buzzed. Reaching the wall of the building, he leaned against it and pulled his phone. "Hello?"

"Rob, it's Nick. He's struck again."

"He's stru…?" It took a moment for Rob to realise what Nick was talking about. "Oh, shit. The couple in the photo?"

"Yeah. We got a tip-off from someone who thought they recognised them. We raced over there right away as we couldn't get in touch, but we were too late. He'd already taken them. We even have the kidnapping on video."

"Does it show the killer?"

"Kinda. His face is covered."

Rob resumed his walk to the door, unlocked it, and stepped inside. "Of course it is." He closed the door behind him, glad to be out of the chill air. "Okay. Thanks for letting me know. You did what you could…"

"Are you okay?" Nick asked. "You sound… odd."

"Don't worry about me. I'll tell you about it tomorrow." Rob started up the stairs. "I take it we have people trying to track the killer?"

"Yeah. He used a van. I've got people going through the traffic cams, checking ANPR, the usual. If he slips up, we'll find him."

"Then let them do their jobs and get some rest. I have a feeling we're in for another long day. I'll see you tomorrow."

"Yeah, will do."

Rob hung up as he reached his apartment door and inserted the key. Stepping inside, he heard Mary call out from further in.

"Rob, is that you?"

"Who else were you expecting?"

"Wouldn't you like to know?"

Rob smiled. His head and side still hurt like hell, but the pain had faded a little on the walk up here. He wondered what state his face was in and how Mary might react. On tired legs, he wandered into the main living space to find Mary standing by the island, pouring him a glass of wine.

"I thought you might like…" She stopped when she caught sight of him and froze. "Oh my God. Are you okay?" Forgetting the drink, she rushed over and started to fuss over him. "What happened? Who did this to you?"

"It was Bill." A wash of emotion flooded through him at the mention of Bill's name. It felt good to get it out and to talk about it. Relieved, he thought back over the attack, and the first notes of anger bubbled up deep inside. "He jumped me as I got out of my car, and attacked." Rob sighed. "I can't believe he got the better of me."

"No one's invulnerable," Mary assured him and guided him to the nearby sofa. "Sit." She grimaced and peered at the wound on his head. "I need to clean that. Are you hurt anywhere else?"

"My side, he kicked me."

"Did he punch you?" She leaned in to get a closer visual and hissed through her teeth. "Ooof, that's nasty."

"Yeah. Slammed my head into the car roof, too."

"Christ. Okay, give me a moment." She dashed off to the kitchen, found the first-aid kit, and was back in moments with tissues and warm water. Settling in beside him, she started to clean him up. "You should get this looked at. You might have concussion."

"No, I'm fine."

"I disagree. I think we should go in and get you checked."

Rob sighed. "Maybe. I need to be back at work tomorrow. I'm not leaving this case."

"Fine, but you're no good to anyone if you collapse, are you?"

Rob grimaced. "No."

She grinned at him. "You know I'm right."

"Always."

Chapter 36

Thursday

Rising from the miasma of fitful nightmares and darkness, Darius thought he could hear someone calling him home, drawing him from the endless void of roiling darkness. He could hear his name, somewhere distant, somewhere just out of reach. If he could just pull himself from the thick oily sludge of his unconscious mind, maybe… maybe…

"Darius!"

Suddenly close and loud, the voice yanked him from the shadows into the…

He jerked up, awake, his vision blurry and bright. He shut his eyes. His whole body ached, and his cheek was cold where he'd been lying on something. He shook his head. Memories of pain and fear rushed back. He remembered being forced into the back of a van, being injected and… Fraya!

His eyes snapped open, wide. "Fraya."

She sat opposite him, on the other side of a small square table.

"Darius."

"I'm here. I'm awake. Are you okay?"

"I'm… fine…"

"Where the hell?" He glanced around.

They were sitting in the middle of some kind of deserted warehouse or derelict building. The room was large with a high ceiling and disappeared into shadows every way he looked. They seemed to be alone, sitting on opposite sides of this table and… He tried to move, but his arms and legs were clamped to the chair and table. No, not all of them. His right wrist was attached to a chain giving him a small amount of movement, and Fraya seemed to be in a similar predicament.

"I have no idea where we are," Fraya said. "But that's not important right now. Darius, see this?" She pointed to her neck with her chained hand as best she could. She wore a metal collar with wires and packs of some kind of dull tan substance around it. The collar was attached via a wire to an electronic unit on the table, out of reach of his chained wrist. An LCD clock counted down on its top. It also showed two beating hearts next to the timer. Beside the device, there was a gun and a note scrawled on a scrap of paper.

One must die for the other to live. Choose or perish together.

"What's this?"

The only thing on the table, close enough for either of them to reach with their chained hands, was the gun.

"He wants us to choose," Fraya said. "Or at least, I think that's what he wants. I think it's that killer on the news, the Games Master. I think it's him, and he wants us to play his game."

"That's a bomb around your neck," Darius suggested.

"Same as the one round yours."

He could feel its cold, unforgiving touch as it pinched his skin. He swallowed. "Is that what he wants? He wants you to kill me, or me to kill you? Is that it?"

"I think so."

She'd been crying. Her cheeks were flushed and wet, and her eyes bloodshot. He hated seeing her like this. They needed to get out of here. He couldn't let this happen.

"It's okay, we'll get out of this," he said and tried to jerk himself free from the bindings. "If I can just..."

"Stop," Fraya pleaded. "You don't have time. Look at the timer. Look at the countdown."

He'd purposefully ignored it, preferring to remain hopeful. They had a few minutes left. That was all.

"We have to choose," she stated.

"Choose?"

"Who lives. It's what he wants." She swallowed. "If you kill me, then you will live, and you can tell the police what happened."

"Hell no. No way. I'm not doing that. No. I want us both to live."

She sighed in relief. "But we can't. He won't let us."

"You don't know that," he protested. "If I can break free…" He violently jerked his chair again.

"Wait, no. Don't. You might make the bombs explode."

Darius froze, her words sinking in. He glanced at the wires again and realised she was probably correct. "Aaah, crap. Yeah, he's probably thought of that."

"You think?"

Darius glanced over the table, the wires and collars once more, and then slumped back into his chair, as much as his binders would allow. "So, we're screwed. Either one of us kills the other, or we both die."

"That's what it seems like."

"I don't want to die, and I don't want to live without you."

"Thank you, I feel the same," Fraya agreed. "I love you."

"I love you, too."

She smiled, and fresh tears sparkled in her eyes. "It was the perfect night, last night. The perfect way to end things, if... if this..."

"It was," Darius agreed.

He reached for her hand, and she reached back. Their fingers touched above the gun.

"I'm not shooting you," he said. "I'm just not doing it."

"I *can't* do it," she answered. "There's no way I could live with myself."

"Me neither. So, how about we wait and see what happens? It might all be a bluff."

"A game. A sick, sick game."

"It makes sense," he confirmed and glanced at the timer. They didn't have long left. "I can't believe this is happening."

"I've been so happy with you."

He smiled. "And me you."

"I love you so much." Her tears flowed freely.

Darius cried, too, as the seconds ticked down.

Three, two, one...

Chapter 37

Thursday

Scarlett left early for work, having planned this detour the day before. Coming here again was potentially something of a stretch, although not totally out of the realm of possibility.

So, after using some rather unorthodox techniques of information gathering and feeling grateful that Calico was on her side, the next logical step was to return to the sprawling estate near Mansfield that Carter Bird called home.

She'd been here a few weeks ago chasing up Owen Mason's location but had left empty-handed. And now here she was again, doing the same thing. Carter was a known associate of Owen's, so it wasn't too much of a leap, but she felt it was still best to keep this visit off the books, just in case. She didn't want to jeopardise her investigation any more than she already had.

At some point, she'd find Owen, and there was no way she'd let him off the hook. She had a personal vendetta against him for what he'd done to Ninette, and she was determined to get her revenge.

Driving through the gated entrance and up the long countryside road that was also the property's driveway, she was reminded of the serious money that criminality of this kind could bring. Was it any wonder that people did these things when the rewards were so huge?

It was risk versus reward, she guessed, and a very personal choice for anyone tempted by this lifestyle.

As she drove, the rustic collection of buildings that made up the main estate came into view. It was the kind of place where you'd find people shooting pheasant and walking about in tweed jackets.

She'd never gone in for that kind of thing, although plenty of her family had over the years down in Surrey. But this place hid a much darker secret, one she was determined to uncover one day.

She parked up at the front of the property and noted the surrounding cars. Land Rovers, a Jeep and a Bentley. She nodded appreciatively. At least they had good taste in motors. But she wasn't here to admire Bird's collection of vehicles and marched towards the front door. She approached, and two large men in black woollen coats stepped into view.

"Can I help you, Detective Williams?" one of them asked.

They remembered who she was.

She inclined her head. "I want to speak to Carter."

"I don't know if he's in, but I can check if you want to wait just here?"

"Please do," she confirmed and planted herself to the spot, crossing her arms. She wasn't going to be fobbed off. She needed to see him.

Scarlett waited for nearly ten minutes before the large security guard returned, with the much slimmer Carter in tow. The man sauntered out of the building with his hands in his pockets, relaxed and unconcerned about her visit.

"Mrs Williams," he greeted her. "To what do I owe the pleasure? Anyone would think you were stalking me."

"I wouldn't dream of it," she replied.

"Of course you wouldn't." He walked by and wandered towards the edge of the gravel, where he stopped and gazed out over the grass to the rolling farmland and patches of trees in the distance. "I sometimes wonder what this landscape would have been like, back in the days of Robin Hood, you know? Have you ever wondered about that? As far as I am aware, it would have all been woodland. Endless forests covered this part of England, from coast to coast. Incredible, right. Think about how much of that land we've lost. How many trees and woodlands."

"You're an environmentalist now?" she asked, giving him the side-eye.

"I'm as concerned about what we're doing to this planet as anyone else, maybe more so than the average person. I have a lot of land to manage, you understand."

"You do have quite a sizable estate," Scarlett agreed. "Plenty of space to hide stuff, or people."

"Aaah. I suspected as much."

"Is he here? Owen Mason? Is he somewhere on your estate?"

"If he is, I have no idea where." He seemed calm and unconcerned.

"And you're sure of that."

He turned to her. "What are you accusing me of?"

"Really? I thought that would be obvious."

"Spell it out for me." There was a threatening undertone to his words.

"I think you're aiding and abetting an escaped criminal, Mr Bird, and I'd very much like to have a look around your property."

"Do you have a warrant?"

Scarlett balled her fist. "I do not."

He shrugged. "Then I'm afraid the answer is no. My apologies. However, do feel free to return once you have the proper documentation, and I will be only too pleased to accommodate you."

His fancy word play was annoying. He clearly thought a lot of himself, and it made her skin crawl.

"I certainly will."

"Good day to you, Detective." With a flash of a smile, he turned and started to walk away. "I trust you can find your own way out."

He was lying to her, she was sure of it, but there was little she could do.

Chapter 38

Thursday

"The report came in a few hours ago. There was an explosion, so we had to wait while the bomb squad made sure it was safe before sending forensics in."

"It's him again, isn't it?" Rob replied as Nick drove them towards the warehouse district south of Lenton in Nottingham. The call had come in while Rob was still at home, and Nick had offered to pick him up.

"We think so, yes. It all fits from what I've heard."

"Wonderful, and we're still no closer to catching him either."

"Nope."

Rob grumbled in frustration, annoyed by their lack of progress.

After several seconds of silence, Nick pointed to his face. "So, are we not going to talk about this?"

Rob glanced at Nick. "I think you're very handsome."

"Piss off. You know what I'm talking about," Nick answered. "Looks like someone took a violent dislike to your face."

Rob grinned. "That's one way to put it." He sighed and prepared to launch into the story. "I got jumped when I got home late last night."

"Jumped? You were attacked? By who?"

"Bill."

Nick stared at him in shock. "What?"

"Yeah. It seems he wanted to reassure me that he'd not forgotten about his vendetta."

Nick's top lip curled in disgust. "Well, I guess it's kind of him to think of you like that. I'm sure you were very concerned."

Rob enjoyed Nick's sarcasm. "Oh, undoubtedly. I was never fond of the quiet life. I slept so much better last night."

"Have you reported it?"

Rob shrugged. "Why? He's already wanted for murder. Roughing me up won't add much to his sentence once we get him."

"You should at least write up a report."

Rob grunted. Nick was right. "Yeah, I know. I will."

Making their way into the industrial estate, they soon found the scene of the crime and parked up.

"Huh," Rob muttered. "I could get used to these warehouse district crimes. Fewer reporters and gawpers."

"Always searching for the silver lining."

"Something like that." Rob led the way through the outer and inner cordons, where they donned forensic gear before making their way towards the warehouse which was at the centre of activity.

Alicia joined them, having been here for a while already.

"Bomb Squad gave the all-clear an hour ago, so we've not had long," she said. "We're still in the early stages of processing the scene. It's a huge space so..."

"Take your time," Rob replied. "Do it right."

"Always. I'm just managing your expectations."

"And it's very much appreciated, Aston," he answered, following her into the building. "So, what do we have?"

"Two bodies," she answered.

They crossed the floor of the building to where a tent had been erected. People in full-body white overalls flitted around it, like moths to a flame. "They were both killed by explosive collars that detonated when the timer hit zero."

Rob frowned. "Both were killed?"

"I can only surmise that they refused to play his game and suffered the consequences."

"They called his bluff," Nick remarked. "Except, he wasn't bluffing."

Rob followed Alicia into the tent, where the headless remains of two people, a woman and a man, were still sitting in their chairs on either side of a small square table. The bodies were a mess, and even now, over a decade into his career, seeing these gory remains churned his stomach. It was the smell, mainly.

Rob averted his eyes and regarded the table, noting the electronic device, the gun, and the note. "I see what you mean. He wanted them to choose, for one of them to kill the other."

"But they refused," Nick added.

"Love conquers all?" Rob asked.

"Hell of a way to go."

"In a way, it's kind of sweet," Alicia remarked.

Rob raised an eyebrow at her. "You've been doing this job for too long."

"Now, that is true. Far too bloody long."

Rob turned back to the table. "Do we know if it's them? The couple from the photo? The people you were tipped off about?" He eyed Nick.

"Hard to tell." Nick crouched to get a better look at their clothing. He withdrew his phone and checked the recording of the kidnapping. "The clothes appear similar to the security camera recording, so it could be, sure."

"He's not tried to pull a fast one on us yet with his victims, so I think we can make a working assumption that it is until we get positive ID."

Nick nodded. "Sir."

Rob addressed Alicia. "Was there anything else we should know about?"

"Actually, yes, there is. This way." Alicia led them out of the tent and across the open floor space to an office room at the side of the building.

There were more forensic officers going about their work in here as well. Alicia led them inside and over to a whiteboard. The two officers who had been studying it and dusting it for prints, stepped away, revealing words scrawled across it.

If you were given a gun and told to kill someone, because the person you love most would die if you didn't, who would you kill?

Tomorrow, we'll find out who Jennifer chooses.

Rob read the text through a few times, committing it to memory. "Who's Jennifer?"

"No idea," Nick replied.

"How many Jennifers are there in Nottingham?" Alicia asked.

"If his target is even in the city," Rob added. "They could be in one of the towns or villages, or even further afield. We can put something out on the news again, but there's no telling if it would change anything."

"That's not a reason not to do it," Nick urged.

"No, it's not."

"Are you losing faith?" Nick asked with a knowing raise of his eyebrows.

Rob grimaced, annoyed at himself for allowing his mood to get the better of him. Last night's attack had got to him more than he wanted to admit in front of his coworkers. Bill's appearance after months without seeing him had hit him hard. He needed to snap out of it and focus on the job at hand. The families of the victims and the mysterious Jennifer were relying on him. "I'm just frustrated. We need a break. We need a lead. A solid lead. Not something like this." He waved at the board. "This is little to no help."

"Right," Nick agreed. "So let's get to work."

Rob nodded once to his friend. "We do all the usual. We speak to people who might have been working close by, who might have seen something in the weeks leading up to this. We check CCTV, and we also poke into the financials of the building. All the usual angles, and keep your fingers crossed."

"Fingers and toes, guv," Nick agreed.

Chapter 39

Thursday

Lucas pulled up outside his son's home and parked. He applied the handbrake and stared over at the modest house with its uncared-for garden and wondered if he wasn't going a little crazy. Somehow, with money Lucas couldn't account for, his son had bought it several months ago and moved in.

For weeks his concern had been growing, steadily and slowly. He, his wife, or both of them, would visit occasionally, and their son would grudgingly put up with them, making it clear he didn't want them there and would very much prefer it if they left.

But they'd only recently got him back and were only too aware of the mistakes they'd made with him as he grew up. They really didn't want to make those same mistakes again now that they had a second chance. A chance to make things right and hopefully turn their son into a productive member of society.

They tried to get him out of the house, help him meet people, maybe go on some dates, broaden his horizons, but it didn't seem to matter what they said or did, he just wasn't interested in anything they had to offer.

But there was no way they were going to give up on him. Not this time. Not now.

Lucas sighed and glanced at the double garage beside the house. Their son spent so much time in there, toiling away on his secret projects, whatever they were.

Lucas had tried to take an interest and find out more about whatever it was he was making, but their son just didn't want them anywhere near.

Lucas looked away, up the street. Maybe he should just go home and forget the fears brewing in his mind. Fears that had been bubbling away under the surface. There, but not yet fully formed. He'd told himself he was imagining things. For weeks he'd found excuses and explanations for everything their son had been doing, but every time he thought he knew what was going on, it proved to be wrong. So maybe he really was just conjuring demons where there really were none.

But the news reports these past few days, the stories of these ingenious killings, the games that this so-called Games Master was putting his victims through... Something about all this seemed eerily familiar.

Surely it couldn't be him. Surely.

Lucas clenched his fists, his nails biting into his palms as he wrestled with his conscience.

"Damn it," he cursed and got out the car, slamming the door behind him. Staring up the driveway, he steeled himself, hoping and yet fearing that he might confront his son and find out the truth.

But Lucas wasn't sure if he really wanted to know the truth, not if what he feared was true.

But what if it was? What if he was the only person who knew the truth, and the only person who could put an end to it?

Felicity would no doubt tell him he was being silly and seeing things that weren't there. She often sided with their son and would talk Lucas down, reassuring him that nothing was wrong and their son would never go back down that road again.

But Lucas wasn't so sure. There were just too many unanswered questions, like, how could he afford this house? He'd never done anything with his life, certainly nothing that could enrich him to this extent. And yet, here he was, the proud owner of a potentially nice home, if he would just care for the damn thing.

With his jaw set and teeth gritted, he marched down the driveway and stormed up to the front door. He banged on it, loud enough that it wouldn't matter where their son was in the house, he'd hear it.

Shaking with fear, his adrenaline pumping, Lucas waited.

But no one came to the door.

Silence reigned over the property.

With a frustrated frown, Lucas banged on the door again, but still, no one answered.

With a grimace, he moved to the windows and peered inside, convinced he'd see his son sitting in a chair, smiling at him from the shadows. But no one was home.

He cursed to himself, curling his lip in disgust.

Until a thought occurred to him. He turned to the garage and the window on the side of it. Stomping over, he peered through the grimy glass, cupping his hands around his face to get a better view. The inside of the garage was clear. There'd been a... thing. A contraption. Something that his son had been working on in there the last time he'd visited. But it was gone.

A chill ran down his spine. His eyes adjusted to the light, and he made out curious graffiti daubed onto the walls. Were they stars or something? Like, a whole load of arrows pointing out from a central point. What on earth were they?

Whatever they were, he didn't like the look of them.

His phone rang, making him jump and snapping him out of the dark thoughts running through his head. Fishing the phone from his pocket, he checked the caller ID. It was his wife. He answered.

"Felicity? What's up? Is something wrong?"

"Yeah, there is something wrong. You're not here. Where are you?"

"I just… I went out." He wasn't sure he should tell her the truth. Not yet anyway.

"Come home, please."

"But…"

"Please. Where have you gone?"

"Just… to the shops."

There was a pause. She didn't sound convinced. "You're not at…"

"No. No, I'm not. I'll be back soon, okay?"

He hung up and glared reproachfully at the garage, sensing a darkness that hung in the air like a malignant stench. He shivered and turned away.

He needed to think.

Chapter 40

Thursday

"From what I've heard, they got their arses handed to them," Guy remarked, smirking at the thought. "Serves 'em right, storming into a Mason-controlled pub like that, thinking they could get some revenge. I tell you, these kids are as thick as pig shit."

"You're not wrong," Oli agreed and took a slow sip of his pint.

They were sitting in the beer garden of a pub in Arnold, Nottingham, waiting for the rest of his crew to arrive. It had only been a few days since their deal with the Hyson Green Killers' gang, but they needed to pass them some info, and soon to keep their trust.

"They're getting desperate," Guy remarked. "The Masons are better organised and have more resources. The Killers will get some lucky shots in, sure, but if they don't sort themselves out, they'll end up signing their own death warrant."

"And you think this garage is the place to do that?"

"I think so, sure. They need a win, and this would give them one and could be quite useful. A strike at the heart of Owen's organisation and their money-making ability is just what the doctor ordered. It might also lure Owen out from the shadows."

Oli shrugged and nodded. "You never know. How's things going with Bill? He's not who I thought you'd work with on this."

"Neither did I. He was a right royal pain in the arse when I was in the force and had an unrelenting vendetta against one of the detectives in our unit."

"Loxley, right?"

"Aye. That's him. I couldn't give a shit about Rob, but Bill caused problems for the unit as a whole, and I had to be particularly careful."

"Worked out in the end, though."

"Aye. As it turns out, he's been quite useful, overall." Guy smiled to himself, remembering how he'd manipulated Bill. He'd struggle to do that now, of course. Bill clearly didn't fully trust him, which was as it should be, admittedly.

"Silver linings and all that. So, where's this garage then?"

"All in good time. I don't want to get too deep into what I want to do until everyone's here. No need to get ahead of ourselves."

"Sure thing, mate. No worries."

Guy sipped his drink. "Have the Masons been in touch since all you separated from them and joined us?"

"I've had a few calls, but nothing I can't handle," Oli remarked. "We weren't exactly a key part of their operation."

"No. I guess not."

As Guy took a swig of his own lager, the rest of the crew appeared from around the corner. Bruce led Declan, Kris, and Murrey into the beer garden. They were chatting merrily, carrying their drinks, and greeted Guy and Oli happily before joining them around the picnic bench.

"How's things, lads?"

"All right, yeah," they chorused.

"Did you come here together?" Oli asked.

"Nah, we met up in the car park," Bruce answered.

"And the bar," Murrey added.

"I see you started early, like," Kris said, nodding to their drinks.

"We ain't waiting for you slow coaches," Guy said.

They descended into a round of friendly insults and jibes.

There was no need to rush into talking business, and it was good to bond with them again. He hadn't really seen them in years until just the other day, and that bonding would take time.

Guy laughed at the latest insult, and something caught his eye. He turned to see another group of men walking into the beer garden. They stormed towards them without hesitation, scowling in their direction.

Guy recognised the burly-looking man at the front and jumped up from the bench, much to the surprise of his friends.

"Shit. Owen," Guy grunted.

His friends stood, joining him.

"There you are, you little shit," Owen growled and pulled a knife. "I'm gonna cut you up."

"Whoa, whoa, calm down, there's no need for that," Guy cried, raising his hands.

The two groups were roughly evenly matched, but Guy was unarmed and not in the mood for a one-sided knife fight.

"I think there's every need. Plucking these turncoats from us and then joining forces with the Killers? You make me sick. And after everything we did for you?"

"Your dad threw me out. What did he expect?"

Owen took a step closer. "A little loyalty?"

"When he showed me none," Guy spat. "When he threw me to the wolves? Screw that."

"You're scum." Owen lunged for him and grabbed Guy by the throat, pressing the blade against his neck.

"Knowledgeable scum, though," Guy replied. The cool blade bit into his skin. "Knowledge I can give you and your dad, right now."

"What are you talking about?"

Guy resisted the urge to smile. He'd got him. "Back off, and I'll tell you."

"Tell me, and I'll *think* about backing off."

Guy allowed the smile to creep onto his face. "I'll give you a taster. It's about Erika, Rob's neighbour. I know something you don't. Something your father would *love* to know. Something you could take to him."

Owen leered at him for several seconds, before he leaned in, getting right into his personal space. "This better be good." His spit splattered into Guy's face.

"It will be, but I'm not speaking with a knife to my throat." Guy narrowed his eyes and waited.

Owen sneered and then relented. He pulled back but remained within range of a swift strike should he change his mind. "What do you know?"

"I know who Erika's father is."

"Her father? Why would I care who her father is?"

"Because your dad would certainly care. And because of who it is, that's why." Guy waved Owen back, urging him to move further.

Owen grunted and then took a few steps away from him. "Tell me, then."

Guy curled his lip, then glanced at his men and the garden surrounding them. They were alone, giving them a modicum of privacy, which worked both in his favour and against it. Checking his exits, he briefly made sure he had a route out should this turn south. He felt reasonably sure he could escape should he need to and decided to risk it.

"Erika's father is John Nailer. DCI John Nailer. Rob's boss." Guy peered at Owen while taking a few small, retreating steps.

Owen nodded to himself, folded the flick knife away, and pointed it at Guy. "A deal's a deal, but the next time I see you, all bets are off."

Guy nodded. "Understood."

Owen turned and left the beer garden, sending several pregnant stares back towards Guy before he disappeared from view.

Guy relaxed, took a breath, and wondered how that piece of information would change things. He shrugged. It wasn't his problem.

Chapter 41

Thursday

As Rob finished reading another report from the day's endless and seemingly futile hunt for the sadistic Games Master killer, he sighed and discarded the file onto his desk. Slumping back into his seat, he pressed his fingertips into his temples and attempted to massage away the growing headache that was bearing down on him. Once again, he'd been dealing with interviews, statements, and reports of all kinds while juggling phone calls and delegating tasks to all those involved, and yet, it all seemed so utterly pointless.

He felt no nearer to finding this psycho and saving anyone whose life was the target of this killer. They'd released some details of the previous killing to the press, along with the threat he'd made to an unknown woman called Jennifer, warning anyone bearing that name to be careful and vigilant.

But once again, Rob wasn't sure it would be enough and feared that by the morning, another life would be lost.

With his eyes closed and the weight of the world on his shoulders, he focused on his breathing and tried to summon the energy to be optimistic and hopeful.

Feeling watched all of a sudden, Rob opened his eyes to find Scarlett standing over him, her hands in her pockets and a curious expression on her face.

"That bad, huh?" she asked.

Rob nodded. "That bad."

"Right then. Come on. Come and get a drink with me. I need a coffee, and you look like you need one, too."

Rob glanced over to the tiny kitchenette in the corner of their office that was little more than a counter with a kettle, a microwave, and an eclectic collection of mugs. "You take me to all the best places."

"Damn right. Come on. You can tell me all about it, and I'll fill you in on the shitshow that is my hunt for Owen. Deal?"

"Sure, why not," Rob agreed and forced himself to rise from his chair and follow Scarlett across the room.

She quickly busied herself with the task of making their drinks while Rob leaned against the wall, drained.

"How's Mary?" she asked.

"Mary?" The question took him by surprise. "Um, yeah. She's fine. We're fine. She was at the press conference I did yesterday."

"Did that seem odd?"

"A bit. It was nice, though. Nice to see a friendly face in the crowd, you know."

"Mmm. You've always hated those things, haven't you."

"Yeah. So this made for a nice change."

"You want to be careful of any conflict of interest."

"I know. I've spoken to Nailer about it, and I've had frank conversations with Mary. She knows I can't talk about anything and never asks any probing questions. She's very good. She gets it."

"That's good, then. As long as she understands."

"She does. I'm not sure her boss is too happy about it. He'd like the inside scoop, I believe, from what Mary's told me."

"Sounds about right. Well, hopefully she can resist it and separate work and home life. Here…" She handed Rob his mug and led him over to a collection of well-worn sofas that sat in the opposite corner, surrounding a small, low coffee table. They were usually used for informal meetings during the day and occasionally as makeshift beds for anyone pulling overtime.

Scarlett perched on the edge of one seat, and Rob sat close by, holding his mug in two hands.

"Go on, then, you start. I heard about the latest killing. The two who died in the warehouse. How's the investigation going?"

"Not well," Rob muttered. He shifted his position. "We've followed the usual angles, as always. The building was once again linked to the same dead ends as the previous warehouse, with payments routed through offshore shell companies that no longer exist, so that was a waste of time. We've been hunting for Jennifer by cross referencing what we know about the killer and his previous victims to try and narrow things down, and we've alerted the public as best we can, but again, there doesn't seem to be much we can do on that front. And anyway, it's likely he's ready for this and has backup plans in place. I know I would if I were him and giving hints to the police.

"We've been looking into the two victims, talking to their friends and family, but there's nothing there that would give us any concern, and they don't know anyone who'd want to hurt them.

"And then there's forensics, but as of yet, there's been nothing useful. The guy knows what he's doing and is clearly meticulous about not leaving any trace. We have DNA we've retrieved from the scenes, but those results take time to come through, and have not yielded anything useful so far. Time will tell if we pick up anything further down the road that will be useful if this ever goes to trial.

"But, what we do have is plenty of CCTV of the killer, his van, and even of some of his kidnappings. He's clearly not shy about showing himself, although it's always with a mask, and I can only think that this is because he feels supremely confident in his skills to remain uncaught."

"He knows what he's doing," Scarlett remarked.

"He does, yes. His killings don't follow any pattern and seem utterly random. Chaotic, you might say, which fits his ideology."

"Then I suggest that is what he's doing. He knows patterns will always lead back to him, showing his hand. But by being chaotic, he can lead you on a merry chase knowing he's always one step ahead of you."

"Oh, I know. I have no doubt that this is the case. His pattern is to have no pattern at all. To be as chaotic as possible because that chaos protects him and hides him. It's clever, that's for sure."

She took a sip of her drink. "Well, I don't know if anyone's said this to you before, but I have full confidence that you will find this guy and stop him. I know you won't give up, no matter how many low points you hit, and either sooner or later, you will find and arrest him and bring him to justice."

Rob smiled and flushed a little. "Thank you. I appreciate it."

"Any time."

Rob sighed. "Go on then, how's things going with your hunt for Owen?"

"You've been very good, you know, keeping your nose out of the case and letting me do the work. It is your brother I'm hunting down, after all."

"I know. Although, I don't really think of him as my brother."

She shrugged. "Fair point." She paused for a moment. "Well, I find myself in a similar position as you, honestly. I don't have many leads. Just plenty of dead bodies. Casualties of the war between these two groups who insist on destroying each other."

"So, no leads at all?"

"Well, right now, I suspect Carter Bird. I'm convinced he's involved somehow, have been for a while. So, I visited him this morning on a hunch, and he was his usual unconcerned self but refused to let us look around his place. I've applied for a warrant, but that was on flimsy grounds. And with Carter's connections, I have my doubts it'll be granted. He'll tie it up or blackmail someone, and I'll never be able to have a nose round his house."

"He has a record, doesn't he?"

"He does," she confirmed. "But he's been clean for a while now, claims to be a businessman, but we all know that's crap. He's part of the Mason firm and answers to Owen."

"And you think Owen's hiding out on Carter's property, I take it?"

"I do, yes." She shrugged. "Time will tell, I guess. We'll get there, sooner or later. I'm sure of it. We just need to hold firm to our principles and remain defiant in the face of this darkness."

"Wow." Rob smiled. "Thank you. Did you rehearse that?"

"No, I'm just naturally awesome," she answered with a wry smile, clearly pleased with herself.

"Remind me never to cross you, Scarlett."

She beamed at him as he rose from the seat and returned to work.

Chapter 42

Thursday

"So, all in all, that's a big score for us."

Isaac nodded. Lenny finished up, pleased with this latest bit of business.

"Excellent work. I presume you'll bring in the relevant people," he replied.

"Of course."

"Good. We need to get it out there quickly. All this crap with that Nottingham crew is pissing me off."

"It's nothing, sir. They're idiots. They've got no clue how business is done. A group of them turned up at the Hangman's Noose the other night, trying to make trouble. They soon learned the error of their ways."

"Naturally." Isaac generally agreed, but even idiots could cause untold damage to an operation such as theirs.

There was a knock on the door.

"Come," Isaac called.

"Sir. It's Owen. He's on the line. Says he needs to speak to you." He brandished a mobile phone and wiggled it.

"Come in, Spencer. I'll take it here." Isaac turned to Lenny. "Thank you."

Lenny had already risen from his seat and was gathering his things.

"Of course, sir." Lenny made his way out. "Good evening to you."

Spencer handed Isaac the phone, before retreating from the room after Lenny and closing the door behind them, giving Isaac some privacy.

With them gone, he put the phone to his ear. "Owen?"

"Dad, hi."

"You wanted to speak to me?"

"I did. I, um. I have some news for you."

"Really?" Isaac sighed, wondering what his wayward son had got involved in now.

From the reports he'd been getting over the last few weeks, Owen had been leading the fight against the Hyson Green Killers. On the one hand, he appreciated his son working to protect the family from an aggressive competitor, but on the other, it was Owen who had initiated the war in the first place, and they wouldn't be in this mess if he hadn't let his temper get the better of him.

"This better be good," Isaac said.

"I think you will be interested," Owen answered. "I've heard from a source that Erika, Rob's neighbour, is actually the daughter of John Nailer."

"Huh," Isaac muttered and let the news sink in. "So, your suspicions about Erika being linked to Rob have born some fruit."

"It looks that way."

"And how much do you trust this source of yours?"

"I trust they know what they're talking about," Owen replied. "They were connected in the right places, and… it feels right."

"I agree." Isaac couldn't quite put his finger on why it felt right, but it did. "Who was this source?"

There was a long pause from Owen. "Guy Gibson," he said eventually. "I caught up to him, and he used this information to bargain for his life."

"I see. Hmm. You're right. He was well placed to know this. He dated her for a short while."

"He did. Which means he kept this from you."

"Indeed. I'll need to thank him for this one day." He grunted to himself as a thought occurred to him. "I take it you spared his life?"

"I did. He might be useful in the future and might know even more, so…"

"Good call. Okay, thank you for this. I appreciate it."

"No worries. Bye."

Owen hung up, leaving Isaac to contemplate the revelation that Owen had just dumped on him. He chewed on his lip and thought over the details of what Owen had told him. He'd been right. Erika was indeed linked to Rob, through Nailer, who was like some kind of mentor to Rob.

But how had Nailer kept her secret from the world? Isaac had investigated Nailer on several occasions over the years, and this was the first hint of him being anything other than a bachelor.

Isaac placed the phone Owen had called on to one side and pulled out his own mobile. Opening up the photos, he scrolled to find some of Erika that his team had sent him and enlarged one of them.

He eyed the young woman for a while and scrolled through the photos. She was pretty, that was for sure, and there was something familiar about her he couldn't quite put his finger on.

Frowning at one of the better photos of her, he focused on the facts. Nailer was her father, but she had much lighter skin than Nailer. He guessed she was likely of mixed race, meaning she had a white mother.

Something about that clicked into place.

Isaac lowered his phone and thought back to the early days of his dealings with John Nailer. He'd been a fairly constant thorn in their side and seemed to have a personal vendetta against him and his family. Nailer clearly hated the Masons and everything they stood for, spearheading several operations against them as he tried to destroy their organisation.

He'd failed but scored several wins, allowing him to move up through the ranks of the police. But Nailer had always kept one eye on the Masons.

Isaac remembered meeting Nailer a few times, back in the day, back before Rob had left them. They'd bumped into each other at some community charity events that involved the local police, and Nailer had made a point of introducing himself.

Isaac had assumed that Nailer wanted to know his enemy, but was there an ulterior motive?

With a grunt of effort, Isaac got to his feet and crossed the room to a cabinet in the corner. A collection of framed photos covered the top of it. Reaching out, he plucked one from the back and lifted it out. He held it up and peered at the face in the image and then at the photo of Erika.

Was there a resemblance?

Could it really be possible?

He had a sinking feeling that he was onto something, something that could change everything.

Isaac's grip on his walking stick tightened, then the glass in the frame cracked when he squeezed a little too hard.

Chapter 43

Thursday

Lucas couldn't help thinking about what he'd seen at his son's house, a house he shouldn't be able to afford. The image of the vacant garage was seared into his brain, and he couldn't let it go. What had he been building in there? What was his son up to?

Something was severely wrong, he was sure of that. But did it marry up with his fears? Was he right about this, or was he once again off on some kind of wild goose chase that would lead him nowhere?

And those symbols painted on the wall in the garage. What on earth were they all about? What was his son up to?

Every time he closed his eyes, images and thoughts that chilled him to the bone flashed before him. He could hear news reports, talking about someone terrorising the county, and the authorities asking people to come forward. But was he right, or were his fears unfounded?

He sighed and stabbed his food in annoyance. If only he knew. If only he could find out, somehow.

"Lucas," someone said, far off, in the distance.

But he ignored them. He had for more important things to think ab—

"Lucas!"

He snapped his head up and glared across the table at his wife. "What?"

"You're doing it again."

"Oh, sorry."

"You need to leave it. Forget about it. You're wrong."

"But what if I'm not?"

"You are. We have him back. We're doing our best, and he'll come round. He will. Trust me."

"No. I think… I think I need to tell someone…"

"Don't you dare. Do you want to lose him? Do you? Because that's what will happen if you go through with this."

"So, you think he has…"

"No, I don't. But you know his history. They'll suspect him. You know they will, and I just can't lose him again. I can't. I just…" She broke down, tears falling.

Lucas sighed and reached out, taking her hand in his. "Okay. Okay, let's sleep on it. Maybe I'm wrong."

She sniffed. "Thank you."

Chapter 44

Thursday

Rob stared at the TV. The news reporter finished talking about the Nottingham killer forcing his victims to play sick games and the police response. They showed a clip of today's press conference, where DCI Nailer issued a warning to anyone named Jennifer in Nottinghamshire, or the surrounding counties, and how they should take extra precautions in the coming days.

Rob sighed. The knot of frustration in his chest tightened.

If the killer held true to his pattern, he'd be out again tonight, on the hunt for his next victim.

"How's it going?" Mary asked. She sat close by, curled up in the corner of the sofa with a blanket over her.

The news presenter moved on to another story.

"Hmm?"

She nodded at the TV. "The investigation."

Rob smiled. "You're breaking our rule."

"Rule?"

"About leaving work at work."

She shrugged. "They're more guidelines than rules, aren't they?"

Rob inclined his head and nodded. "I suppose we do regularly break that rule whenever it suits us."

She grinned. "So, how's it going? You looked… annoyed, during that piece on the news."

"Is it that obvious?" Rob asked, a little concerned that he was so transparent.

"I can read you like a book, sweetie. It's my job, after all. Besides, I was at that press conference, and the one before, and I can see what it's doing to you. You're frustrated."

He nodded in resignation. "I am, yes. Very. He's been one step ahead of us this whole time, and it doesn't seem to matter what we do, we just hit dead end after dead end, and he's not even shy about showing himself. We've got him on multiple cameras. Admittedly, always behind a mask, and the pictures are never very clear, but still." He took a deep breath and exhaled slowly. "Scarlett's convinced I'll get him, eventually."

"And she's right, you will. I know you will. You won't give up, and you'll go the extra mile when everyone's given up."

He smiled. "You sound like she did."

"Great minds and all that." Mary grinned.

"You're too modest."

"It's a character fault of mine. I'm trying to rectify it."

Rob sighed again and let his head fall back on the sofa. "He's good. Whoever he is, he's very good. I'll give him that. He leaves no trace. He's cruel and inventive and he's being actively random with his victims. Other than the method of the killing, it's difficult to find a pattern."

"And he's left another clue? This Jennifer?"

"Yeah. His next victim will apparently be someone called Jennifer. We have no idea who that is, and there's just no way of reaching out to all the Jennifers in the county, so… I don't know. I'm just not sure how we're going to find him."

"I guess it comes down to what are you willing to do. What are you going to do to find him?"

"Well, one idea I've been texting Nailer about is another press conference. A bigger one this time, where we show the press more of what we have on him. Open up the books, so to speak, to see if anything clicks with people. We'll release more CCTV of him, that kind of thing, just to see if something hits."

"Sounds like a plan to me," Mary answered, nodding encouragingly. "You need to get everything out there, show the world what you have. You never know what might generate a lead."

Rob grunted. "I know. And I know we'll find him. I have full confidence of that. It's just a question of when, really."

"Hmm. And how is Scarlett? She's still on the Mason case, right?"

"She is. She's neck-deep in gang violence at the moment, hunting for Owen. I'm trying to keep it at arm's length, in all honesty. I feel like the less I'm involved with that, the better. I'm not sure I can remain impartial, and I don't want to be seen to be going after my own family." He shrugged. "I suppose there's some self-preservation involved with that, but I think it's the best thing for the case."

"I think you're right," Mary agreed. She shuffled over and wrapped her arms around him. "You know, you can talk to me anytime. I want to help. I want to be there for you."

"I know. Thank you."

Chapter 45

Thursday

Something slammed into Jennifer's side and then hit her again, yanking her in a rude fashion from her slumber. With her vision swimming and her mind a chaotic mess of terrifying thoughts mixing with memories of the fading dream she'd been enjoying, she turned to her husband.

"What the...?"

She'd been about to scold him for waking her up, only to discover they weren't alone in their bedroom. Someone was on top of Will, one hand over his mouth while his other hand stabbed him in the arm with a syringe.

He bucked and jerked where he lay, trying to fight the intruder off, but it was too late.

She screamed.

Jennifer scrambled to release herself from the bedsheets that were being held down by the man, and swung a fist at him that she managed to free from the covers.

The attacker growled. William's erratic movements faded; whatever drug it was took effect.

"No!" Jennifer yelled.

The man grabbed her hand and jumped over onto her, jabbed his knee into her sternum. He suddenly hit her across her face, and she doubled up in pain.

"Jen… Jen… Don't…" Will muttered beside her then lost consciousness.

When she looked back up at the man, he'd pulled a gun and pressed it into her cheek. "Shut your face and you'll survive the night."

Jennifer stopped screaming and glared up at him with hate-filled eyes. Whoever this was, and whatever he wanted, she'd find a way to make him pay.

"I'm going to get off the bed, and you're going to lie there quietly, understand? Nod if you understand."

Seeing no other option, she nodded. He slowly climbed off the bed under her watchful gaze. Nightmarish thoughts flooded her brain. She instantly had visions of him raping her at gunpoint and desperately scrambled to think of a way out, a way to save herself and her husband, but found herself struggling.

She glanced left, at Will. He was out cold and of no use at all. She was on her own. Turning back to the man as he rose to his full height, still pointing his gun at her, she narrowed her eyes. "What do you want?"

"For you to do as I say," he said, taking a second syringe from his pocket. He bit the needle cover, pulled it off, and held it between his teeth, watching her. "Roll over," he ordered.

Jennifer's heart sank. It really did sound like he was going to have his way with her. But again, she saw no other option and did as he asked. Once she was on her front, he grabbed the hem of her pyjama bottoms and yanked them down, over her bum.

She gritted her teeth, only to suddenly feel the sharp pin prick of the needle. It only lasted a moment, and then it was gone.

Seconds later, the world around her faded, too, and she fell into the void of unconsciousness.

Chapter 46

Friday

The dark visions of violence and terror retreated into the inky void. Jennifer rose from her involuntary slumber. Dreams of violations and of being controlled and manhandled faded, and she rose back to consciousness.

Awareness returned, and she woke from her nightmare-filled sleep, becoming acutely aware of the surrounding room.

Something was making a god-awful racket.

Was it her alarm?

Weak from whatever drugs had been pumped into her, she rolled to her left side and twisted her head, forcing her eyes to open. She focused on the other side of the bed.

William was gone.

Her husband, the man she loved and adored, had vanished. The sheets were a mess on his side, but he was nowhere to be found. Terror and fear washed over her, and she sobbed.

"You stupid…" She shook her head, angry with herself for not doing more, and reached out to where Will usually lay and gripped the sheets. "Will. Oh God, where are you?" Squeezing her eyes shut, she shuddered and cried. Fury rose from deep down. "You bastard!" she yelled, before burying her head in the sheets.

Her phone kept ringing. It clawed at her brain, raking its nails over her skull. "Shut up," she snapped. But the phone continued its rude awakening.

Her strength returning, she rolled the other way and flung her legs over the side of the bed. Once upright, she noticed she was already dressed but felt uncomfortable. "What the hell?"

Exasperated she ran her fingers through her hair, and fidgeted with her clothes, sighed, and glared reproachfully at her phone. An unknown number was calling her.

Was it him?

A shiver rippled up her spine at the thought and what he might have done to her. She felt violated but not intimately. She got the feeling that whoever their attacker was, he hadn't raped her.

That was something, at least.

Grabbing her phone, she answered the call. "Hello?"

"Good morning, Jennifer." The voice was distorted. Disguised. But it was him, she was certain of it.

"What do you want? What have you done with Will?" She wiped tears from her cheeks and forced her emotions back. She needed to focus.

"I have taken your husband, and if you want to see him alive again, you will do exactly as I say."

"You're that Games Master, aren't you," she stated. She'd seen the news reports and discussed it with Will the night before. They'd locked up early last night, just to be sure. Not for one moment did she actually think she would be his next victim. "I saw the news reports."

"That is of little consequence to me, and it shouldn't be to you either. You need to focus on the task I am going to set you."

"I'm not doing anything until I see William. I need to see him. I need to know he's alive."

"Of course. Accept the video call request."

With a grimace, she lowered her phone and did as he asked. The screen flicked to a live video feed of her husband. He'd been stripped to his underwear, gagged, and tied to a chair. He'd also been beaten.

Jennifer sobbed and clamped a hand over her mouth to stop herself from becoming hysterical. "Will. Oh God, Will. What has he done to you?"

"William is alive, for now," the man said from offscreen. "But, you see that collar he's wearing?" He approached her husband and lifted William's chin to reveal a metal collar with wires trailing from it.

Will's eyes were wild with fear and anger.

Her breath caught in her throat to see him like that. "Oh God," she gasped.

"That is a bomb that I can trigger from anywhere, with this." The man held up a black plastic box with a couple of switches and buttons on it. He flicked one, and it beeped.

Jennifer jumped, fearing he was going to hurt Will. Instead, a red light illuminated on the collar.

"I've armed the bomb. If you don't do as I ask, if you fail to fulfil my request, or if you try to speak to anyone else about all this, I will trigger that bomb. Do you understand? If you speak to the authorities, your family, friends, anyone, he dies. Got it?"

"I understand," she replied. "What do you want me to do?"

"You have until six p.m. to kill someone. That's twelve hours. It can be anyone. Anyone at all, but you need to kill someone. If you don't, I will kill William."

"And how do I do that? How do I kill someone?"

"Use the gun."

"Gun?" She scanned the room quickly and then spotted the ugly black firearm that had been placed on her dressing table. "Oh."

"Yes. That gun. And please don't try to grow a brain or do anything clever. I *am* watching you."

"What? How?"

"Look up."

She did and spotted the fresh addition to her room. A black camera had been stuck to the ceiling in the corner of the bedroom.

"Wave," the man stated. "You're on *Candid Camera*. But that's not all. Open the front of your shirt, and you'll see you're wearing a wire, and there's a tracking device on the gun."

Jennifer tugged at her blouse, releasing a button, and saw the mic and the trailing wire.

Feeling her heart sink, she glanced back at the pistol. "Do I have to use the gun?"

"You do, yes."

"Okay." She wasn't sure what else she could do other than to agree to his demands. In her head, a rough plan started to form. She'd agree to his demands and then spend those twelve hours working out what she should do. There had to be a way through this, a way to save William and not kill anybody. There just had to be. "Okay, fine. I'll do it. Just… don't hurt William."

"Well, that really does depend on you, doesn't it? Good luck." The man hung up.

Jennifer felt sick to her stomach. What on earth could she do? She felt lost, alone, and utterly at sea.

With some effort, she rose from the edge of the bed, walked over to her dressing table and stared down at the gun. She'd never seen one up close like this before. Gingerly, she reached out and touched the grip. She recoiled from its coolness and the weight of the thing. It was designed only to kill, and it looked the part. Brutal, angular, and unforgiving. Still feeling uncomfortable, she turned away from the camera and opened her shirt to get a better view of the microphone she was wearing. Taped to the centre of her chest, the trailing wire ran under her bra. A sinking feeling gripped her; she opened the front of her trousers and noted how it also trailed beneath her knickers, too. With a shiver, she realised she'd been naked when he'd wired her up, and then dressed her, like some kind of weird full-sized doll. Gross.

Rummaging around, she adjusted her clothes to feel less odd and buttoned up her clothing again, before peering nervously at the gun.

Her phone buzzed. The text came from an unknown number. She read it.

Tick, tick. Time's passing. You'd better get going.

She squeezed her fist in annoyance and fear. He was right, she needed to do what he had asked. Steeling herself, she reached down and picked up the gun.

Chapter 47

Friday

Reaching for his coat, Rob took his phone out again, finding it unbelievable that no one had called. But the notifications had barely changed, and there were no missed messages or calls.

"Stop checking your bloody phone and take the win," Mary admonished him. "Maybe he was having a night off. Even serial killers need a break every now and then."

Rob allowed a smirk to play across his face. He slipped his phone back into his pocket. "Maybe we have another day before he kills again."

"That's more like it," Mary agreed.

Rob turned away as they made for the door to his apartment, and grimaced. Somehow, he didn't believe it. The killer had worked quickly so far, and he'd left a clue at the previous killing, so why wasn't Rob being called to a crime scene somewhere to deal with the aftermath? It didn't feel right. Something felt off, wrong.

The killer's message to them suggested Jennifer would be forced to make a choice, to kill, or see a loved one killed. But how long would the Games Master give her? Minutes? An hour? A day? Maybe there was a Jennifer out there right now, desperately trying to work out who she should kill to save her partner?

The thought chilled him to the bone.

"Come on, slow coach," Mary said. "I've not got all day."

Aware he'd been daydreaming, he apologised and made for the door. "Do you want dropping off?"

"Nah, I'll take my car," Mary said while he locked the door. "I never know when you'll be back. But if you are, do you fancy a takeaway?"

"Yeah, sure," Rob confirmed. "What were you thinking?"

"Chinese?"

"Ooh, yes," he cooed. "Crispy chilli beef, please, and egg fried rice. Lovely."

"The usual, then."

"Always."

"No problem," she answered.

A door across the landing opened. They turned to see Erika step out of her apartment.

"Rob. I was hoping to catch you," she said, crossing the landing. "Oooh, ouch." She eyed the bruises on his face and went to reach up but drew her hand away before she touched him. "I heard that something had happened, but... Who did this?"

Rob shook his head. "Don't worry about it. It's not important."

"But you're hurt."

"I'm fine, honestly."

"This wasn't because of me, or," she mouthed the word *mum*, "was it? This wasn't our fault?"

"What? No! This has nothing to do with you."

She sighed, clearly relieved. "Oh, okay then."

"You thought that what? It was the Masons, come to rough me up to get to you or...?" He let the word hang, unsaid.

"Well, I didn't know. But, yeah, the thought had occurred to me. I was concerned, and I didn't know how bad it was. It looks bad."

He waved her concerns away. "Seriously, I'm fine. A little bruised, sure, but my pride took more of a beating, in all honesty."

"And we all know that the male ego is a fragile thing," Mary added.

Erika smirked.

"Oi." Rob turned to Mary. "I thought you were on my side."

"Case in point." She gestured to Rob.

He rolled his eyes. "Seriously, no. You have nothing to worry about. This was part of a long-standing feud that's reared its head again."

"Oh, you mean Bob?"

"Bill," Rob corrected her. "Of course, you encountered him, didn't you."

"Briefly, yeah, in my kitchen." She raised an eyebrow and screwed her mouth up. "A delightful man."

"Yeah, well, he jumped me outside and did this."

"He's wanted for murder, isn't he?"

"Yeah. But he gave me the slip, so…"

"I'll keep an eye out," Erika replied and gave him a mock salute. "I remember what he looks like."

Rob smiled at his half-sister and pulled her in for a hug, something they'd only recently started doing following the revelation of their family connection. "Thank you."

"Take care out there." She stepped away. "Bye."

Rob watched her go and then glanced at Mary once Erika's door was closed.

"Aww, that was nice of her," Mary remarked.

Rob shrugged. "It is a little odd. I don't think I've quite got used to her as a sister yet."

"You will," Mary reassured him and then led him from the building. "Let's go."

Chapter 48

Friday

The gun was surprisingly heavy. Jennifer handled it hesitantly, taking care to keep her fingers away from the trigger. She didn't want to accidentally fire it. Turning it over in her hands, she noted it had clearly been modified with a small black box bolted to the butt of the grip. A red LED glowed on it. She guessed this was the tracking device he'd mentioned.

She knew little about guns, other than what she'd seen on TV shows, but was aware that some or all of them had a safety on them to stop them from being fired unintentionally. Did this gun have one of those? It was kind of boxy in shape and seemed to have buttons and things built into it. She noticed some words engraved on the side of the barrel and angled the weapon so it caught the light.

It was a weird logo, but it looked like Lock or Glock, maybe, with the number 17 beside it. She had no idea what that meant but guessed it was the make or model of gun. Next to that, it read: Austria. She grimaced.

Unable to find anything that said safety or something similar, she gave up and assumed it would fire when she pulled the trigger, and decided to be careful.

She turned and glared up at the camera in the corner of her room and stared at it. Hatred swelled in her chest. Narrowing her eyes, she raised the gun, pointed it towards the camera, and pretended to fire.

She sighed and relaxed again, letting her arm drop to her side. What was the point?

Her phone buzzed. She checked it to find another text from the Games Master. It was a photo of a screen, showing the view from the camera as she pointed the gun at it.

Beneath it, she read:

You need to point that gun at someone other than me if you want to see your partner again.

Jennifer grimaced, and as she moved towards the door, raised her middle finger at the camera.

Stepping out from her room, she crossed the landing. She needed a wee. In the bathroom, she saw another camera and cringed. She briefly considered holding her need to pee, only to change her mind. Screw him, she thought, and relieved herself anyway. Downstairs, she found more cameras, at least one in each room.

In the kitchen, she put the gun down and leaned over the counter, wondering what to do. She glanced at her watch. Time was marching on, and she needed to either do as the man asked or find another way through this. She couldn't do anything in here. There was no one to kill, and she was under constant surveillance, which meant she needed to get out and about. She needed space and time to think, and she needed to at least seem like she was doing what he wanted her to do.

She glanced along the corridor towards the front door. That's where she needed to go. She needed to get out of here and try to save Will and herself. Reaching for the gun, she paused; her stomach rumbled.

She was hungry, but as she glanced at the toaster, she hesitated. Would she be able to keep down what she ate? Did she even want to eat anything? Was it a waste of time? No. She had no idea how long this day would last, and she'd certainly need the energy for what was to come.

She should eat.

Jennifer spent the next twenty minutes making marmalade on toast, drinking some orange juice, and brewing a cup of tea. Pleasingly, she felt a little more human after all that, and more confident that she'd find a way through this, one way or another.

On her phone, she opened Google Maps and worked out a rough route of where she could go. Their house was close to the centre of Nottingham, within walking distance, so it made sense to wander into town. She could think things through without being watched, and if she chose to follow through with this psycho's demands, maybe a chance would present itself.

With her handbag in hand, she carefully placed the gun inside and left the house. The walk into town would take forty minutes or so from here, but she could take her time and explore a few diversions to draw it out. There had to be a way through this, to free William and save herself from having to kill someone. Surely.

Walking north through the West Bridgeford estate where they lived, she soon found herself behind and passing other people, going about their day, unaware that she was carrying a gun in her bag and was under orders to kill someone.

She crossed the road, came in behind a man walking in front of her, and she wondered if she could somehow kill him and get this over with. She reached into her bag to check the gun was still there, before carefully wrapping her fingers around the grip.

But there were other people around, in front and behind her. Her heart raced, and she gave serious consideration to the deed. Maybe she could duck down a side road or between two houses and get someone to follow her in there? Or maybe she should knock on a door and force her way into a house? Maybe she should kill a homeless person, or a delinquent youth? A criminal?

Sweat beaded on her forehead. She considered the possibilities, but when she went to lift the weapon from her bag, she found she just couldn't. She couldn't bring herself to do it. It was impossible, at least for now.

Disregarding the idea of actually going through with this, she dropped the gun into the bottom of her bag and pressed on. She soon reached the Trent Bridge.

Exhausted already, she veered left into the small park beside the river and walked down to the bank. She stood for a while, staring out over the rolling waters meandering by, under the bridge. On instinct, she reached into her bag to grab her phone and read any messages. Her fingers brushed past the gun. She shivered. Plucking her mobile out, she checked it. There was nothing interesting on there.

She grimaced, stared out over the river and back down at her phone again.

Could he see her now? Would he know if she tried to call or text the authorities?

Turning on the spot, she scanned over the small area of grass and nearby buildings. There were plenty of people around. Any of them could be the killer, watching her, making sure she stuck to the rules. The tunnels under the bridge! She froze and fixed her gaze on them.

Perfect.

Jennifer stalked towards them. There were two. One tunnel was the main walkthrough where the path led, but the other was up on the grass and was often where kids hung out at night. She remembered that someone had been kidnapped in there a few months ago.

Undeterred, she marched up onto the grass and into the tunnel that passed through the bottom of Trent Bridge. Halfway through, she stopped and glanced back and forth, looking both ways. No one was around.

A small grin to passed over her face, as she gripped her phone and navigated to the call screen. Briefly, she contemplated calling the police but hesitated. Calls could be tapped into, so maybe he could do that? He could listen to her call the police and then kill Will.

She closed the call screen and stared at the apps arrayed before her. Her phone seemed to be running a little slow today, she noted, before disregarding the thought. Maybe WhatsApp? Messages were encrypted on that app, so maybe that could work? She needed a number, though, and didn't have one to hand. Annoyed, she opened her browser and searched for the Games Master press conference and found a number she could text. Perfect. She copied it and opened a new chat. She started typing and was about halfway through when her phone buzzed. A notification appeared at the top of the screen.

I know what you're doing. If you send that text, Will dies.

Jennifer's blood ran cold, a sinking feeling gripping her gut. Somehow, he was watching her and knew what she was doing on her phone.

A wave of anger and frustration rose inside her. She cursed, let out a wail of anguish, and stamped her foot in pure annoyance. Her fingernails bit into her palms as she squeezed her fist.

Cursing to herself, she deleted the half-written text. She was about to close the app but hesitated. She might need that number later. After a quick rummage in her handbag, she found a pen and copied it to the back of her hand. Maybe there was another way…

As she closed the app, she again noted the phone's delayed response to her taps and swipes.

Her breath caught; she realised she'd heard of people cloning phones to watch what someone else was up to. Had this man cloned hers? Was he watching everything she was doing on it? Was that causing it to lag?

Ever more creeped out, she dropped her phone into her bag like it was infected with something and shivered.

Feeling more trapped than ever, Jennifer wandered to the mouth of the tunnel and glared across the small park and the various people in, or moving through it. Was he here? Was he watching her right now? She didn't spot anyone acting suspiciously, though, and sighed.

Reluctantly, she walked back to the road and made her way over the bridge, heading north again, into the city.

Chapter 49

Friday

"So, what you're saying is, we've got bugger all," Rob said, following the briefing from the team, updating him on the investigation so far.

"That's not really what we said," Tucker replied.

"Yeah, we don't have nothing," Nick said. "Just…"

"Okay, fine," Rob cut in and waved his hand dismissively. "We have nothing actionable right now. Is that better?"

"Much. But yes, we have no solid leads on the fucker at this time," Tucker agreed.

Rob sighed. "Brilliant."

"You sound as frustrated as a horny celibate monk in the *Playboy* house."

Rob smirked. "Something like that, yes. Okay, so let's go through it again. The family and friends of…" he checked his notes, "Darian and Fraya, all agree that they can't think of anyone who'd like to kill them or cause them harm. They were a calm, friendly couple who wouldn't hurt anyone, according to them."

"Correct," Nick confirmed.

Rob continued. "We're still going through the footage from CCTV, but there's nothing conclusive there yet, and forensics is still working on stuff. There's little new from the previous crime scenes. Also, we've looked into the number of people called Jennifer, and there's a fair few in the county, so contacting them all is going to be tricky, if not impossible."

"Right," Tucker confirmed. "But hopefully the news reports got most of them."

"Which ultimately brings me to where I think we need to go with this," Rob remarked. "We need to use the public more. We need to use them to get ahead of this even more than we already are. I think we need to release as much of the footage of the killer as possible in the hope that someone recognises him."

"Do you think he's already got to this Jennifer he named?" Nick asked.

"Probably. She could be out there somewhere trying to find someone to kill, which means we need to find a way to help her."

"Sounds like a plan," Nick remarked.

Tucker nodded and stood. "I'll work with the digital team to collate the footage, get the best clips we've got edited into a single video."

"Awesome. I'll talk to Nailer and get this set up," Rob said. "Let's make this one count."

Chapter 50

Friday

Following the three cars filled with members of the HGK gang, Guy drove towards a Sutton-in-Ashfield industrial park. He did his best to keep up, as did the following van, which they planned to load up with anything of use, but they were breaking the speed limit most of the time and bullying other road users out of the way.

The whole idea was for this to be a lightning raid on a Mason operation, to take the people there by surprise, quickly gain the upper hand, and send a message to the Masons. Guy just hoped it worked. The one thing he was less sure of was being here with the gang while they did it.

"Are you sure about this?" he repeated, voicing his trepidation again.

"I'm sure," Bill answered from the passenger seat beside him. They took another corner at speed. "They need to see that we're all in on this and that we're not gonna screw them over. Besides, I want to see what this drug operation is all about. Might turn out to be useful."

Guy shrugged. He couldn't argue with that. The info on this operation had come from one of their contacts, who alerted them to its existence and a recent shipment of drugs they were cutting. Apparently, it was one of the more important locations used by this arm of the Mason firm, run by Carter Bird, who worked for Owen Mason.

But despite this, he still didn't enjoy having to do this raid alongside the Hyson Green Killers. They were unpredictable to say the least, and Guy didn't trust them. Theirs was a truce built on very shaky ground, and it could fall apart at any time.

Guy followed the lead three cars into the edge of a commercial property that resembled an old garage that had ceased trading, and yet there were several cars parked up outside. The Killers pulled in and skidded to a stop. Doors were flung open before the vehicles had parked, and the crew was jumping out. Brandishing lethal blades, bats, and improvised weapons, they rushed towards the nearby building. He could see guns tucked into the belts, but they were a last resort. Gunshots were bound to summon the police, so it was best to do this quietly and avoid the pigs turning up entirely.

Guy stomped on the brake, parked, and followed the others as they jumped out of the four-by-four. Bruce handed him a baseball bat, and they fell into position behind the last of the Killers.

Shouts and yells already came from inside the unit. It sounded like chaos in there.

Here we go, he thought, and stepped in through the doorway.

The Killers had gone to town on the Masons and their workers, beating and stabbing them. Fights were happening all around them, while the dead or injured littered the floor.

The gang moved fast, focusing on those putting up a fight and overwhelming them with sheer numbers. Further in, the lead group moved into the offices at the end of the building.

With his baseball bat ready, Guy stalked through the room, noting the rows of tables where they'd been cutting drugs with other ingredients and bagging it up.

As they'd prepared for this, he and Bill had been keen to emphasise that there was no need to kill everyone inside the building. Many of them would be useful either as converts or informants, so the gang were under strict orders to take as many hostages as they could.

Guy nodded approvingly at the number of people who were being forced to their knees and having their wrists zip-tied behind their back. As they moved through the space, three men came charging out from behind a car, wielding various metal tools as weapons.

Guy turned and swung his bat. Its length worked to his advantage, reaching the thug before he got close enough to use the wrench he was carrying. Catching him on the side of his head, he dropped the man to the floor with a thud.

With his blood running hot, Guy stepped in and swung again, bringing the bat down on his attacker's head for a second time. The brute fell still and didn't move again. Others tackled the remaining two. They were quickly subdued.

"Oi! Mate," called someone from the offices at the back.

Guy looked up.

One of the gang members waved them over. "Cold wants to see you."

Bill turned to Guy and gestured to the offices with a jerk of his head. "Let's check it out."

Guy nodded in confirmation and fell into step beside Bill. They marched across the workshop. In a messy back office, Guy found two people on their knees with their hands up, but he only recognised one of them.

"Carter Bird," he muttered in slight shock. "Shit." He had not expected to find such a high-ranking Mason here, but he guessed it made sense. He was keeping an eye on the operation, making sure the drugs were properly processed. This was an unexpected bonus.

"Well, well, well, Carter Bird," Bill said. "And Councillor Clayton. This is a surprise."

A councillor? Guy raised an eyebrow. It appeared that Carter was making use of his time by taking meetings with corrupt officials, too.

"Thought you might be interested in these two fucks," Watts said and then leaned in towards Carter. "Especially this one." He jabbed Carter in the chest with a knife.

"That I am," Bill confirmed.

"You're getting fuck all from me," Carter spat. He was calm and self-assured, unlike the councillor.

"I'll do whatever you want, just don't hurt me," Councillor Clayton pleaded by way of contrast. But that wasn't surprising. As a member of the local council, he likely wasn't used to seeing extreme violence and was probably terrified.

Bill laughed and addressed Carter. "We'll see about that."

"What do you want to do with them?" Watts asked.

Bill pointed at the two gangbangers standing guard. "Watch them," he said, before beckoning Guy and Watts out of the room. Once they were far enough away, he turned to guy. "Do you think he'll know where Owen Mason is?"

Guy nodded. Similar thoughts had occurred to him. "Very likely, yes. He worked directly for Owen and was his closest crew member. If anyone knows, it's him."

"Then I suggest we take this opportunity to find that out." Bill faced Watts. "If this works out, you might finally get your revenge."

Watts nodded. "Don't be too long. I'm sure our arrival hasn't gone unnoticed."

Bill nodded and ordered Carter and the councillor out onto the main shop floor, where they placed his fingers in a vice and started asking questions about Owen's location.

"Where's Owen?" they began.

"You always were a disappointment," Carter stated, staring at Guy. "You gave Isaac everything, your whole life, doing as he asked and living a lie for years as part of the police, and still you didn't live up to any of his actual sons, including Rob. You're pathetic. And now look at you, turning on the only family you've ever known. Isaac was right to kick you out."

"Screw you." Enraged, Guy punched him.

Carter glared at Guy. "Do your worst. You'll get nothing from me. And if anyone in here does talk, they'll have Isaac to answer to."

From then on, he said nothing. Carter was immoveable as stone. He didn't answer any of their questions and only grunted and hissed with pain when they slowly crushed his fingers. Following that, they took a hammer to his feet, pulled out several fingernails on his other hand, and beat him to a pulp before they finally gave up. He wasn't speaking, and there seemed to be little they could do to change that.

In the end, Bill asked for Guy's baseball bat and smashed his skull in. Guy watched on grimly, disgusted at what the Masons had made them do. He blamed them for all of this.

Nearby, the councillor sobbed as they made him watch.

Bill pointed to one of the nearby men they'd captured. "Him. Bring him here." He addressed the room. "We're going to find out what you all know, one way or another."

"Um, excuse me? Yeah, hi. I, err, I'd like to help."

Guy turned as one of the Killers backhanded the speaker. The man fell to his side and spat blood on the floor. The whole room was watching.

"What did you say?" Guy asked, approaching.

"I can help," the man said. "I've worked for Carter for a while, and I, err… I know where Owen is."

"Shut it, Ramsey," another captive hissed at the speaker.

"Piss off, I'm not dying here," Ramsey said.

"You do?" Guy pressed.

"Yeah. I saw him." Ramsey seemed excited to share what he knew.

"Stinking traitor," the protester barked. "You'll fucking die for this. I'll make sure of it."

"Shut it, Foster, the adults are talking," Ramsey answered.

"Where?" Bill asked Ramsey, stepping up beside Guy. "Where did you see Owen?"

"If I tell you this...?" the man began, giving them a knowing look.

"If you tell them..." Foster shouted angrily.

Annoyed, Bill stormed over to Foster holding a dagger and slammed it into the side of his neck, ripping it out. Blood spurted from a severed artery. Foster gurgled, fell to the floor, and writhed in pain.

Guy watched for a moment, a little shocked by the man Bill had become, then he returned his attention to Ramsey. "If your info is sound, then you'll be free to go," Guy agreed, unsure if Bill would honour his word.

Ramsey thought for a moment and then nodded. "All right, fine. He's at Carter Bird's place."

"What?" Bill exclaimed, perplexed. "No he isn't."

Guy stared back and forth between Bill and the informant. "We checked that out weeks ago, he's not there," he added. "It was the first place we checked, before we approached HGK."

"Have you been this week?" Ramsey asked. "In the last few days?"

"No," Guy admitted.

"He's there," Ramsey confirmed. "He's there now. He moved in a couple of days ago after being in hiding."

"Shit."

"Right under our noses," Bill stated and kicked a chair in a rage. "Fuck!"

"Do you believe him?" Watts asked.

Guy gave the informant a cool glare. "Why should we believe you?"

Ramsey glanced over at the bloody mess they'd made of Carter and then back to Guy. "I either tell you now or get tortured and tell you later. I know which I prefer. And besides, I like my fingers just the way they are."

Guy nodded and asked Bill, "What do you think?"

"We take him with us," Bill replied and spoke to the other members of Guy's crew. "Bring the van around."

Chapter 51

Friday

Standing at the side of the room, Rob watched Nailer lead the press conference, talking to the assembled journalists about the case and what they were hoping to get from this.

"We have previously released footage of the killer, hoping someone might recognise him, without success. But as the suspect continues his killing spree, it's become clear to us that we need to do more, which has led to this unprecedented release of evidence," Nailer explained. "It's standard practice only to release a small amount to protect the legal process, but the nature of these crimes, their cruelty, their brutality, and the speed the suspect is operating at has forced our hand. So we now ask that the public take a close look at the footage and screenshots we have made available, because to delay this arrest further would put more lives at risk."

Nailer continued, and Rob sensed some movement to his right and turned. Mary edged past other journalists to stand beside him.

"Hey," she whispered, leaning in.

"Hi." He smiled back.

"You're not on the desk this time?"

Rob shook his head and pointed to the scabs and bruises on his face. "We agreed it wouldn't be good for me to do this with my face resembling a punching bag.

Mary nodded. "Fair point. You might scare some people off."

"Aye."

"I take it there hasn't been any major developments this morning then?"

"Nothing worthwhile, no," Rob confirmed.

"Damn."

Nailer came to the end of his presentation, talking about a reward they were offering for information that led to an arrest, and proceeded to take a handful of questions before he finally wrapped it all up.

"Hopefully this will make a difference, though," Mary said.

"I certainly hope so."

"Fraternising with the enemy, Miss Day?" a male voice stated from close by.

Rob glanced up to see journalist Vincent Kane a short distance away, a smug expression on his face.

"I'm not sure that's allowed, is it?" Kane continued.

Mary spun. "Piss off, Vinnie, before I ram my foot where the sun don't shine."

Kane seemed momentarily offended. "Don't tease me." He stepped closer. "Nice bruises, Detective. Who gave them to you?"

"None of your business."

"I beg to differ. You're the lead detective on this case, and it seems like you're out getting into fights. That's not a good look for someone with your family connections. Would you care to comment?"

Rob clenched his fists and gritted his teeth but resisted knocking the man out. "And what do they have to do with anything?"

"Trust, reliability, conflict of interests… I could go on."

Mary stepped between them. "Right, that's enough, Kane. Get lost."

"Why should I?"

Mary stepped closer. "Don't tempt me."

Kane stared into Mary's eyes for a few seconds before he backed off and laughed. "I was only having some fun." He gave a mock salute to Rob. "I'll see you around."

Rob watched him walk off and muttered to himself, "Not if I can help it."

"Ignore him," Mary suggested. "He's an idiot."

"Agreed."

She smiled. "You'd better get to work. I imagine you'll be inundated with calls now that you've offered a reward."

Rob sighed. "You have no idea."

Chapter 52

Friday

Having wandered for hours around the same few city centre streets surrounding the Old Market Square, hunting for a way out of this nightmare, Jennifer was feeling ever more desperate. She needed to bring this to an end. But how? What could she do?

She contemplated calling friends or family and somehow asking them for help, but how could she do that without risking William's life? The killer was watching her every move, cutting her off from her entire support network.

Besides, her mum would just panic, and her dad wasn't the most practical of people, and she really didn't want to drag them into this nightmare anyway. What if the killer then went after them, too? She'd never forgive herself if her actions led to them being harmed.

The same went for her friends. She discounted several of them without a thought, believing them to be more of a liability than an asset. Besides, she had the same fears about getting them involved, too.

But maybe there was a way through this, if she picked the right victim. She'd seen the news reports about the previous victims and how that man had killed his wife but likely wouldn't face jail time because of the circumstances of the act.

Maybe they'd see this in the same light?

She was being blackmailed and had little choice. What was she to do? Let the love of her life be killed by this psycho? No one in their right mind would allow that to happen.

Walking through the Old Market Square again, she noticed some youths sitting near the water feature, making a nuisance of themselves. She watched them catcall a passing girl. Then they tried to provoke a man as he went too close by barging into him, only to shout obscenities at him as he strode away.

She watched and touched the gun in her bag. She'd only need to shoot one of them. It would be so easy, and then her partner would be safe, and the world would be better off.

Everyone hated anti-social behaviour. She'd be doing the city a favour.

Beyond the kids, a moped parked up, a man sitting on it, staring in her direction. He wore a helmet, so she couldn't see his face, but she recognised the bike and his outfit. She'd spotted him a few times before and had started to think he was following her around.

Was he the killer? Was he the one doing this to her? Or was she imagining things?

Gripping the gun, she marched towards him, staring at him. But he sped off as she approached.

She watched him go and shook her head. Maybe this was all in her imagination. Maybe she was seeing things that weren't there because of the stress she was under.

Of course the man fled the scene! Anyone else would do the same if a crazy woman confronted them... wouldn't they?

Shaking her head, she meandered through the streets. Maybe no one deserved to die. Maybe she should just walk up to the police station and to hell with the consequences...

She wandered along another street, glanced up an alleyway, and spotted a homeless man. He sat up against the wall, his arms wrapped around his knees with his head buried. He looked cold.

Jennifer stepped into the alleyway, staring at him. No one would miss him. If he had anyone to love him, he wouldn't be out here sleeping rough. He'd be staying with a friend or family member, or in a shelter somewhere.

She reached into her bag and wrapped her fingers around the gun again, feeling its weight. It would be so easy, she reasoned.

Glancing back towards the street, she crept up the alleyway, wondering if she could make a quick getaway. She'd need to run, but she could do that easily enough. It was just a few seconds, a quick action, and then William would be safe. He'd be free to go, and she could continue living her life. No one would deny her that, right?

This was it, her way out. A solution.

Her phone buzzed, and the man gazed up.

She dropped the gun back into her bag and fished her phone out instead. Under the man's watchful gaze, she turned away and checked the notification.

It was a text from her friend, Loren.

Are we still on for tonight?

"Shit," Jennifer cursed. She'd forgotten all about that. She was due to meet her for a meal out later.

Her mind reeled from the spiral of dark thoughts that had been running through it as she quickly tapped out a reply.

I need to postpone.

She considered leaving it there but reconsidered. Maybe Loren could help her? She was a level-headed and practical woman, after all. Jennifer added a second sentence.

I might need to text you about something later.

She hit send and watched it go. It got two blue ticks instantly, meaning that Loren had seen it. Then her friend replied.

OK.

Jennifer smiled to herself. She walked towards the end of the alleyway before suddenly remembering that the killer might have seen her text. She cursed, stuffed her phone in her bag, and stormed out of the alleyway.

"Damn it, damn it, damn it," she muttered, annoyed with herself and her stupidity.

He'd call her. The killer would call and tell her she messed up and that William was dead. She knew it. Of course he would. She'd expect nothing less. She'd broken the rules and would suffer the consequences.

Minutes passed. Five, then ten, then fifteen, and there was no phone call.

Huh?

She stopped in the middle of a pedestrianised street and wondered what was going on. Had he not noticed? Had her texts with her friend got through without him seeing? She had been down an alleyway, out of view. Maybe he'd been busy trying to catch up to her and watch what she was doing? He couldn't be watching a cloned phone the whole time, especially not if he was driving around on a moped, trying to keep her in sight.

Maybe there was hope after all.

She needed a plan.

Chapter 53

Friday

Rob replaced the phone back into its holder and rose from his seat. Nearby, Nick and Ellen glanced up.

"What's going on?" Ellen asked.

"Something come up?" Nick added.

"Maybe," Rob replied. "This one sounds interesting, if one of you wants to join me."

The pair looked at one another.

"You go," Nick said and waved her off. "I'm balls-deep in these calls."

Ellen jumped up from her chair. "Eeew, but awesome."

Pulling his jacket on, Rob made for the door. "Let's go."

"What's going on?" Ellen asked as she fell into step beside him, straightening out her own jacket.

"Someone's in reception, claiming to know the killer."

"Our killer? The Games Master?"

"Apparently so," Rob confirmed. "They asked to talk to the detectives on the case."

"More pranks or…?"

Rob grimaced. From the moment they'd put out the latest footage and offered that reward, the phone lines had gone crazy, and it had been all hands on deck. They'd all been taking calls as the system got overwhelmed in the hour right after the conference until things started to finally ease off a little.

It would be like this for days, though. Even if they caught the guy today, it wouldn't stop as people tried desperately to get that money.

He hated offering rewards for info, as it always meant they were bombarded with scammers trying to fleece the system and people who just wanted to cause trouble for the police. But he saw no other options. They were desperate for help with no other way of getting it.

It was easy to troll and prank over email or phone calls, but doing it in person was much less likely, however. Something that raised his hopes when he'd got the call from reception.

"Hopefully not. I doubt it anyway. Someone would need some serious balls to come here and prank us to our faces."

"I think you underestimate the youth of today," Ellen remarked.

Rob grunted. "Yeah, maybe."

They walked into the reception of Sherwood Lodge and were quickly pointed towards a middle-aged couple. Sitting to one side of the room, they were talking quietly between themselves.

Rob approached. "Mr and Mrs Shaw?"

"Yes?" the man said.

He was a little more confident than the woman, who seemed sheepish.

"I'm Inspector Loxley, and this is Constable Dale. You wanted to speak to us?"

The pair rose from their seat.

"Yes, we did," Mr Shaw answered. "I think we might know who you're looking for."

"I see. Well, before we get into that, how about you come through to a room where we can sit and talk in private?"

They agreed and followed Rob through the security door to a meeting room with soft furnishings.

Ellen made drinks while Rob got them settled and avoided the subject of the case. Instead, he focused on small talk about the weather and traffic, until they were all ready to get to the point.

"All right, so, you said you think you know who we're looking for? I take it this is about the so-called Games Master case?"

"That's right," Mr Shaw answered. "We think we know who the killer is."

Beside him, his wife visibly cringed and squeezed his hand. Mr Shaw glanced at her.

"Are you sure?" she began. "I just..."

"It's him. I know it." He sighed. "I wish it wasn't, but it's time we face the reality of the situation. You know it as much as I do. You know the truth."

"But..."

"Felicity," the man said. "We need to do the right thing. You saw the news report. You saw the videos. It's him. You know it's him."

She squeezed her eyes shut, and tears fell over her cheeks. "I just... I don't want to believe it."

"I know." He sighed again and turned to Rob. "We think it's our son. Fletcher."

Rob fixed the man with a glare. "Your son?"

"It all fits," Mr Shaw said. "I don't want it to, but it does. There's no way around it. It just does."

"Okay, and do you know where he is now?"

The man shook his head. "That's what scares me, because no, I don't. I went round his house these past few days, but can't find him and can't reach him. I have no idea where he is."

"Okay, let's start at the beginning. Tell me about your son."

Chapter 54

Friday

After the call came in, Scarlett wasted no time jumping in a pool car with Tucker to check out this latest scene of gang violence. They were endless, always brutal, and from the little she knew, this seemed like a major one.

As she sped towards Mansfield, Scarlett glanced over at Tucker in the passenger seat, who was watching a video on his phone.

"What are you doing?" she asked. "Is that a cooking video?"

"What? I'm hungry," he protested.

"Is that on YouTube?"

"Yeah, a local guy, I think. Calls himself the Pit Wizard. He does all these barbecue and smoker meals. This one's about Burns Night Burgers."

"Oh, right. Do they look good?"

"Well, if my rumbling tummy is anything to go by, then yes, they look incredible."

"Okay. The Pit Wizard. I'll check it out. Might be something on there I can cook for Chris."

"Probably."

"Awesome. Right, that's enough of that. Time to get your head in the game," Scarlett warned. She pulled into the former garage on the edge of an industrial estate in Kirkby-in-Ashfield and stopped short of the outer cordon.

They jumped out and quickly made their way through the outer and inner cordons, where they donned forensic suits and walked into the building with Sergeant Alex Soto.

"It's the usual bloody mess," Alex explained.

They hopped across the stepping plates put down to preserve the crime scene from trampling officers.

"We've got the remains of drugs and what could be a cutting operation that was going on. There's cocaine over everything."

"Yum," Tucker muttered.

"We've also got a whole load of bodies which we're working to identify, but there's at least one I think you'll recognise."

"Oh, and who's that?" Scarlett followed Soto, pausing every so often to peer at the scene and make mental notes of what she saw.

"He's over here."

Soto led them towards the centre of the room where they found a blood-covered corpse tied to a chair. His head had been caved in. But even so, she recognised the face. She'd seen it many times, including face to face when he was alive.

"Carter Bird," she murmured. "Well, well, well. They finally got to you."

"Shit," Tucker exclaimed. "He's one of the leaders. Works directly for Owen Mason."

Scarlett stared at the ruin of the man and considered what this could mean for her investigation. He'd probably been tortured, suggesting they'd been trying to get information out of him. But had they been successful? Because, if they had, it might lead the Killers directly to Owen Mason.

She hopped back to another stepping plate and scanned the room. To the left of Carter, her gaze came to rest on another face she recognised. "Crap."

"What now?" Tucker asked.

She nodded towards the body she'd spotted. "Recognise him?"

Tucker moved closer and crouched beside the body. He sported a huge wound in his neck and lay in a pool of his own dried blood. "That's Foster Cook. The guy we arrested at that crack house and had to let go."

Scarlett nodded. Tucker was right, but what he didn't know was that Calico, under Scarlett's direction, had tortured Foster into giving up the location of Owen Mason. With a grimace, she glanced between the two bodies, and her chest tightened. Here were at least two dead people who knew Owen's location, one of whom had been tortured. It wasn't by any means conclusive, but it seemed extremely likely that the HGK gang had found out exactly where Owen Mason was, and if they knew that, it was likely they would be on their way there right now.

Time was running out.

If she wanted to find and arrest Owen, bring him to justice, she'd need to move fast, but she wasn't sure if she could justify what she would need to do. There wasn't exactly a clear trail of evidence leading to Owen Mason that had been properly recorded and logged. But right now, she wasn't sure if she cared or not. The Hyson Green Killers might go in there and kill him, which wasn't the worst result but not really what she wanted, or their attack might force him back into hiding.

She couldn't allow that to happen. She needed to bring him in, now, ideally before the Killers got to him.

Scarlett approached Tucker and leaned in. "Come with me," she urged and led him to a quiet spot outside.

"What is it?"

She took a moment to herself to think about what she was about to do. Telling another officer about some of the dodgy shit she'd been up to was a risk, but she felt sure she could trust Tucker and the rest of her team from Rob down to keep her confidences. After a moment's consideration, she decided to tell him. "I think I know what's happened here, and I think I know what they're going to do next."

"Who? The Killers? The Masons?"

"The Killers. I think they know where Owen is, and they're probably heading over there."

"Over there? Over where?" Tucker frowned at her. "Do you know where Owen is?"

"I believe he's staying at Carter Bird's place, or at least, he was."

"How do you know that?"

"I had Calico extract that information from Foster Cook after we let him go."

"You what?"

She shrugged. "I needed to know."

"I see." He stared at her for what felt like an eternity. "So that's why you've been heading over to his house recently?"

"Correct," Scarlett confirmed. "And we need to get there now, quickly, before the Killers do. We can dream up a trail of evidence later, if we need one. But I just need to bring Owen in."

He stared at her for a long moment. "This isn't exactly by the book."

Scarlett shifted uncomfortably from foot to foot. "Yeah… I know. Sorry. I just… I needed to do this…"

Tucker sighed. "I get it. Your friend. I know." Putting his hands on his hips, he looked back up at her. "All right, let's do this. Let's go get him. Have you got a plan?"

Chapter 55

Friday

Half an hour had gone by, and the killer had so far not said a word about the text Jennifer had sent her friend. Had she actually got away with it? Had the killer missed that little interaction on his cloned phone?

Jennifer wondered about this for a while until, as she wandered the streets in something of a daze, she finally got another text from the killer.

Time waits for no man... or woman for that matter. You're running out of time.

She stared at the screen of her phone and found a glimmer of hope there, where she'd expected to find none.

He didn't know.

He can't have known. He'd have killed Will if he'd noticed the text. She smiled to herself.

It meant she had a chance. It meant, if she could avoid being watched, she could do all kinds of things. She just needed to avoid speaking because he was clearly listening to her via the wire strapped to her chest, and he was doing his best to monitor her phone, but that seemed to be patchy. She guessed that if he wasn't watching his cloned phone when she used hers, he missed it entirely.

She could use this. It was valuable knowledge, and if she played her cards right, she might be able take advantage of it.

But how? What would be the best way? How would she know when the killer wasn't watching his cloned phone? She couldn't have loads of text messages coming into her phone, because even if he missed some of them, he'd notice them eventually, and that would blow her cover.

A woman swept by, stuffing her mobile into the back pocket of her jeans.

Jennifer stared at it.

She needed another phone. She needed one that wasn't compromised, that she could use freely without fear of it alerting the killer. But that left her with two options. Either buy a phone, such as a pay-as-you-go cheap thing, or steal one.

As she roamed the streets, she spotted a phone shop and briefly considered seeing what she could buy, but hesitated. Was he watching her? Could he see what she was doing right at that moment?

Turning on the spot, she peered into the crowds, and after a moment spotted that same moped she'd approached earlier, and grimaced. No, he'd see where she was going, and he'd hear her talking to the shopkeeper. It wouldn't work.

Silently, she cursed to herself and abandoned that idea.

No, she'd need to steal one. It was the best and safest way but presented its own unique challenges at the same time. Any phone she nicked would probably be locked, so she'd need to have a way in. She needed to see someone enter their code or pattern. A fingerprint was too secure. But this would mean she'd need to visit shops, following people with their phone out, watching to see if she could make note of their security code or pattern, and then steal their phone.

Probably not an easy thing to do, but at least she'd look like she was hunting for someone to kill. He shouldn't suspect what she was doing.

With her mind made up, she headed for the department stores and shopping centres, places where there would be lots of people and she could hunt for a suitable mark.

She wandered around the shops and she found herself drawn to women, and usually younger ones who would walk around, often with their phone in their hand, texting or scrolling while browsing and talking to their friends. The men tended to keep their phones in their front pockets, whereas the girls would either slip them into a back pocket or their bag.

It wasn't long before opportunities started to present themselves, and it surprised her how often she found herself in a position to easily steal a phone. In fact, if that was all she needed to do, she could have had one within forty-five minutes of beginning her hunt. It was amazing how free people were with their devices.

But getting a phone wasn't enough. She needed to know how to unlock it, too, otherwise it would be useless.

She picked out each target and watched to see how they handled their mobile. Were they letting it lock and then unlocking it again, and if so, how were they doing that? Anyone who used their fingerprint she discarded and moved on, looking for people using codes, or even better, patterns.

The minutes turned into hours, and she soon approached her first chance, feeling sure she'd memorised the pattern. When the moment came for her to grab the phone, she hesitated, not quite believing that she was doing this, until she'd successfully plucked the device from the bag and walked away without the girl noticing. Pleased with herself, she quickly tried the pattern, but it wouldn't work. She frowned and tried it again, but still, it wouldn't unlock. Had she used the wrong code? She tried a couple of variations, but the device remained stubbornly locked.

Frustrated and annoyed that she'd misread the pattern, she walked by the payment desk and surreptitiously left the phone on the end of it, in the hope it would be found, before leaving the shop entirely.

It was pointless being upset, though, it didn't help anything. Annoyed but impressed with herself, she moved on, continuing her hunt.

Another forty minutes passed before she had a second chance. This time, she knew she was right. She'd seen the pattern several times from several angles and couldn't be more sure.

This time, when the moment arrived, there was no hesitation. She dived straight on in, plucked the phone from the young woman's bag, and hurried swiftly away.

Once again, she tried the pattern and easily unlocked the device. It had a cracked screen, but she didn't care and stuffed it into her pocket.

With that hurdle crossed, she entered the street and considered the next stage, and realised she needed to copy her friend's phone number into her stolen phone. However, that came with a degree of risk, because he might see her access her contacts on his clone.

Unless... was there a way to distract him?

Jennifer stopped in the middle of the street, she turned and hunted for the man she'd seen following and watching her from his moped. She couldn't see him right away, so she wandered in the direction she'd last seen him.

It didn't take long before she spotted him again. He was getting onto his moped. Smiling to herself, she took a long, cleansing breath and marched towards him.

Come on, run, she thought, urging him to flee.

He spotted her from a distance, and after watching for a moment, spun dismissively away and gunned the engine. In seconds, he was off, the moped wailing as he accelerated.

As soon as she thought she could get away with it and he wouldn't see her, she took out the two phones and copied the number over. It took seconds but felt like an age. What if she'd got it wrong and the killer was someone else, or he circled back before she was finished?

She closed the phone book app, put her mobile away, and marched up the street.

The next stage would take a little longer, and she needed to be careful.

He'd start to suspect something if she kept approaching him and forcing him to flee. Besides, he was out of sight now, and it might be ages before she spotted him again. She needed to act now.

Nearby, she spotted a much smaller store that would be perfect for her plans, and walked inside. It was a New Age shop filled with crystals and Gothic art. Quiet and serene. She seemed to be the only customer. But that could work to her advantage. He was unlikely to follow her into such a place and get that close to her. It also had a stand in the middle of the shop floor that she could just about peek over and watch the door while hiding what she was doing with her hands.

Positioning herself behind the stand, she pulled out the stolen phone, keyed in a text to her friend, Loren, and hit send.

God, she hoped this worked.

Chapter 56

Friday

"All right." Rob addressed the small group that had gathered around him, including Nick, Ellen, a couple of uniformed officers, and three bomb squad officers who were already fully decked out in their protective clothing. "We've cleared the surrounding houses and got everyone back behind the cordon." He turned to the sergeant leading the bomb squad. "Are you happy with everything?"

"I am," Sergeant Selina Ellison replied. "I've been through the briefing, and I'm aware of the case so far. I'll go in with my boys, and we'll scout out the place. He's already shown us that he's a skilled bomb maker on his previous killings, so I think it's reasonable to expect that he might have laid a trap in the house in case we found it. No one follows us in until we're sure that the house is clear."

"Understood," Rob said. "You have full authority on this."

"You can watch on the screen." She pointed to a nearby thick black plastic case with an open laptop inside that was being manned by another officer. "We all have body cams. I'll talk you through anything we're seeing."

"Thank you, Sergeant," Rob said. "In your own time."

Rob backed away and moved over to the case that was set up in the back of one of the bomb squad's vans. The noise and activity in the street, coupled with the heightened stress the county was already under due to the killer, meant that there was already a crowd and a few reporters watching. Rob did his best to ignore them, though, and focused on the screen.

"What do you think we'll find in there?" Nick asked, leaning in.

"God knows. Depends if his parents are right in their suspicions, but if they are, I'd expect to find Chao's symbols and evidence of his crimes."

"And the parents seemed convinced?" Ellen asked.

"The dad, Lucas, especially. He said he was here the other day and saw odd symbols on the walls, and the contraptions he'd been building in his garage had gone."

"Well, Fletcher Shaw has a criminal record." Ellen read the notes in her pad. "He was sent to prison a few years ago for attacking someone. It was the latest in a string of such attacks, and his victim was left with life-changing injuries. He served six years before he got out at twenty-five years of age. He was released early for good behaviour and what was seen as genuine remorse for his actions."

"And look how that turned out," Nick said.

"Did his parents say much else?"

"They said he was always playing cruel games while he was growing up, forcing his school mates and even his parents to make impossible choices. He'd torment and torture animals, too."

"Oh, Jesus," Ellen said. "He really is a dick, then."

"An intelligent one, too," Nick added. "Apparently his dad said he was always interested in how things worked and would spend ours building things and making stuff."

"It all fits," Rob remarked. "Intelligent, but cruel, with an interest in playing games and building stuff. It couldn't be a closer match."

"How did we miss him? We went through criminal records..." Ellen said.

"I know," Rob muttered. "But his previous crimes were nothing outlandish. No games, no bombs, nothing.

There was nothing to link anyone to these recent crimes. Also, he clearly knows what he's doing when it comes to avoiding the police and keeping crime scenes clean."

"Do you think he had help?" Ellen asked.

"Possibly," Rob answered. "If he's linked to the same movement of chaos killers we've been seeing recently, then it's likely he's been in touch with this Ashen King we've heard about. I think that's where the money came from."

"His dad mentioned that he wasn't working but seemed to have more money than ever before," Nick said.

"Sounds like this Ashen King is enabling these killers, backing them financially and who knows what else," Ellen remarked.

"Agreed," Rob said.

The officer manning the computer got their attention. As Rob watched, the bomb squad were approaching the buildings, heading for the garage first. They reached the window and peered inside, the cameras on their helmets adjusting to the murk and boosting the light as they pointed into the gloom of the garage.

Inside, Rob could make out an open space surrounded by tables littered with tools and bits of metal, wood, and electronics. On the walls, he spotted the same chaos symbol daubed in black paint over and over again.

"Shit, yeah, I think we're at the right place," Rob muttered.

"No one seemed to be in there," said Selina over the comms.

"Move on to the house," Rob suggested.

"Copy that," she answered, turning to one of the other two who were with her. "See if you can find a way inside and start your investigations."

"On it," the officer replied.

Selina pressed on and approached the house with the other officer who was with her. They moved to the doors and windows and squinted through the dirty glass. They avoided trying the doors or pressing the doorbell for the moment, just in case anything triggered any traps. Towards the back of the house, Selina peered through another window and spotted a laptop set up on a desk.

"I've got a computer in here," she said. "It's on, too. I can see some kind of video feed, maybe? Like security camera footage."

"Can you see what it's of?"

"It's difficult to make out at this distance, but I think there's someone in the pictures, maybe sat on a chair in a large open space?" She sighed. "Aaah, shit. I can see wires and I think... That's got to be a bomb in there, under the laptop."

"Similar to the others," Rob said, more to himself than anyone else.

"Yeah," Nick said anyway, agreeing.

"Ma'am," one of the other bomb squad officers said over the comms. "I'm getting a reading on the door, or on the other side of it. I think this place might be wired to blow."

"I agree," Selina answered.

"Damn it." Rob grunted and frustration. "How long will this take?"

"As long as it takes," Selina confirmed. "Looks like we've got work to do."

Chapter 57

Friday

"Let's get there in one piece, shall we?" Tucker said over the sound of the engine.

Scarlett checked her speed and eased off the accelerator. She'd been going a little too fast in her eagerness to get to Carter Bird's house.

"Sorry," she muttered. On the next straight, she reached out and tapped her phone in the holder, placing a call. It started to ring over the speaker.

"Calico?" Tucker asked from the passenger seat.

"We need backup," Scarlett replied. "These guys don't mess about."

"Good call. I hope she can make it."

Scarlett grimaced and nodded in agreement. She hoped so, too. Her mind raced as she waited for the call to connect, running through ways she could plausibly explain why they'd gone to Carter Bird's home.

She'd returned there the other day and based that visit on plausible suspicion. He was a well-known part of the Mason operation, and it wouldn't be the first time an officer of the law had spoken to him simply because of his connections, including herself.

But she settled on a better idea this time and smiled to herself, the idea crystalising in her mind. He'd been murdered, so it made perfect sense for them to go to his home and inform the next of kin. It was only a short leap to them saying they'd seen Owen through a window and moved in for the arrest.

Pleased with her plan, she settled into the car ride.

The call connected.

"Scarlett?" Calico said over the speaker.

"Hey. You're on speaker. I'm with Tucker. We're going to Carter Bird's place. He was just killed in what could be another gangland murder, and I'm convinced that Owen Mason is living in Carter's house. So, we're heading over there. We'd love to have you along for the ride."

"You're going there now?" Calico asked.

"Yep. We think the Hyson Green Killers found out the same info about Owen, so we want to beat them to it."

"Shit. Okay, do not go in there without me, okay?"

"How long will you be? This can't wait..."

"It can, and *you* will. Wait for me, Scarlett. Do you hear me? Do not go charging in there."

"Okay... sure," she answered, trying to sound as authentic as possible.

"Scarlett!"

"I'll wait..." she exclaimed.

"You'd better." The call ended.

Scarlett stared at the road ahead and could feel Tucker's eyes boring into the side of her head as she drove. He knew full well what was going through her mind. "Stop staring at me."

"You're not going to wait for her, are you?"

"I'll wait," she said through gritted teeth.

"For Calico to get there?"

"I'll wait for her to get close," she answered, her cheeks flushing.

He grunted and looked away.

She glanced at him and then back at the road, frowning. "What?"

"Nothing."

"You think I should wait, don't you?"

He shrugged. "Does it matter what I think?"

"Well... I just... I thought you'd try and talk me out of it."

He smirked. "Did you? And why would I do that? You and I both know that when you set your mind to something, there really is no stopping you, is there?"

She smiled. "I… can be persuaded… sometimes…"

"Yeah…. Right."

"I can."

"Bullshit. You're the firecracker's firecracker. When you set your mind to something, it's going to happen, one way or another. I've worked with you long enough to know that by now."

"Am I that bad?"

"Oh, don't feel guilty about it. It's what makes you, you. So, you just focus on the road ahead and get us there in once piece, yeah?"

She nodded and concentrated on navigating her way through the countryside on the outskirts of Mansfield, until she finally found the entrance to Carter's estate and turned in. She sped up the long driveway and peered ahead, expecting to see the gang already here but hoping they weren't.

The house came into view, and the driveway seemed quiet.

"Yes!" she hissed and veered onto the grass a short distance away from the house. Parking in a mostly concealed spot on one side of the property, she jumped out and opened the boot.

Tucker joined her, and they both pulled on stab vests and checked their gear.

Grabbing a baton, she felt all too aware that she was bringing it to what was likely going to be a gunfight, and felt suddenly vulnerable. But there was no time to worry about that right now. They had a job to do and a man to arrest.

"We go in, grab Owen, and get out. That's it, okay?"

"If he's still here," Tucker remarked.

Scarlett grunted and glanced up at the house. She stared at it for a few seconds, squeezing her baton. "He's here," she muttered. She wasn't sure how she knew, but she did. She felt quite confident that Owen was in there somewhere, hiding.

"I hope you're right, and I hope this is quick. I don't fancy getting caught in a gang crossfire."

"Agreed," Scarlett said and glanced around. There was no sign of Calico, and she likely wouldn't get here for a while. She briefly considered waiting but found herself aching to get in there and find Owen. The Hyson Green Killers would be here soon, she felt sure of it. They would know the police would pay a visit to Carter's house once they'd found his body, so they'd want to get here before them. There was no way they'd jeopardise their revenge on Owen and let him be taken away. Scarlett had made up her mind. They had to get in there right now. Calico could follow them in later. "Right, let's go. We can't wait for her."

"I was afraid you were going to say that," he said, falling into step beside her as she started towards the house. "How do we get in?"

"Any way we can." Ignoring the front door, she led Tucker round to the side and started checking the windows when she passed them, hoping for a way in. Ahead, wooden gates led to a rear courtyard. They were open, so she slipped through, checking the way ahead before moving into the space beyond.

There were more cars in here and a few doors alongside the windows. "Come on," she urged under her breath.

"I'm coming," Tucker answered.

They moved along the wall, and she checked each window to make sure no one was inside, and if not, to see if it was open. None were. At the first door, she tried the handle.

It opened.

"Yes!" she hissed and eased it open. Beyond, she found a pantry or utility room with a single exit and crept inside.

Tucker followed her in and closed the door behind them.

Sneaking to the door, she peered through and moved into an empty kitchen beyond. The house was generously proportioned, and the kitchen was state-of-the-art. But there was no time to admire the fittings. Two doors led deeper into the house. She paused to listen but heard nothing to indicate which way she should go. In fact, the entire house was silent. She glanced at Tucker. He shrugged.

She mimicked his gesture and pointed to one door.

He nodded.

Satisfied, she crept through it into the next room. A feeling of being watched grew in her chest. Something didn't feel right. Or maybe she was worrying over nothing? It was possible that Owen wasn't here, after all.

Maybe he'd already heard about Carter's death and had made a run for it.

The door slammed shut behind them.

Scarlett turned.

Owen stepped out, pointing a gun at them. "Pretty sloppy, Williams." He grunted. "I thought you were better than this."

She sighed and raised her hands. "Sorry to disappoint you."

"That's all right, I'm used to it. I'm consistently disappointed by the police. So, what's the reason for this visit, then? Hmm?" He narrowed his eyes. "Did…? Did something happen to Carter?"

"I'm not at liberty to say, other than you're under arrest, Owen Mason, for…"

"Shut up," he barked. "Get on your knees."

With no other option, she did as he asked and lowered herself to her knees. Tucker did the same.

"You do not have to say anything. But it may harm your defence if you do not…"

"I'll harm your fucking defence." Owen backhanded her across her face and sent her sprawling to the floor.

Pain exploded across her cheek, and she fell, gasping.

Tucker called her name.

She turned to see Owen punch him in the face. Tucker dropped to his hands.

"No," she yelled as he kicked Tucker in the ribs.

Beyond him, she spotted several more thugs wandering into the room, also armed. They'd seen them coming and laid a trap. She cursed to herself.

Owen glared at her and smiled, before he kicked Tucker again, dropping him to his side.

"Leave him alone."

"You'd rather I focus on you?" he asked and stepped closer.

She backed away, scooting across the floor on her bum, only to back into another thug. She glanced up. The brute planted his foot onto her back and threw her forward onto her hands.

"You won't get away with this," she spluttered.

"Oh, I very much think I will," Owen said. He was suddenly close and kicked her across the face.

She hit the floor in a daze, her vision swimming from the pain.

She rolled to her front to protect herself, only to hear footsteps come rushing into the room.

"Boss. We've got company," someone said, urgency filling their voice.

Chapter 58

Friday

Rob and the police cordon were far enough away from the house that he could hardly see it from where they were standing. Half the street had been evacuated and were standing behind the fluttering blue-and-white tape behind him, while the bomb squad went about their business. They'd identified several potential bombs around the property and were doing their best to find the triggers and work out ways to neutralise them.

They'd been here for over an hour, and it seemed they were no closer to getting into the house.

"This better be worth it," Rob muttered, annoyed at the delay.

They needed to find the killer, and time was passing all too quickly.

"Give them time," Nick reasoned. "We're making progress."

"I know. I'm just eager to find the guy and bring this to an end."

"Aren't we all," Nick agreed.

Rob's phone rang. He pulled it out and noted it was a call from the Lodge. He stepped away from Nick and answered. "Loxley."

"Rob, it's Nailer. We've had a call from someone called Loren, who claims to be a friend of Jennifer, the next victim of the killer. Apparently, Jennifer got a message to Loren from a stolen phone because the killer is watching everything she's doing. She's in Nottingham, and she needs help."

Rob frowned as he considered the message. They'd had a thousand calls from people since the press conference, and most of them were either well-meaning but useless, or just wastes of time, including from people either claiming to be the next victim or claiming they knew the victim. "Okay, and what makes you think this one is genuine?"

"I've spoken to Loren and confirmed a few things, got her to text and ask Jennifer questions, and so far, it's all holding up. This feels right to me. I think we've found her. We need to follow this up."

Rob nodded to himself. "All right. That's good enough for me. We're coming in. They don't need us here."

"How's the bomb squad doing?" Nailer asked.

"They're working on it, but it'll be a while."

"Okay. See you soon."

Rob hung up and turned to look for Nick, only for his phone to ring again. It said Calico on the screen. He answered it with a frown as Nick glanced up.

"This is unexpected."

"Scarlett and Tucker are going after your brother, Owen. They know where he is, and they've called me in as backup."

Rob grimaced. The timing couldn't be worse. "Are they in danger?"

"I don't know," Calico answered. "I've asked them to wait for me before going in, but... You know Scarlett."

"Of course. Where are they?"

"Carter Bird's house."

Rob took a moment to consider his options before making a choice. "I can't help you. Scarlett knows how to handle herself, and I have a lead on a victim that I can't pass up."

"Are you sure? This is your brother we're talking about."

Conflicted feelings gripped his mind, but every time he thought it through, he knew what the right thing to do was. Jennifer needed his help. "I know, and honestly, it's probably best I'm not there. I'll just complicate things. And as I said, while she might be a little hotheaded, Scarlett is a capable and formidable woman."

"No shit. All right, as long as you're sure."

"I am. You're on your way there?"

"Of course."

The only woman who scared Rob more than Scarlett was Calico, so in all honesty, he felt sorry for Owen. "Do what you need to do."

"Always." She hung up.

Rob pulled the phone away from his ear and stared at it for a long moment. He hoped he'd made the right choice.

"Everything okay, guv?"

Rob looked up to see Nick approaching with Ellen in tow. "I think so. We need to get going. We've got a lead on Jennifer."

"Is that all?" Nick asked.

"No. But I'll tell you on the way. Let's go."

Chapter 59

Friday

With Scarlett's hands now zip-tied behind her back, one of Owen's thugs marched her and Tucker to a room at the back of the house. The man held her forearm in a vice-like grip as he shoved her forward, forcing her to keep up with the thug's pace to avoid falling flat on her face.

"Hey, easy, easy," she called.

The man rushed her through a series of rooms towards a set of double doors. He didn't slow on their approach. She flinched away when he thrust her towards them, using her as a battering ram to open the doors.

"Christ," she gasped, before he threw her to the floor of the room beyond. She landed awkwardly on her front and somehow kept her face from slamming into the tiles.

Tucker landed beside her with a grunt, blood leaking from his nose and mouth, and a nice bruise forming on his cheek.

Breathing hard, he met her gaze. "Are you okay?" he whispered.

She nodded. Everything ached. She could taste blood and was in a substantial amount of pain but was far from incapacitated. Twisting, she stared up at the two brutes who turned back to the doors.

"Shut them," said the first and tallest of the two.

She'd heard Owen refer to him as Denzil, and the other as Vaughn.

Vaughn did as Denzil asked. He was shorter, but thicker set, and probably the stronger of the two. But he also seemed to be lower in the gang's hierarchy.

"Should we help?" Vaughn asked. "I want to kick some arse."

"We were told to watch these two," Denzil said, waving at her and Tucker. He glanced down and met her eyes. His lip briefly curled in disgust before he looked away.

"Fuck 'em," Vaughn suggested and reached for something tucked into the back of his jeans. "We should just kill 'em."

"That's not what Owen wanted," Denzil replied. "We wait. The boss will call when he's ready. We need to wait here."

Vaughn shifted from foot to foot, clearly dealing with some excess energy. "I don't want to wait. I hate waiting. Those fuckers are going to be..."

A bang came from the front of the house, like the sound of a door being broken open. Gunfire swiftly followed it. She glanced at Tucker, who appeared equally concerned. Shifting and squirming, Scarlett managed to sit up.

Denzil glanced at her but said nothing. Vaughn opened one of the doors. The sounds of shouts and more gunfire echoed into the room. The Hyson Green Killers were here, and clearly, they wanted Owen dead.

"What are you doing?" Denzil asked and went to shut the door, but Vaughn held it fast in his huge hand.

"Screw this. I ain't baby sittin' no pigs," Vaughn spat.

Denzil put his arm in Vaughn's way. "Owen said to wait, so we wait."

"What if Owen's fucking dead already?" Vaughn asked. "Then what? You gonna stay here and wait to get murdered? Fuck that."

"Vaughn!"

But Vaughn pushed his way through his arm and marched out of the room, leaving Denzil in the doorway, staring after him.

Tucker was up too now, crouched and ready, like she was. Scarlett glanced at Tucker and jerked her head at Denzil, then nodded. Tucker followed her gaze, and then back to Scarlett. He shrugged.

Scarlett grimaced. This was their chance. They couldn't wait. She charged at Denzil, launching herself towards the thug and throwing her whole body at the man. He turned as she reached him but was taken completely by surprise. He fell, landing hard on his back with Scarlett on top of him.

He grunted in agony.

Tucker kicked the gun from Denzil's hand. Scarlett pushed herself up. Denzil, half in a daze, blinking rapidly, spun towards her. Briefly considering her options, with her hands still bound, she saw only one way to attack him.

With a grimace, she braced herself and head-butted him, driving her forehead into the man's face.

It hurt like hell. Denzil's nose exploded, and blood splattered. To her right, Tucker stamped on the man's hand.

Denzil wailed.

He wasn't unconscious. Annoyed, she repeated the attack. Again his head slammed back into the tile he lay on, but this time after a feeble attempt to stay conscious, he fell limp beneath her.

Scarlett sat up, straddling him, and allowed herself the luxury of a few cleansing breaths, then finally stepped off him.

The gunshots from the front of the house had become more sporadic, but they hadn't stopped. They wouldn't have long before one side won out and someone came searching for them. Scarlett crouched and, with a little pain and a lot of grunting, brought her zip-tied hands back to her front, where she could finally break them and free herself and then Tucker, who wasn't able to perform the same gymnastics.

"I've not quite got your flexibility," Tucker remarked.

"Don't worry, I've got you." She walked over to where he had kicked Denzil's gun and picked it up. She ejected the magazine and checked it, slapping it back in. "Fully loaded."

Nearby, Tucker rifled through Denzil's pockets and found a spare magazine, also filled with bullets. He threw it to her and stared at the fallen thug. "Remind me never to cross you, little Miss Hammerhead."

She shrugged. "It was the only weapon I had." She frowned at the pain. "Bloody hurt, though. I won't be doing that again in a hurry." She rubbed her forehead.

"Plan of action?"

"Let's see what kind of mess we're dealing with," she said and stepped to the doorway.

The next room was clear, and so was the wide corridor beyond that. She led the way, holding the gun up and ready. They crossed the first room, and a couple of gunshots rang out, followed by some shouting.

She paused and listened. Approaching the next door, she peered along the corridor ahead. She could make out a body further up, sticking out of a side room, motionless. She recognised it.

"Vaughn ran headlong into an early death."

"Serves him right."

"Come on," she urged and snuck along the corridor, moving at pace.

On their left as they reached the body, a set of open double doors led to a large room and several more lifeless casualties inside. She crouched beside Vaughn and pointed out the discarded gun beside him to Tucker. She stared into the room.

Towards the far side, a young man in a hoody pointed a gun at a kneeling man. Recognising Owen Mason as the man being held at gunpoint, she frowned. Several more gang members stood close by, keeping watch. It seemed the Hyson Green Killers had won this round.

"Shit," she gasped under her breath.

She watched. Two more men were led into the room by a third gang member, and she recognised both instantly.

It was Guy Gibson and Bill Rainault, and it looked like they were on the side of the HGK gang.

"Is that...?" Tucker asked in shock.

"Yeah," she replied in a whisper, fascinated.

"Wait, I'm filming this," Tucker said and pulled out his phone.

Bill led the way over to where Owen knelt and glared down at him.

"What you gonna do?" Owen asked. "Kill me?"

"I am severely tempted to," Bill replied. "But no, *I* won't kill you."

"Pathetic," Owen commented, scorn dripping from his words. "Both of you. I bet neither of you has the guts to kill me."

Bill smirked. "I have no genuine desire to kill you. Not really. Guy might like to take some revenge, but no, he won't be killing you either."

"Cucks, the pair of you," Owen muttered.

"Thaddeus, however," Bill continued and turned to the tall, thin man who was with them. "Thaddeus *will* kill you." He turned back to Owen. "He wants revenge for what you did to his brother when you escaped. I'm sure you remember murdering him in cold blood."

Scarlett couldn't see Owen's face, but she guessed it had dropped once he realised who Thaddeus was.

Thaddeus stepped forward, brandishing his gun. "You killed my bro, my family, my blood," he announced. "Now it's my turn to repay the favour."

"Now, hold on," Owen pleaded, his voice suddenly shaky as Thaddeus raised his gun. "We can talk about this. Let's not be rash."

Thaddeus said nothing. He squeezed the trigger and blew a hole through Owen's head. He dropped to the floor, and the three men just stared at the lifeless body.

"Fuck me," Tucker whispered.

"Jesus," Scarlett hissed, in shock over what had just happened.

She watched for a few more seconds, before sensing something and swivelling, only to stare down the barrel of another gun.

"Drop the guns," the gangbanger ordered

She did as he asked, and so did Tucker.

"Up! Both of you." He held the gun high and sideways, pointing it at her head as he called out, "Oi, boss, look what I found."

Scarlett raised her hands, Tucker following suit. She stared across the room towards Bill and Guy.

"Wow!" Bill remarked. "Today is our lucky day."

"Scarlett, Tucker," Guy added. "This is unfortunate for both of you."

"We saw what you did," Tucker said.

"What we did?" Bill asked. "Why? What did we do?

"Bring them here," Guy ordered. "It seems we need to talk."

Scarlett glanced back at the kid holding them at gunpoint. The kid looked to Thaddeus for confirmation that he should follow Guy's orders, but behind him, back down the corridor, Scarlett spotted movement in the shadows.

Suppressed, rapid-fire gunshots rang out, bullets tearing through the kid with the gun. Blood exploded onto them both before he fell.

"Get down," Calico called out. She hustled up the corridor towards the doorway and the room beyond.

Scarlett ducked sideways, glancing into the room. Bill and Guy ran. Gunfire rang out; the Killers fired wildly back. Calico and her friend, Burton, both carrying suppressed automatic rifles, fired into the room.

Scarlett kept out of the way, but it didn't last long. In less than a minute, the gunfire stopped. Engines roared outside and then receded into the distance.

"Clear." Calico relaxed and stood up in her all-black outfit. She glared at Scarlett for a long moment. "In future, when I tell you to wait, you wait. Got it?"

Scarlett shrugged. "I'll take it under advisement."

Chapter 60

Friday

Fletcher stared at the Ann Summers shop across the street. He could see Jennifer inside, standing behind a display. She kept glancing up from browsing the shelves and nosing around. What was she doing?

It wasn't a huge shop, and he felt sure she'd spot him if he went in. Not to mention how uncomfortable he'd feel walking into a women's lingerie shop. There was also the risk that she'd crack under the stress of the day and use the gun she was carrying on him, something he didn't want to risk, not after she'd tried to approach him when he was on his moped.

Following that second encounter, he'd decided to follow on foot. She'd been hanging around the pedestrianised areas of the city anyway, so there wasn't much point in him using the moped.

Having changed his coat and donned a cap, he'd successfully managed to follow her around without her noticing him, until roughly half an hour ago when she'd stared right at him and given him a curious glance. Did she recognise him?

He'd backed off since then. There was no need to be so close to her when he had other methods for surveillance.

He checked the cloned phone often, but she hadn't used it in hours, and he had heard nothing useful over the mic either. Instead, she'd been moving erratically around the city centre, going from shop to shop, looking around and following people. It certainly seemed like she was hunting for her victim, but time was running out, and six p.m. was swiftly getting closer. She had just under an hour to go before he would need to set off his trap and kill her partner.

Speaking of which, he opened his phone and checked the video feed from the camera he had trained on her partner. He remained secured to the chair with the bomb around his neck, just as he'd left him.

Fletcher smiled to himself. This was working out quite well, although, he'd hoped that she might actually go through with it and kill someone.

The previous game hadn't worked out as he'd planned when the couple decided to wait out the timer and die together. That was a little annoying, but it couldn't be helped.

With any luck, Jennifer would come through for him and deliver the result he wanted. Chaos. He wanted chaos and disorder. He wanted people terrified, and this first selection of games had gone really rather well.

He'd already started work on designing the next few, working through some ideas for what he might try next, but he needed a break first. These things took time and resources, and he needed the police to back off, too. So far, his planning and random choice of victim had worked out well for him, so he hoped to repeat that for round two.

Returning his attention to Jennifer, he checked his watch and grumbled to himself. He tapped out a message on his phone and pinged it over to her.

Ticktock, time's running out.

The message was successfully delivered, and he watched as she fished her phone out and read it. It seemed to annoy her, and moments later, she left the lingerie shop and headed towards the Old Market Square. She crossed the street and entered a shoe shop.

Fletcher switched sides, too, and came to a stop behind an advertising stand opposite, so he could remain partially hidden. He could see her inside, gazing around, picking up shoes, until she left just seconds after a man strode out of the shop ahead of her. Had that man been in Ann Summers too?

Trailing her into the square, he realised she was following this man from the shoe shop. Fletcher's heart skipped a beat. Had she chosen her victim? Was she finally doing it? She'd left it late, but he didn't mind. The hopelessness of her situation must have finally got to her.

In his excitement, he got a bit too close and had to force himself to back off. No need to ruin this delicious moment.

The pair walked around the front of the town hall to the other side and crossed the street. He watched the man turn right into an alleyway between a coffee shop and a Burger King on Cheapside Road. The sign on the cut-through read: Peck Lane.

Jennifer rushed to catch the man up, dodging between other shoppers. She reached into her bag.

She was doing it!

Unable to hide his grin, Fletcher sped up. He didn't want to miss this. He found himself a position where he could see down the alleyway, stopped and stared after the pair of them.

How would she do this?

She jogged, caught up, and tapped the man on the shoulder.

"Excuse me," she said, her voice sounding loud and clear in his earpiece.

Fletcher stepped closer, peering between the people passing by.

The man turned. "Hmm? Yes?" he said, before an expression of shock appeared on his face. "What the hell? What do you want? I have money if you want it, the man babbled.

"There's nothing you can do," she said and fired the gun.

The noise was tremendous. People around him flinched in shock and looked around, hunting for the source of the noise. A handful of people started shouting and running, and then came a couple of screams. People spotted the man in the alleyway falling to the ground and the woman backing away to the main street.

Fletcher just smiled and relished the moment. Utter chaos reigned in the street. People ran in all directions, but Fletcher just watched, proud of his work. This was the best one yet.

Jennifer turned and marched out of the lane, pulling out her phone. She was tapping something into it as she passed by, just a few metres away. He stepped closer to the lane.

He didn't want to get too close. It would seem suspicious, but he needed to make sure she'd fulfilled her side of the bargain. He stared at the man, who lay lifeless in the alleyway, staring into nothing. He certainly appeared dead, and she'd obviously fired the gun. He wanted to go in there and check the pulse, but others were already rushing in. He needed to stay back and hide his identity.

He took one last look at the face of the dead man, a face that felt a little familiar but he couldn't place, before he dismissed his fears and reversed.

With a grimace, he checked his phone to find a message from Jennifer.

It's done!

"It is indeed," he muttered and placed a call to her.

She answered after half a ring. "I did it. It's done. You need to free William. Now."

"Congratulations, Jennifer. You've done well. I'm pleased. And yes, I will now hold up my part of the bargain." He pulled out a small home-made device and pressed one of its buttons. "There, he's free. You can call his mobile if you like. It's in his pocket. And once agai—" She'd already hung up, and he could hear sounds of movement through the mic she wore.

He shrugged. His work here was done.

"Come on, come on," he heard her say. "Answer, damn it."

He smiled to himself. It would take William a few moments to get out of the restraints, even though they'd been remotely released. Pulling out the cloned phone, Fletcher saw the call going through from Jennifer to William and put the device to his ear. He wanted to listen in.

After a tense few moments, the call was answered.

"Jen?"

"Will," Jennifer answered. "Oh my God. Are you okay?"

"Yeah, I'm fine. I'm okay. A little bruised but okay."

"Where are you?" she asked.

"I don't know. In a building somewhere. I'm trying to find an exit... Oh. Here we go."

"You need to get out of the building and away from the bomb."

"I know, don't worry. I'm getting out, and… There, I'm out. I'm on the street."

"Keep going, move away from the building," she said, her tone serious.

Fletcher frowned at her words. Something felt off about them, as if she knew something that he didn't.

"It's fine, I'm okay."

"No, keep going. Move away, now."

Fletcher stopped in his tracks. He could see Jennifer up ahead. She'd stopped, too, and was staring right back at him.

What was going on?

A thought occurred to him. The man she'd shot in the alleyway. He'd felt familiar. Not overly so, but just a little. He turned back, but the crowds were too thick and people were running back and forth.

Several people emerged from the crowd, their attention fixed on him. They pulled guns of their own.

This was a setup.

He'd been conned.

He spun on the spot. More people approached, revealing weapons as they came.

The game was over, and he'd lost, it seemed. Still holding the remote in his hand, he mashed his thumb into the two buttons on the side.

Half a second later, a distant boom sounded across the city. Again, people flinched.

Expecting them, Fletcher turned and ran, only to be tackled to the ground a second later by a nearby officer.

"I am arresting you on suspicion of murder," the officer said, reciting the caution to him. She pulled his hands behind his back and cuffed him while other officers stepped in and helped.

Annoyed and frustrated, but helpless to do anything about it, Fletcher silently fumed to himself. How had he missed the setup? How had she pulled this off? And who was the man she'd shot?

Chapter 61

Friday

Rob pushed himself up from the ground of Peck Lane and leaned against the wall with a grunt. "Aww, bloody hell. That wasn't nice."

"You're alive?" one of the surrounding civilians asked, clearly shocked.

Rob smiled, a tad embarrassed. Moments ago, these people had surrounded him, checked his pulse and hunted for the bullet wound, only to find the ballistic vest under his shirt.

"We thought you'd been shot."

Rob coughed. "I have been shot." His chest hurt like hell.

"All right, everyone, back away, please." Nick approached with several uniformed officers.

They ushered the members of the public back and out of the way, until the lane was clear while Nick crouched beside Rob.

"Well done."

"Thank you."

"You should have let me do it, though. You took a risk."

"I know. But it worked out, right?"

"Yeah, we got him. Jennifer was a great help."

Rob smiled. They'd been in town for nearly two hours, messaging Jennifer on the stolen phone, working out who the killer was, and planning how they were going to save William. The conclusion being that seeing this through to the end, and making the killer think he'd won, was the best way of achieving their goals.

"You did well," Nick remarked. "You were very convincing."

"What can I say, I give good dead."

Nick laughed. "I guess so."

"I heard an explosion," Rob said and got to his feet, stiff and a little battered.

"Yeah. There were two of them, actually," Nick confirmed. "When he realised he'd been caught, he blew up his house and the bomb William had been wearing. No one was hurt, luckily. We'd pulled everyone out, and William was out of the building."

"Good work," Rob said.

He crossed the street to where Fletcher Shaw, the Games Master, was being held, facedown on the ground. He stared up at Rob's approach and scowled at him.

"You led us on a merry dance, Mister Shaw. But it ends now."

"It never ends." He looked away.

"Indeed it doesn't," Rob remarked. He stepped around to where Jennifer Quick was being checked by uniformed officers.

"Jennifer," Rob said. "It's Rob Loxley. Nice to finally meet you."

She smiled. "Thank you for all your help. It's good to put a face to the name."

Rob agreed. They'd been texting back and forth for well over an hour as they'd arranged this sting operation. "We have William, by the way. He's a bit battered and bruised, but he's okay."

"Thank you so much. When can I see him?"

"It won't be long. We'll need statements from both of you, though."

She nodded. "Of course. Thank you."

As he walked away, Nick addressed him. "By the way, there's one other thing I need to tell you."

"Oh?"

Chapter 62

Friday

After the adrenaline of the sting operation, Nick's news about Scarlett and Owen came as a shock and brought Rob back down to earth with a bang. He left the scene immediately and drove north in the pool car, using the lights and siren to bypass any holdups.

The journey passed in a fog of confused thoughts and emotions. He tried to process what this might mean, both for him and his wider family. He felt sure that Isaac would find a way to blame him and the police for it, no matter what the truth of it was.

Christ, he hoped Scarlett wasn't the one to pull the trigger.

Half an hour later, he drove into Carter Bird's estate and found swathes of marked police cars and support vehicles had beaten him there, and the place seemed to swarm with officers.

He navigated his way inside the mansion, past scenes of bloodshed and death where the Masons had clashed with rival gang, the Hyson Green Killers, in a violent showdown, leaving members of both sides dead on the floor.

In a room towards the back of the house, Rob found DCI Nailer watching forensic officers from a distance. They took photos of Owen Mason's body. Scarlett was also nearby, talking to other officers.

Rob walked over and stood next to his boss and mentor. He said nothing and stared at the lifeless corpse of his brother as photographic flashes of white light bathed the scene.

It didn't seem quite real.

"Well, shit," Rob muttered.

"Yeah," Nailer agreed. "That was my reaction, too."

"I'm not sure how I feel about this."

Owen was his brother, his blood, so surely, he should feel sad, but he didn't. He didn't feel happy about it either. In fact, he didn't really feel much of anything. Just felt kind of numb.

He had no relationship with Owen to speak of, or any of his brothers, so maybe that was to be expected? He didn't have any answers.

"I'm honestly at a loss," Rob said.

"That's understandable," Nailer replied. "For what it's worth, I'm sorry this has happened."

Rob grimaced. "Thanks, I guess." He stared at the body for a while longer. "So what does this mean? For us, I mean. For me, Erika, and Mum?"

"I… I don't know. I'm not sure this makes you any safer."

"No, I guess not."

Scarlett walked over. "Hey." She looked sheepish while sporting cuts and bruises that had been taped up and cleaned.

"Hi. Are you okay? What happened?"

She pointed to Owen. "Blame him."

"He did that to you?" Rob felt terrible for her.

"Yeah. To me and Tucker. We're okay, but I might take tomorrow off, if that's okay, guv?"

"Of course," Nailer confirmed.

"So, what happened?" Rob waved to the room. "How did he die?"

"I attended a crime scene earlier today and found Carter Bird's body there. He'd been tortured and killed. So, we made our way over here to let people know, and spotted Owen. We tried to make an arrest, but things got messy when the Hyson Green Killers showed up."

"I see," Rob said. "And who killed Owen?"

"Thaddeus Watts," she replied without hesitation. "The brother of the boy who Owen killed during his escape from prison."

Rob nodded slowly. "Makes sense."

"It does, but it's not the most interesting part of all this."

Rob raised his eyebrows. "Oh? And what's that?"

"Bill and Guy were here, working with the HGK gang."

It took several seconds for Rob to realise his mouth had fallen open in shock. "What the hell?"

"Yeah." She nodded, her smile a thin line.

"Damn!" Rob took a moment to let that sink in. Bill had sunk to even greater depths, it seemed. He snapped out of it and spoke to Scarlett. "Well, I'm glad you're okay. You need to get some rest."

"Thanks. Yeah, I will. I just need to finish up."

Nailer coughed. "While you digest all that, I'll arrange for someone to inform Owen's family about his death." He turned and walked away.

"Good luck with that." Rob stared back at his lifeless brother. Things had changed, and not for the better.

Chapter 63

Saturday

"So, the only question I have left for you really," Rob said, "is why?"

They'd been talking for hours, going over everything, from Fletcher's childhood pranks against his school friends and other children who lived close by, and how he'd intentionally hurt them for his own enjoyment. They'd discussed his incarceration for repeated violence and harm, that culminated in him going to prison for several years, until his eventual release, and then his admittedly inventive killing spree, by putting people in impossible situations or giving them impossible choices.

Through it all, Fletcher had said little but did answer some questions and at least interacted with them, which was more than could be said for some of them.

The only thing he hadn't extracted an answer out of him about was the money. He'd been clearly funded by dark money. An influential backer who helped him embark on this carnage, but all they had on that were ideas. The most obvious being that the mysterious Ashen King who'd funded the previous two chaos killers had done the same with Fletcher. But Fletcher had so far refused to confirm or deny anything.

It didn't help that the explosion at Fletcher's house had obliterated any hope of them finding information from his computer either.

"Why did you do this?" Rob pressed. "Why would you kill all these people in these horrific ways?" He watched the man opposite as he thought something through.

"Chaos," Fletcher said eventually. "To cause chaos, instability, uncertainty. Fear. That's why. That's why we do it. Humans fear the unknown, and chaos is the epitome of the unknown. All your rules and laws, they're pointless. They mean nothing, and they cannot save you. Nothing can save you. You'll see."

"We?" Rob said, smiling. "We? Is this the Ashen King again?"

Fletcher sighed. "This is just the beginning. You realise that, right?"

"It looks more like the end, for you."

Fletcher chuckled to himself. "This is so much bigger than me."

Chapter 64

Monday

"We're rolling up as many of Carter's assets as we can, getting them under our control and seeing what we can do with them," Guy said, referring to his notes on the table. "The sale of all that gear has given us some working capital, so we should be able to use that to our advantage."

Nearby, Bill stood at the window of the upstairs room, staring out over the street below. "I told you it would work."

"I know you did."

Guy looked over at the silhouette of Bill against the window and almost didn't recognise him anymore. He wasn't the same man who had worked for the police for all those years. He'd been stripped down, his outer layers peeled away, leaving behind a raw and cruel shadow of a man who'd stop at nothing to get what he wanted. No longer constrained by the rules and laws of society and the police, he'd become something different and altogether more dangerous.

"Anything on the Hyson Green Killers?" Bill asked. "Are we done with them?"

"We've cut ties," Guy confirmed. "And there's been no hostility from them. They seem cool."

"Good."

There was a knock at the door.

"Yeah?" Guy called out.

The door opened, and Bruce's face appeared. "Boss. He's here."

"Send him in," Guy ordered.

Bruce ushered a man into the room and shut the door behind him. A little overweight, the man seemed nervous and fidgeted with his tie and cuffs. He was well dressed in a tailored suit, which was far too expensive for a local councillor to afford.

Bill turned to face him. "Councillor Clayton. It's good to see you again."

"Th… thank you, yes. It's good to see you, too," he stammered.

"Don't be nervous," Bill reassured him and waved to a chair. "That unfortunate business at the garage with Mr Bird was a necessary action. But I am sorry you had to see it. Hopefully we can leave that firmly in the past and move on, however."

"Of course, yes," the councillor confirmed and took the offered seat.

"I hear you're moving up in the world. Is that right? Next stop, Westminster. Right?"

"Well, we'll see." He flushed.

"I'm embarrassing you. I apologise." Bill took a seat. "Right then, down to business. I'd like to know more about the arrangement you had with Mr Bird, and we'll see if we can't improve on things…"

Chapter 65

Tuesday

Checking through his notes, Rob did his best to ignore the flutter in his stomach. He needed to be calm and focused for this, and any nerves would just get in the way.

The sound of Nailer's office door snapped him out of the merry-go-round of intrusive thoughts, and he glanced up. Nailer paused outside his office door before approaching.

Rob stood and went to meet him. He felt certain that Nailer would offer to conduct this interview without him, but Rob had no intention of letting Nailer do that and did his best to project an air of confidence.

"You don't have to do this, you know," Nailer said.

"I know. But I want to."

"Are you sure? I don't know how this is going to go."

"I know. But I'm going to do this. I need to be in that room."

Nailer nodded and seemed to resign himself to it. "All right, if you're sure."

The pair of them left the office and headed down to the interview rooms on the ground floor. The space they would be using was one of the more comfortable ones, not a sparse interrogation room, and their visitor was already in there, having been escorted through by an officer who was waiting outside when they'd arrived.

"Is he here?" Nailer asked the uniformed officer and pointed to the door.

"He is. He's comfortable and has a drink," the officer confirmed.

"Thank you."

Rob followed Nailer through the door, and when Nailer stepped out of the way, Rob's gaze fell onto the man sitting on the comfortable seat, his hands clasped in his lap and his walking stick beside him.

"Mr Mason," Nailer began. "Thank you for coming in."

Rob's father, Isaac Mason, looked up and smiled. "Of course. Happy to be of service." Isaac didn't stand, and his face was impassive. His gaze switched to Rob. "Son. I wasn't sure if you'd be here for this."

Rob shrugged. "I wouldn't miss it." He moved to sit opposite Isaac but close to Nailer who was setting a recorder going.

Isaac nodded. "Well, it's good to see you."

Rob offered him a thin smile but said nothing. The feeling wasn't mutual.

"Firstly, I'd like to offer our condolences for the loss of your son," Nailer began with a sympathetic smile.

"Thank you. I appreciate that."

"Right, well, let's get down to business, shall we?" Nailer suggested. "We asked you to come in today because we needed to talk to you about your son, Owen, and his actions over the last few weeks, and work out how much you knew and see if you can offer any insight into his actions. Okay?"

"Of course, go ahead," Isaac replied.

"I'd like to remind you that, because of your family connection, you will be interviewed under caution. Which means you do not have to say anything. But it may harm your defence if you do not mention when questioned something which you later rely on in court. Anything you do say may be given in evidence. Do you understand?"

"I do," Isaac confirmed.

"Excellent. Okay, so, when did you first learn of Owen's escape from custody?"

"When the police called to inform me."

"So you didn't know beforehand?"

"No."

"And when did you take that call?"

Rob sat back and watched Isaac carefully as Nailer worked through his questions, asking how much Isaac knew about Owen and his movements before, during, and after his escape. He asked about the Red Room case and what he knew about that, and all the violence that had happened after Owen's escape leading up to his death in Carter Bird's mansion. In every instance, Isaac claimed to know nothing at all about the criminal activities of his son, other than what he'd learned from the police and through hearsay and rumour.

He expressed dismay and disgust for his son's actions during both the Red Room case and in the more recent gang violence. He was also apparently shocked that Owen was capable of such things and wanted little to nothing to do with Owen once he'd found out the truth.

Through it all, Isaac remained calm and stoic, only giving the bare minimum of information and rarely expanding on any given topic. He didn't seem rushed and took every question in his stride.

Rob was actually impressed with how he handled the interview, even though they got nothing of any use or interest from it.

In the end, the whole thing became rather annoying. Nailer turned off the recorder and moved to wrap things up.

"Okay, thank you so much for your time, Mr Mason. You've answered all our questions, and I can't think of anything else that we might need. We appreciate your time."

"Of course. It was my pleasure. Next time I see the commissioner, I'll be sure to sing your praises to him."

Rob gritted his teeth at the veiled threat and smiled through it.

"Thank you," Nailer added. A note of annoyance laced his tone. "I appreciate that."

"So, am I free to go?"

"You always were. You're not under arrest, Mr Mason. This was all entirely voluntary."

"Aaah, yes, of course."

Rob wasn't falling for it. Isaac had known that from the start. The police had interviewed him enough times to know how these things worked.

"So thanks again," Nailer said as he shifted in his seat. "We will be in touch if we need anything else."

Rob went to stand beside Nailer.

"Happy to help," Isaac said and looked at Rob. "Oh, and I meant to ask. How's your mother?" His eyes flicked to Nailer. "How's Annabelle?"

Rob froze to the spot, his whole body going rigid from the shock of what his dad had just said. He stared at the man opposite, unable to speak.

Nailer paused, too, but he recovered faster. "I'm… not sure what you mean? She's been missing for twenty years."

Isaac stared at them both, his eyes cold and suspicious. He said nothing for far too long.

And then he smiled suddenly and waved dismissively. "Of course. I don't know what I'm saying. How silly of me. Please forgive these senior moments." He used his stick to stand.

Still in shock and not believing a word that Isaac had just said, Rob found himself rooted to the spot and unable to move. Nailer, meanwhile, rushed around and asked the officer outside to help Isaac out of the building.

"Thank you, and good day to you both," Isaac said, before he disappeared.

They both stared at the door as it slowly closed, and then Nailer turned to Rob, an expression of shock on his face.

"What the hell was that?" Rob asked. "Does he know?"

"I think we need to assume that he does from now on," Nailer suggested. "He's obviously been sniffing around, sending private detectives out to poke into things, so I think he's had his suspicions for a while."

"Shit. He did that on purpose then. He was waiting for a reaction, and… he kind of got one. From me, at least. You handled it better."

"Nothing was confirmed by either of us, but at least we know now. We know he's at the very least suspicious. We need to be careful."

"I don't like this. I don't like it one bit."

"Neither do I," Nailer confirmed.

Rob grimaced and glanced back at the door, an uneasy feeling building deep in his gut.

THE END

Detective Loxley will return…

Author Note

Thank you so much for reading *Just a Game*, the seventh book in the Loxley series. I really appreciate it.

Originally, I'd planned for this book to be something else and feature a completely different main crime story, but as I went through the early stages of planning, it became clear that I needed to do more research before I could write my original idea, so I switched to this.

I'm very pleased with this book, but I realise I didn't have the usual trope of having the killer show up early in the book and then reveal him later on. But I felt it was kind of unavoidable given that I had this idea of the killer doing everything in his power to keep from being found, such as choosing his victims at random. This made it difficult to have that typical reveal at the end feel credible.

Instead, I was forced to have a different reveal, when we learn it was Rob who'd been shot but that he's totally fine and this was all planned.

Hopefully you will forgive me for making this change.

I am thrilled with this book, though, and hope you enjoyed it, too.

In Chapter 54, Scarlett noticed Tucker watching a cooking video on YouTube, by someone called The Pit Wizard. Billy the Pit Wizard is a real person and YouTuber who I know, and you can find him on YouTube.

Check him out and give him a subscribe.

youtube.com/@ThePitWizard

I will write book eight in the not-too-distant future, because I'm not done with tormenting Rob yet, but I might take a brief break to write something else first before I return to Loxley and friends.

Stay tuned.

Thanks again.

Andrew

Come and join in the discussion about my books in my Facebook Group:

https://www.facebook.com/groups/alfraine.readers

Book List

https://www.alfraineauthor.co.uk/books